THE CIRCUS
AT THE END OF THE SEA

THE CIRCUS

AT THE END OF THE SEA

Lori R. Snyder

HARPER

An Imprint of HarperCollinsPublishers

Library of Congress Control Number: 2021935323
ISBN 978-0-06-304710-5

21 22 23 24 25   GV   10 9 8 7 6 5 4 3 2 1
❖
First Edition

For my mom, Judie Snyder,

who taught me to see the magic that is all around us.

✳

All her life, Maddy Adriana had felt *pulled*.

In her twelve years of being alive, that feeling had gotten Maddy into far more trouble than anything else. After all, group home leaders didn't much like it when you wandered off after something no one else could see or hear. Probably they liked it even less than real parents—although, to be fair, Maddy had never had real parents, so her knowledge of them could be measured as either exactly zero or as what she saw in the movies, which was basically the same thing. And even though she didn't like getting in trouble, didn't like it at all, it was hard to stay put when you felt as though you had a rope around your heart pulling you toward . . . something.

Maddy loved that feeling. It was perhaps her favorite thing in the world, that moment of knowing there was magic right around the corner and it was calling her. Of course, she didn't tell anyone what she saw, not anymore. It turned out that no one actually wanted to hear about magic, even if they loved it in books. And it wasn't as though the other group home kids ever liked her that much to start with. She was always the weird new kid.

And now here she was, being sent to yet another group home. This time, though, it was because she was sick. Maddy tried to push that thought out of her mind and instead wondered what everyone else would be like. Maybe she could start fresh, make some friends? Then again, maybe all the other kids at this home were sicker than she was. Maybe they stayed in bed all the time. Maybe the people who ran this home would make *her* stay in bed all the time! That thought was the worst one yet.

The problem was that no one knew what was wrong with her. She had already spent two terrible months in bed while a team of exhausted county doctors discussed her as though she weren't there. In the end, they had shrugged their collective shoulders, written "heart murmur" on her medical form as their best guess, and prescribed pills for her to take when her heart raced and her vision went dark. Then they advised the county to transfer her to the Venice Beach Home for Children, which was designed for kids who, like Maddy, were sick and deemed to need Extra Attention.

Maddy hated Extra Attention.

So now here she was, sitting on the county bus on her way to the home for sick kids, staring out the open window. She twisted the silver bracelet around her wrist as she watched the scenery go by. Her skateboard, by far her most prized possession after her bracelet, was tucked protectively under her feet. The bus driver knew her, so he didn't even bother trying to put her skateboard into the luggage hold below the bus. He always called Maddy "Hot Rod"—which wasn't at all who she was, but she liked it nonetheless.

It was a glorious summer day, the very best kind of day to not spend on a bus, and the sidewalks were packed with people on their way to or from the beach. The sun beat down through the bus window, burnishing the brown of Maddy's shoulders and turning the black of her thick, wavy hair into a blanket of warmth. Everyone outside was laughing, happy, calling to one another. The air smelled of sunblock and ocean, and whenever the bus crept through an intersection, Maddy could see flashes of glittering blue sea. She listened to the rhythm of the traffic swishing by and wondered if the Venice Beach Home for Children would be close enough to the beach to walk. She listened to the rhythm of her own flawed heart. She tried not to listen too closely to the rhythm of all the happy people outside, with friends and families of their own.

"Do all new homes do that same introduction game?" came a small voice next to her. Maddy started and turned to the girl sharing her bus seat, whose name was something pretty that started with a T and had a rhythm like a waterfall. Waterfall T was much younger than Maddy and clearly nervous; she sat on her hands and bounced a little in her seat. Maddy smiled at her.

"You mean the one where you have to remember everyone's name and say what they're bringing to the picnic?" asked Maddy. When the girl nodded, Maddy replied, "Not all of them, but a lot do."

"Oh," said Waterfall T quietly. "I like that game." And then she blinked hard, twice. Maddy knew that blink. That was the blink that said, *I had friends at my old home, and a life, and now they are sending me someplace where I don't know anyone. What if they yell? What if no one likes me?*

That blink was one of the worst parts of being a group home kid.

"Want to play a game I made up?" asked Maddy. She hardly ever played Something Perfect with anyone else, not since she'd realized that she could see and hear things that others couldn't. While she could usually recognize magic right away, every now and then something that was magic looked normal, and something that was normal looked magic. She loved that she could see the magic, but she didn't love the way other kids treated her when they couldn't, so she had learned it was safer to not mention it. But Waterfall T looked so sad. Maddy would just have to be extra careful to only choose things that were clearly, plainly *Not Magic*, things she was sure everyone could see.

Waterfall T stopped bouncing. "Okay," she said.

"Here's how you play," said Maddy. "We both look out the window and find one thing that we think is perfect. Then we tell each other what it is and decide which one we like best. Okay?"

Waterfall T chewed her lower lip. "Like what?"

Maddy paused. What Something Perfects had she seen lately that she knew for sure weren't magic? "Um . . . like a flower growing out of the sidewalk. Or, um, a plastic bag that's floating in the air like a parachute. Things like that."

Waterfall T grinned and pointed out the window. "Like that dog with a purple collar?"

"Nice job!" said Maddy. "See? You're a natural."

Maddy turned back to the window to take her turn. A man rode by on a bicycle, a battered surfboard tucked under one arm and his hair in dark ropes down his back. His bike frame, wheels, and handlebars were decorated with furry yellow fabric, and purple lights flashed from his spokes.

"There," said Maddy. "That bike."

Waterfall T leaned halfway across Maddy to look and then nodded vigorously. "You win! Now you go first."

And so it was that Maddy was looking carefully out the window when the bus crawled past a sign that read *Welcome to Venice, CA*, which was right next to a low concrete wall with blue waves painted across the bottom. So it was that she noticed when the biggest cat she had ever seen jumped to the top of that wall. So it was that she was paying close attention when the cat turned to look right her, as though on purpose.

Maddy leaned eagerly toward the window. Even from here, she could see the cat was magic. The cat's nose was flat and broad, its tail thin and tufted, and the fur around its head was long enough to maybe count as a mane. Running along either side of its spine were twin ridges of fur, like a punk feline haircut. Most of all, its eyes were round like a person's, not slitted like a normal cat's. Something feral and ancient stirred within them.

Maddy had once lived in a suburb near the mountains, where bobcats hunted at night. This cat looked a little like that . . . and a little like nothing she had ever seen before.

"Did you find something?" asked Waterfall T, who showed no sign of seeing the cat.

"Not yet," said Maddy slowly.

And then, as though stenciled by an unseen hand, small, neat letters appeared on the wall just beneath the cat. They were midnight blue in color and written in a beautiful flowing script, one letter at a time, to spell out two words:

why
not?

Quietly but distinctly, Maddy's heart went, *tug.*

At the same time, the bus—which had been rickety at best the entire trip—shuddered mightily, backfired twice, and came to a complete stop. The cat jumped down from the wall, trotted past a mural of cartoon bunnies inexplicably bursting out of the neck of a tuxedo jacket, and then disappeared behind a building. Maddy craned her neck, trying to see where the cat had gone, but a small whimper next to her snapped her attention back.

Waterfall T looked a little frightened. Maddy knew that look, too, the look of everything being out of your control. She tore her mind away from the magic outside and nudged Waterfall T with her shoulder.

"Look at that," said Maddy, pointing at the bunnies in the mural. She leaned in close so the other girl could hear her over the whoops of a bunch of bored kids on a bus that had just broken down within walking distance of the beach. Waterfall T rubbed one hand across her nose and looked where Maddy pointed. Her face folded into confusion.

"Why are there rabbits in that suit?" she asked.

"Just because, I think," said Maddy, relieved that Waterfall T could actually see the mural. She had been a little worried that something so wonderful had to be magic. The cartoon bunnies were adorable, giant ears attached to black button eyes and little black noses. "That's what makes it perfect."

Waterfall T was saved from having to reply by the bus driver, holding his phone in one hand, announcing that yes, the bus was broken down, yes, he was calling for a replacement, and no, they weren't going to stay on the bus and swelter in this heat. Maddy grabbed her skateboard and followed everyone off the bus as the driver, phone to ear, tried to keep kids from running off. When she stepped out, he looked at her over his phone and mouthed, "Hey, Hot Rod, you got your pills, right?"

Maddy nodded, and—because she knew that grown-ups liked to be reassured—patted the pocket where she kept her heart medicine. The bus driver gave her a thumbs-up and then returned to his call.

Waterfall T was now talking to someone else, so Maddy stood alone next to the bunny mural. She couldn't see the beach but she could feel it, like a deep, salty invitation. A strange fluttery feeling settled into her stomach.

why not?

A pack of teenagers, half of them in board shorts pulled too low around their hips and the other half in shorts and bikini tops, came toward her, joking loudly with each other. She stepped out of their way and almost got plowed over by a smiling family with two tottering kids holding plastic buckets and shovels.

Maddy was way too old to still think her parents were out there somewhere, coming for her someday. Even so, she couldn't help feeling a small, sharp pang whenever she saw a family like that. She looked away and blinked, the same blink Waterfall T had done earlier.

She didn't want to go to a new home, either. She didn't want Extra Attention. What she wanted—what she had always wanted—was to follow the magic.

why not?

The words circled through her mind. Behind her, the other kids goofed off while the bus driver yelled at them to *keep it down, will ya, I'm on the phone!* Maddy closed her eyes and let it all resolve into a rhythm, the kids and the bus driver and the sounds of vacation and beach and boardwalk. It washed over her, bringing with it a damp coolness that hadn't been there a moment before. Something had shifted; she could hear it in the rhythm around her.

She opened her eyes. Sure enough, a patch of white fog that hadn't been there before was drifting toward them like an exhaled breath on a cold day. Pale tendrils curled over the sidewalk as it floated closer, wispy and nebulous. Where the sunlight hit it, it looked aglow.

Maddy glanced at the bus driver, who was now yelling into his phone, "I can't be responsible for twenty-three kids—in VENICE BEACH, no less—what are you *thinking*?" And then she glanced back at the fog.

It was definitely Something Perfect.

It was also definitely magic.

Tug, went her heart.

Behind her, the bus driver was shouting, ". . . twenty-three kids! TWENTY-THREE!" over and over, as though that would somehow make the person on the other end of the phone hurry up and do something.

The strange white fog was tumbling faster now. It flowed past Waterfall T and the other kids, straight to the bus driver. For the briefest of moments, it rose up to wrap him in a foggy hug, and the air smelled suddenly of salt and wildness, of dusted cinnamon sugar and fried dough. Maddy inhaled deeply, chills dancing down her arms. Then the fog burned away, as quickly as it had come.

"Twenty-two kids!" the bus driver was yelling. "TWENTY-TWO!!!"

A quiet roar filled Maddy's ears.

The bus driver hung up the phone. Heart pounding, Maddy watched as he gathered up the other kids and herded them back onto the broken bus to wait, yelling over their protests that he had to, that insurance said so, that it wasn't his fault. She watched as he marked each child against a list on the clipboard he held in his hands. She watched as he double-checked his clipboard, did a last head count, and climbed onto the bus without ever once turning back.

Maddy's chills turned to wave after wave of warmth, as

though she were drawing heat from the sun-drenched pavement beneath her.

why not?

Waterfall T sat by herself in the same place on the bus, chewing on her fingernail, not even looking for a seatmate who had disappeared. And then the bus started up, the driver giving a muffled exclamation of surprise. Maddy wrapped her arms around herself and squeezed as the bus began to inch forward, her pulse so strong she could feel it against her arms.

No one on the bus so much as turned around to look at her. No one shouted, "Hey, you forgot the girl with the skateboard!" No bus driver said, "Hey, Hot Rod, get your behind up here!"

Maddy put her skateboard on the ground and stepped onto it with one foot. She knew what she *should* do. Of course she did. She should yell and wave her arms and run after the bus. She should remind the bus driver that he was supposed to take her to the home for sick kids. She should turn away from Something Perfect, from the magic that had appeared in glimpses her whole entire life but that now seemed to be kicking the door wide open for her, and she should pretend she hadn't seen it at all.

But she had. For a moment, *want* battled *should*.

And then, somewhere down by the sea, a drumbeat began.

It was followed by another, and then another, the rhythm ricocheting off the buildings. At the same time, a movement by Maddy's feet caught her eye. More words were forming next to her skateboard, words of the same midnight blue as the words on the wall.

you
are
here

Her skateboard seemed alive beneath her feet, willing her to move, to *go*. Maddy Adriana stood up straighter. She patted her pocket to be sure her of pills—because the truth was, grown-up worry was contagious. And then, heart fluttering like wings, she pushed off toward the sound of the drums, so overwhelmed by the sudden taste of caramel and buttered popcorn in her mouth that she didn't even notice the dozen pairs of black painted bunny eyes that followed her movement down the street.

2

The last time Maddy had said the word *magic* out loud, she had been eight years old. A magnificent golden butterfly the size of a dinner plate had landed on her arm. It had tickled and made her laugh, and she had followed it when it fluttered away. It wasn't until later, when she tried to explain why she had run off from the group home picnic, that she realized no one else had seen the butterfly. Nor had anyone seen the others just like it that were swooping around her when the group home leader found her three blocks away. Before this, grown-ups had written off Maddy's stories as imagination, smiling indulgently and patting her on the head. This time, she had been sent to bed early after a scolding on how she was old enough to know better and a lecture on why lying was bad.

But she *didn't* lie, and she *did* know better. She knew better than anyone that magic was real. After all, she had worn it on her wrist for as long as she could remember.

Now, as she steered her skateboard down the Venice boardwalk through throngs of tourists and street vendors, past a mural of an animal that looked like a cross between a cheetah, a wolf, and a unicorn, and by a man wearing a tiara that flashed green and blue lights, Maddy glanced down at her silver bracelet. It glimmered in the bright beach sunshine, and her name—*Madeline Adriana*, which was engraved on it in lovely flowing letters—caught the light. Her bracelet had been her only identification, or so she had been told, when she was found as a one-year-old on the doorstep of a county office.

She still had the bracelet—or, rather, it still had her. One unbroken piece of silver with no hook or clasp, it had grown as she grew, stretched as she stretched, and it cradled her wrist the way Maddy imagined a mother might cradle her child. It looked like a regular bracelet until you knew it didn't come off, and it reminded her that someone, somewhere, had cared about her enough to write her name on a piece of silver and make sure she always had it with her.

She loved it more than anything.

Not having to explain about the bracelet was the only good thing about moving so many times: she was never in one place long enough for anyone to ask. If they had, she wouldn't know what to say. She had studied every book about magic she could find, searching for any hints or clues. She had found stories of changelings and Fairyland and flying carpets; stories of furniture that transported you to other worlds and stories of creepy button-eyed families. But nothing about a bracelet you couldn't take off.

Now, as Maddy followed the sound of the drums, a strange lightness filled her. She had transferred from home to home enough to know that every place had a different feel. Some places were full of rush and push and hurry, so that the very air could barely catch its breath. Some places were sleepy and didn't like to be disturbed. But a place where everyone was laughing and there were murals on almost every wall was like a parade, a place to get happily lost and watch the world as it wandered past.

Maddy loved parades.

Along one side of the Venice boardwalk were shops that sold T-shirts and food and books and crystals; along the other were tents with henna tattoo artists, jewelry makers, and fortune-tellers. Past the boardwalk was a bike path that snaked through the sand, jam-packed with cyclists and skaters, and past *that* was the sparkling blue ocean, the beach thick with sunbathers. Something about it felt like a memory to Maddy, as though she had dreamed about this place a very long time ago. Her skateboard wheels made their own rhythm as they hit each crack in the buckled pavement: *cla-chunk, cla-chunk, cla-chunk,* and she clicked off a counter-rhythm in her head: *badum cla-chunk badadum cla-chunk badum cla-chunk badadum cla-chunk.*

Now Maddy could see the drum circle on the sand, the drummers themselves hidden by a huge dancing, swaying crowd. She came to a rolling stop, grabbed her board, and hurried across the beach toward them. Soft, hot sand squished into her flip-flops and oozed between her toes.

At the edge of the drum circle the sound was deafening and wonderful. Maddy wanted to see the drummers, to watch how they were making the rhythm happen. Doing her best not to bump into any of the dancing, sun-warm bodies, she snaked her way through the crowd, the smell of sunblock and sweat stinging her nose. She squeezed between two people in sarongs and bikini tops and then she was there, near the drummers at the center. At least twenty of them strutted and played. Some had drums held in straps that went over their backs or across their shoulders; some had drums they hit from both sides; some made their drums sound like talking. The breeze picked up the rhythm and flung it through the air, weaving it together like a perfect, Maddy-sized hammock where she could rest.

It was the most glorious thing she had ever heard.

Maddy set her skateboard on the sand, tapping her leg to keep time and singing along under her breath. The beat ebbed and flowed, now loud and now soft, fast to slow to fast again. It was as though someone had reached into her heart and pulled out exactly how she felt, the longing and wonder and worry and magic, and put it all into a rhythm. One of the drummers caught her eye and dipped his head at her, and Maddy smiled back. It lasted only a split second—the drummer saw someone he knew and turned his attention elsewhere, yelling, "Yo, Skeeter Chen!" —but it left Maddy feeling warm and welcome.

She followed the drummer's gaze to see a boy about her own age, who yelled back, "Yo, Anthony M.!" Like her, the boy— Skeeter Chen, Maddy guessed—had a skateboard. Unlike her, he held his board by one hand so it dangled at his side in a stance of careless-cool. In fact, this boy was all skater-boy cool, from his black clothing to his short, spiked black hair. Kids who looked like that, like they knew exactly who they were and where they belonged, made Maddy a little nervous. Just then, though, the boy noticed Maddy looking at him and flashed her a grin, his whole face becoming friendly and open. Maddy flushed, then shyly smiled back.

The drummers played a complicated little riff, like ten rhythms at once all piled on top of one another, and Maddy's attention snapped away from the cool skater boy and back to the drummers. The one who had nodded at her seemed to be the leader, and his hands moved in a precise rhythm, never stopping. Sometimes he would yell out a formless word and play a short, fast beat, *da-da-da-da, da-da-da-DA,* and then everyone would change rhythm all at the same time. Maddy could tell it was coming when his arms, muscled and coated with a thin sheen of sweat, would bunch up. She kept her eyes on him, trying to find the secret that told everyone what rhythm he wanted them to play.

If she hadn't been watching so closely, she might not have noticed when he raised one callused hand and tossed a handful of sand into the air.

The rhythm rose. Someone shouted. Someone else blew a whistle, shrilly, three times.

The sand he had thrown was snaking through the air, forming the vague, glimmering outline of a person . . . then two people . . . then five . . . then seven. Maddy drew in a quick breath and rose to her tiptoes, her hand on her bracelet. Slowly, the sand outlines filled in to become seven people—all just a little older than Maddy. At first they were shimmery and translucent, but then they became solid. Their skin was lightly striped the color of the ocean at night, and their hair—the same steely blue but with more of a silvery sheen—cascaded over their muscular shoulders in twists that reminded Maddy of sea serpents. Their eyes shone dark brown and aqua, wet rock gray and deep teal. When the sunlight caught their striped skin, Maddy could just make out fine, silvery scales.

And then they began to dance.

Their feet touched down lightly on the heads of the drummers, their movements sinewy and fluid, arms flung wide and graceful as they wove through the air like eels. They found each beat and tangled it into something syncopated and gorgeous before freeing it to meet itself on the other side. Then, slowly and with excruciating beauty, they started to slide their bodies into shapes so impossible, so completely boneless and astonishing, that Maddy couldn't help but cry out in delight. Each one was more flexible and each pose more unimaginable than the last.

Maddy tore her eyes from the dancers and glanced around. Could anyone else see this? Her eyes locked with the skater boy's across the circle, and his grin grew wider. *Right?* his grin seemed to say. *It's amazing!*

One of the sand dancers put her hands on the lead drummer's shoulders and lifted up into a handstand above him, her back curving into the shape of a crescent moon until her legs extended by her ears, practically resting on her shoulders with her toes pointed out in front of her. Then another dancer leaped up, his hands on the first girl's shoulders, and gracefully took the same pose . . . and then another, and another . . . until all seven of them were stacked into a tower of curved spines and scales, shimmery hair and sunlight, all balanced on the lead drummer's shoulders as he played. Silhouetted against the sunlight, the dancer on the top shifted all her weight to one arm, extended the other arm out to her side, and straightened her legs into the splits. She opened her mouth and grinned. Row upon row of sharp teeth like a shark's lined her jaws.

Maddy felt as though she might float away with the beauty

of it, as though her heart might fly out of her body. She couldn't help it. She started to clap.

The deep gray eyes of the girl in the splits went wide with shock, and seven heads swiveled to stare. For the space of a heartbeat nothing stirred; even the rhythm seemed to hitch. Then all seven of them pushed off into the air, somersaulting in prisms of color over the heads of the crowd.

Without thinking, Maddy grabbed her skateboard and turned to push her way out of the drum circle after them. They were waiting for her, ribbons of sand sloughing from their skin to form little mounds on the beach. Maddy raced up and then stood there, unsure what to say.

Finally, one of the dancers spoke, and his voice was like faraway waves. "You can see us?" he asked.

"Yes," Maddy said, a little breathlessly.

All but one of them—the tallest one, who was standing in front with crossed arms—broke into peals of laughter that sounded like the clicking of lobster claws. The dancer who had spoken to her did a pirouette in the air, landed gracefully on another's shoulders, and bent down to kiss the top of Maddy's head.

"Come, hurry!" he cried. "Before we are gone!" The dancers turned as one—all but the tall dancer in the front, who frowned at Maddy first—and ran, leaping through the air in long, wide-legged ballet leaps, shedding glittering sand as they began to dissolve.

Fireworks exploded inside Maddy. This time, she wasn't

going to let something magic get away. She took off after them, not even caring that her heart was racing or that her vision might start to go dark at the edges, not even caring that what she was supposed to do when this happened was stop and take a pill and lie down until she felt normal again.

But she wasn't normal. If she was honest with herself, she had never been normal. For it was only then, with a strange but familiar rhythm pulsing through her veins, that Maddy was drenched with the unshakable certainty that she had been here before.

3

Maddy caught up to the sand dancers at the mouth of a pier that jutted out over the water like a long runway with a rounded end. All seven of them were in deep discussion, huddled together in the kind of circle that Maddy had learned to avoid in group homes. The dancers were dissolving steadily now, so from certain angles they looked simply like swirls of sand. Maddy stumbled up to them, holding her side and panting, her feet burning and tired. Running in sand was hard!

"Um . . . hi," said Maddy, the words fumbling out of her. She had never actually had a conversation with magic before, and suddenly she didn't know what to say. "That was, um, that was amazing!"

The tall dancer, the one who had frowned at her, stepped forward, her lovely features pressed into a look of distrust. "We can't talk to you," she said flatly. Sand poured from her.

"But, Josi," said the one who had spoken before. "She can see us! She should go down the pier, just in case—"

"Be quiet, Emmon!" snapped Josi. "You know we're not supposed to interact with anyone new. We're probably already in trouble. We'd better get Vanessa."

The other sand dancers murmured uncertainly. But Emmon shook his head and said, "No. I'm tired of waiting. She can *see* us!" He did a flip and landed in front of Maddy, the smell of sea on his skin. "Go down the pier," he said softly. "Just . . . just try."

Maddy glanced at the pier. It was long and keyhole-shaped, with tall iron gates marking its entrance. The gates were wide open, but chains dangling from them told her they must be locked at some point. The pier had short concrete walls topped with wooden railings and was lined with lampposts, seagulls perched on top of almost every one. A blue wooden lifeguard station on stilts stood just inside the gates. Beneath the pier, surfers bobbed in the water near the pilings, watching the waves.

Maddy turned back to the dancers, about to ask what was special about the pier, but where Emmon had been there was now a small pile of sparkling sand.

"Wait!" cried Maddy as more of the dancers disappeared. She had so many questions! "Are you . . . is this . . . you *are* real, right?"

It wasn't what she had meant to ask, of course. As soon as

the question left her lips, she wished that she could grab it back. There was so much else she wanted to know, so many better questions than that one, but it was too late. Only Josi remained now, and she leaned in so close that Maddy could count the ragged rows of pointed, bluish teeth. Maddy took a step back.

It was the first time she could ever remember stepping *away* from magic. She wasn't sure she liked it.

"Define *real*," said Josi, and then she winked out and was gone.

Maddy stared at the spot where Josi had been, and then turned to look down the pier. She was still a little shaken, but the pier looked perfectly normal, the way it should look on a crowded summer weekend. Tourists snapped photos, skateboarders and inline skaters wove through openings in the crowd, and fishermen leaned on the railing to watch their lines in the water. At the end of the pier, where it opened into a large circle, two benches sat back-to-back. And just past the end of the pier, a fog bank was drifting in, strange and white like the fog that had enveloped the bus driver.

Tug, went her heart.

The fog crept closer, playing tricks with the sunlight. It made the end of the pier look as though it were bathed in a soft magenta light. A shirtless lifeguard in red shorts and a whistle around his neck came down from his tower and explained to a family with a gaggle of small children that yes, there was a fog bank coming in, but no, they didn't have to worry as there were never summer storms in Venice.

The lifeguard was wrong. Maddy could sense the storm coming by the way the rhythm of the air had changed. A wisp of fog swirled by her like drifting smoke. At the end of the pier, the odd magenta glow shifted to indigo.

A thrill of anticipation raced up Maddy's spine. She loved storms. Hugging her skateboard, she stepped through the iron gates onto the pier.

"Theydies and gentlethems . . ." whispered a voice.

Maddy froze. A cool breeze lifted her hair from her shoulders and picked up bits of fishing wire and plastic and tinfoil from the ground, spinning them into miniature tornadoes. She took another step.

". . . elders and wee ones . . ."

Maddy could hardly breathe now, and her heart pounded against her ribs. One more step.

". . . and especially those between and betwixt and more than the sum of their parts . . ."

Without really knowing why, Maddy broke into a run toward the end of the pier. At the same time, the storm hit, the summer storm that Venice never had. Waves that had been light and playful were suddenly at full roar, crashing into the pier, sending spray onto Maddy's skin like a damp kiss. Wind buffeted her and her feet slapped out a rhythm on the concrete; people around her jumped out of her way, shouting, "Slow down!" and "Look out!" The lifeguard had grabbed a red buoy from the side of the tower and was rushing people back to their cars, alternating between blowing his whistle and shouting directions.

Maddy ran faster, shivers running across her whole body as she pushed against the people streaming the other way. Her feet played a backbeat against the concrete, a drumbeat of expectation. Below her in the now-choppy sea, surfers climbed out of the water, their wetsuits shining like sealskin. She ducked around a balding man as the wind lifted his baseball cap from his head. For a moment, Maddy could swear it became a top hat.

The wind and fog engulfed her and she leaned into the feel of the storm on her skin. The last of the people fishing at the end of the pier hurried past, their poles whipping in the wind as a wave crashed over the railing. Maddy sidestepped the water and kept running. At the end of the pier, the light turned a deep, perfect purple.

Behind her, something yowled.

Still running, Maddy looked back. A low shape was swirling out of the fog, taking form as the huge tawny cat she had seen earlier from the bus window. It was hurtling toward her at full speed. She had just enough time to think that a cat in a storm was perhaps the strangest thing yet—didn't cats hate water?— but then the cat began to grow. Its body filled out, becoming more and more muscled, and the fur around its head darkened into a thick, majestic mane. Its face broadened and took on a sleek fierceness. The two ridges of fur along its back stretched and feathered, forming copper-colored wings that beat against the wind—once, twice, three times—easily lifting what was now a winged lion into the air. Maddy gasped as it overtook her, flying so close that she could see the water droplets beading like miniature worlds on its fur. Its paws were the size of tires, its tail a tufted whip.

"Wait!" cried Maddy, flinging out one arm to . . . do what? Grab a gigantic flying lion in midair? The lion soared past, smelling of musk and wetness. It did not wait.

Maddy's skin felt electric, as though it might light up of its own accord, and she was almost ill with excitement. Moisture from the fog gathered on her eyelashes and sent rainbow prisms dancing in her vision. A trash can tipped onto its side, shreds of paper and plastic flying from its mouth as it rolled. Off in the sea, a swell like a wall of water began to form.

The light at the end of the pier turned a rich gold.

"Wait!" screamed Maddy again. But the storm ripped the word from her mouth as the winged lion flew straight over the pier railing and into the wall of water barreling toward them, disappearing behind it.

Maddy raced to the end of the pier, heaving for breath as she let the railing catch her. Wind and fog and salt water clawed at her eyes, but even so she could see the immense wall of water building above her—the immense wall of water that was about to crash down on top of her. She dropped her skateboard and tucked into herself as everything flashed into slow-motion dreaminess: the rolling of the wave as it crested, the small fish silhouetted inside of it, the blue of the water changing to a translucent green.

And then it crashed. Maddy cried out as the wave broke on top of her, as the force of it tore her from the railing and tumbled her into the center of the keyhole end of the pier and drenched her in . . .

. . . glitter?

Wincing, Maddy slowly uncurled herself and rose to stand, shedding blue and silver sparkles. The fog had settled into a dome around the end of the pier, cutting off the rest of the world. She could still hear the wind, still feel the pier shake as wave after wave slammed into it, but the storm itself was outside, distant and muted like a watercolor version of itself.

For a moment, nothing stirred. And then a pop like a muffled firecracker sounded, and another, and another. White lights blazed to life around the pier railing until the entire circular end of the pier was ringed in lights.

It looked like nothing so much as the round stage of a big top.

"Welcome . . ." The whisper floating on the fog was marred with static. *". . . to a world beyond your wildest dreams. To spellbinding feats and astonishing deeds, to wonders of land and wonders of sea, all offered for your amusement and edification."*

Maddy pushed her hair, wet with fog and salt water, out of her eyes, and her hand came back coated in glitter the color of the sea. More glitter eddied in circles at her feet.

"What is this?" she asked quietly.

The wind died as fast as it had come, sending shredded trash raining down like confetti. In the sudden quiet, an arc of white lights flashed to life in the sky above her:

IL CIRCO DELLE STRADE RINGMASTER: THE EMINENT SIGNOR ZAVALA

"Close your mouth!" screeched a seagull that had swooped in out of the fog. "Where were you raised, a barn?"

Maddy snapped her mouth shut. At the same time, a few of the white lights sputtered and died, and then a few more.

"Um," said Maddy. "Right. Um. Hi." She pointed at the lights above her. "Do you know what that says?"

"The Circus of the Streets," said the seagull. "It's Eye-talian, dummy. Ain'tcha got no culture?"

Then it pooped on her.

"Ew!" cried Maddy as the gull took off again. Scrunching her face, she looked around for something she could use to clean her arm, finally settling on a piece of shredded napkin. In the distance, she could hear the seagull laughing.

"It's not funny!" Maddy yelled into the fog.

"Ha, is too!" came the gull's voice. "Oops! Here comes Vanessa. Gotta scram before she puts me to work. See ya, wouldn't wanna be ya!"

Roller-skating toward Maddy was an incredibly tall woman, as tall as the lampposts and almost as skinny. She wore a cropped white tank top, dark blue short-shorts, and light blue leg warmers that were pulled all the way up her legs like unfinished knitted tights. Glittery water splashed from the wheels of her blue skates, which were decorated with bright white lightning bolts on the sides, and her wavy blond hair flowed around her shoulders and danced across her turquoise eyes as though caught in an underwater current. Her skin was pale with a light golden tan . . . and she was also somewhat transparent. As she drew closer, the woman shrank in height, so by the time she reached Maddy, she was only as tall as a very tall person.

"Hello!" said the woman in a high, sweet voice.

Surreptitiously, Maddy tried to wipe the last of the seagull poop from her arm. "Um . . . hi," she said.

"You should leave that, you know," said the woman. "It's good luck."

Maddy stared at her doubtfully. "It's gross."

"Sometimes luck is like that," said the woman. "Besides, you lit the marquee, so you must be lucky! However did you do it?"

They both looked up at the marquee. More of the lights had burned out, so now it read:

IL C CO ELLE STR DE R MA TER: THE MIN T S GNOR I ALA

"I didn't do anything." Maddy looked around for a trash can, but all of them had tipped over. So instead, she placed the napkin carefully on the ground. She felt bad about littering, but not bad enough to keep holding that napkin. "The, um, mark-thingy lit on its own."

"Nonsense." The woman wasn't entirely transparent after all; it was more as though someone had started to erase her but had gotten bored halfway through. "The marquee only lights when there's going to be a new show. It's been dark over a year now, ever since the Ringmaster went away. A year, I tell you! It used to light all the time, practically every day and night. But now, well, the performers have completely lost heart, poor things, and I can't even tell you how terrible I feel about that. After all, I'm the Muse of Venice. I'm supposed to bring inspiration. But how can there be inspiration when we can't have any new shows?" The woman stuck out her hand. "I'm Vanessa. Pleased to meet you."

"I'm Maddy." Maddy shook Vanessa's hand. "What's a muse?"

"You've never heard of us?" Vanessa sounded a little sad. "Muses are responsible for all the inspiration in the world!

Without us, nothing gets created. We suggest new ideas, bring flashes of insight, conjure up feverish visions and brilliance. Are you *sure* you've never heard of us?"

"Oh, *that* kind of muse," said Maddy hastily, not wanting Vanessa to feel bad. "I guess I just forgot. Um . . . you're who the sand dancers went to get, right?"

"Sand dancers? Oh! You mean the Ichthyquilibrists!" It sounded like ick-theee-QUILL-uh-brists. "Aren't they spectacular? It's their spines, you know, cartilage and not bone. Way more bendy. Yes, that's me. They told me you could see them, and so of course I had to come right away. And now you've lit the marquee! So tell me, Maddy . . ." Vanessa clasped her hands together eagerly. "Who *are* you?"

Maddy shook her head, confused. "I'm Maddy," she said.

"Well, of course you are," said Vanessa. "That's not what I mean, though. I mean in terms of the circus, who are you?" The muse shifted her weight to one foot so her hip stuck out like a supermodel pose. "Performer?" she asked, ticking things off on her fingers as she spoke. "Audience? Maybe maintenance?"

One of the bulbs in the first letter C exploded, sending a faint scorched smell into the air.

"Alrighty, then," said Vanessa, just as cheerfully. "Not maintenance. Food service?"

"No . . . I mean, I don't think so. I don't think I'm any of those things." Maddy waved her hand, taking in the marquee, the pier, and the tall, semitransparent muse herself. "What is all this? Where am I?"

Vanessa tilted her head to one side. "It's the circus. What did you think it was?"

"Venice Beach," answered Maddy truthfully. She hadn't meant to be funny, but Vanessa laughed.

"Oh my, of course it is! They're one and the same, Venice and Il Circo delle Strade." Vanessa said the name of the circus with an Italian accent, so it sounded like *ill chair-co della straday.* "It's just that everyone can see the city itself, but only those who truly love this place can see the circus *inside* the city. Il Circo is like . . . oh, let's see, how can I explain?" Vanessa began skating in slow, thoughtful circles around Maddy, her hands clasped behind her back. Maddy had to keep turning to watch her. "Il Circo is the city within the city, the show within the show. The streets are our stage and the Ringmaster is our leader. It's the true heart of this city, that's what it is."

"So . . . you're all part of a circus?" A lightness was growing inside Maddy. "You, the drummers, the Ickthee . . . um, the Ickitee . . ."

"Ick-theee-QUILL-uh-brists," Vanessa sounded out helpfully. "From the Greek *ichthus,* meaning fish, and the Italian *equilibrato,* meaning balanced. I helped name them. Don't you love it?"

"Yes," said Maddy, and the lightness gave way to something else, something that fizzed through her bright and sharp: a fleeting, unfamiliar taste of belonging. "I love everything here.

Is that why I can see the circus but other people can't? Is *that* why the marquee lit?"

Vanessa turned to skate in the other direction, reversing her circles around Maddy. "Well, now," she said. "That's a tricky question. Normally I would say yes, of course, because that's how it works. Anyone who wants to see the circus, who really looks for it, can see it. But before the Ringmaster left, he decreed No New Acts and No New Audience. Which is why I asked who you are, since no one new has seen us in so very long. If the Ringmaster were here, he'd probably be able to tell just by looking at you. Me, I'm not much good at categorizing and organizing, but I'll try. Let's see . . . are you feeling particularly inspired right now? Because if you're a performer, you would probably find being around a muse inspiring."

Maddy wasn't sure what inspiration should feel like. She had some vague idea that it was like a bulb lighting up in your head. Even so, she was fairly sure she wasn't a performer. She wasn't remotely daredevil-y; she had never even done a single trick on her skateboard and didn't want to. And once, one of the group homes had put on a concert and she had refused to come out from behind a potted fern the entire time. She had just sat there, hidden from everyone, and drummed along quietly, using the plant leaves as cymbals.

Performing involved a lot of Extra Attention.

Maddy wrapped her arms around herself, suddenly realizing how cold she was. Her tank top and shorts, which had been perfect for the sunny day she had expected, were far too thin for standing in damp fog. "Can I just be audience? I think I'd like that."

"To be honest, I don't even know why I'm asking," said Vanessa sadly, coming to a stop. "The truth is that you can't be anything as long as the Ringmaster's decrees are in effect. It's been just dreadful! I do so love Il Circo, and I do so love being a muse. It's just that . . . well, a circus with its Ringmaster gone, with no newness or innovation or anyone to plan shows or schedule acts or warm up the audience, is hardly a circus at all. We are on the verge of being . . . oh, I can hardly stand it . . . *boring*. Look!" Vanessa held out her arm. Maddy could see right through it. "I'm positively fading away!"

"You're not supposed to be like that?" asked Maddy.

"Supposed to be see-through? Dear me, no! Muses need to be visible so people can recognize us. Sure, sometimes we show up in flashes and sparks—that *is* fun—but mostly we appear because someone's invited us by working hard, by committing to what they are doing. It would be wrong to disrespect them by being only"—Vanessa looked down at herself and sighed—"partial. You can't have a circus without inspiration, you know, so if I disappear, well . . ." Her voice trailed off and she pushed a tendril of hair out of her face. "If I disappear, so does the circus."

"Forever?" asked Maddy, horrified.

"Forever," answered the muse.

Years in group homes had taught Maddy that it was usually

wiser to stay quiet and act as though you didn't care about anything, so she didn't have much experience at getting involved in things on purpose. But she took a deep breath and tried anyway.

"Maybe, um . . . maybe I could help?"

"Help?" Vanessa sounded confused.

"Help you fix whatever's wrong with the circus," Maddy rushed to explain. "So you can be solid again. I'm not sure what I can do, but if there's anything . . ." Maddy paused, alarmed. Vanessa's eyes were filling with sea-blue tears. "I'm sorry! I didn't mean—"

"No one ever asks a muse if we need help," said Vanessa, sniffing. "It's always, 'Muse, why don't I have any good ideas?' or 'Muse, why hast thou forsaken me?' when probably we're just out getting groceries or visiting a friend, same as you might on your time off." Three blue tears ran down her cheeks, plopped on the ground, and became three teeny tiny octopuses that tentacled across the pier, up the short wall, and over the railing to tumble into the sea. Maddy stared after them, openmouthed, as the muse continued. "Not that I'm complaining, mind you. I love my job. But for a human to offer to help one of *us* . . . well, that is just about the kindest thing I've ever heard." Vanessa picked up the crumpled seagull-poop napkin and blew her nose loudly. "If only you could bring back the Ringmaster. Ever since he left, nothing has been right."

Maddy wrenched her gaze away from where the tiny octopuses had been. "What exactly is wrong with the circus?"

"Well, that's part of the problem." Vanessa balled up the napkin and threw it up into the air, where it made a perfect arc. As if on cue, a seagull dove out of the fog, grabbed it, and took off with four other seagulls in hot pursuit. "We aren't really sure. It started a while ago . . . I'm not sure how long. Muses aren't very good at tracking time. We don't care about that, you see. Anyway, at first it was barely noticeable. The normal wear and tear, a set malfunctioning, an act falling apart. Performers taking ill or quitting unexpectedly. Nothing you'd really notice by itself, of course, but taken all together it was worrying. Il Circo was zigging when it should have zagged. This happens sometimes; you get off beat for a while and then you find your rhythm and lock back into place. Usually, I just send a nice blast of inspiration and all is well, but this time nothing seemed to help. I started fading, the audience dwindled to almost nothing . . . and the poor performers! They grew positively listless. Of course our Ringmaster was beside himself. We chose him to be the Ringmaster all those years ago because he loves the circus so. It's his job to protect Il Circo, to make sure it's strong and dynamic and extraordinary. Anyway, he set forth the decrees of No New Acts and No New Audience and then he left to bring Il Circo back to its full glory. He's been gone ever since."

After a lifetime of rules, Maddy couldn't help but be a little disappointed that there were such things as Circus Decrees. She had rather thought a circus would be exactly the opposite.

"This circus used to be so loud and merry," continued

Vanessa. "Such daredevils and dancers, such poets and prophets, such *fun*! And our Ringmaster was the boldest and grandest Ringmaster alive! We need him back."

"Maybe if you told him how much you miss him—"

"We can't," said Vanessa. "You see, when you become part of Il Circo, you don't just join the circus. You bind yourself to it for as long as you want to stay. It's an old and powerful magic that keeps the circus safe. Part of the binding is agreeing to follow the Ringmaster's rules. And right now, for whatever reason, he doesn't want to be found, and he's made that a rule, so no one who is bound can find him. It makes telling him anything a bit difficult."

"Everyone is bound?" This was the first thing Maddy had heard about the circus that made her uncomfortable. Suddenly she missed the sunshine, the warmth, the people. "What if someone who is bound wants to leave? Can they?"

"Of course!" Vanessa looked offended. "Everyone *chooses*. It's a circus, not a prison. People choose to be connected, and they choose if they want to leave. Bindings can break, you know. At least, most of them can."

"Are *you* bound?"

"Muses cannot be bound to anything," said Vanessa, "but we belong with our home territory and get weak when we leave. I have tried to go look for him, but every time I do, I get more transparent. You, though! You lit the marquee, and you can see us. As long as you're not bound, maybe you can find him."

"I don't think I'm bound," Maddy said slowly. "How would I know?"

"Do you have a tattoo?"

"I'm twelve!" said Maddy—and then, when the muse shrugged, added, "No!"

"Has a tall stranger appeared to you in a dream carrying a red surfboard?"

Maddy's dreams were vivid and technicolor, often filled with dark caverns or bright bursts of light, but never with surfing. She shook her head.

"Do you have an unremovable piece of jewelry?"

Maddy's hand flew to her bracelet. At the same time, in a dramatic explosion that showered them in white sparks, the rest of the marquee went dark.

5

"I don't understand," said Maddy, trying to get her bracelet off even though she knew it was no use. A lump had formed in the pit of her stomach and the smoke from the marquee smelled like blackened toast. For the first time since she had left the bus, she wondered if she had made the right choice. "How can I have a binding?"

Vanessa took Maddy's hand and looked at her bracelet. "It's not one of ours," she said, a small crease appearing between her eyebrows. "In fact, I've never seen anything quite like it."

Maddy pulled her hand back. Her whole life, she had thought of her bracelet as something special, a magical gift from a mother or father she had never known but who had loved her nonetheless. It had seen her through being parentless, through moving from group home to group home, through not belonging anywhere or to anyone. It had never once occurred to her that maybe the silver band was yet another thing in her life that had been done and decided without her having any say in the matter.

"Don't worry," said Vanessa, although Maddy thought the muse herself sounded a little worried. "I'm sure it's fine. The Ringmaster is an expert at bindings. When you find him, maybe he can tell you what it is."

"*If* I find him," said Maddy. She worked at the bracelet some more, trying to slide it over her hand.

"Here's an idea," said the muse in a pretend cheery voice. "Are you hungry? I'm hungry, and I just know some nice food will work wonders. Why don't you join me for lunch, and then you can meet a few of the other circus folks as well? There's always someone hanging out in the café."

The lump in Maddy's stomach roiled and grew. "Okay," she said in a small voice.

"I'll call the taxis," said Vanessa, still in that same careful, I'm-not-worried-in-the-slightest tone. She reached up, the top of her long arm disappearing into the mist. Immediately there was an outraged squawk as Vanessa pulled a very angry seagull out of the fog.

"Could you call the racing skulls, please?" Vanessa said sweetly to the gull. It replied with some extremely bad words that Maddy had only heard once before, when a group home leader was yelling at her assistant. The gull then tumbled away into the fog.

"The skulls will be here lickety-split." Vanessa leaned against the railing to take off her skates and socks, revealing toenails painted a bright sunshine yellow. She stuffed her socks into her skates, tied the laces together, and then hung the skates over one shoulder by their laces. "And look! Here they are!"

Two enormous skulls, each the size of a small boat, sailed toward them over the water. Maddy stopped fiddling with her bracelet to stare. Their craniums were smooth and polished, shiny in the bright fog, with eye sockets like small caves. One of them wore an eye patch. Eyepatch skull slammed violently into the other one, who retaliated by barreling into Eyepatch's jawbone. Both skulls paused, stunned.

Vanessa smiled. "They're a little competitive. Racing skulls do so love to win, you know. Yoo-hoo! Over here!"

The skulls snapped back into motion, jostling for position and coming to a stop right next to the pier. The tops of their heads didn't quite clear the pier railing.

"All aboard!" said Vanessa, and she hurdled the pier railing like a track star, landed perfectly on the top of one of the skulls, and sank gracefully into a cross-legged position. "I left you the pirate-y one. She's much jollier. To the circus café, please," she said to her skull.

Before Maddy could ask any reasonable questions, such as

how she was supposed to actually *get* aboard, Vanessa's skull had sped off into the fog.

Maddy looked at Eyepatch's smooth cranium and then down at the water. It seemed likely she might end up there, so she pulled her pill bottle out of her pocket and checked the lid. It was supposedly not only childproof but also waterproof. She knew the childproof part didn't work—she could open it easily—but hopefully the waterproof part did. At least it was tightly closed, so she put it back into her pocket and buttoned the pocket shut, just to be safe. Then she picked up her skateboard and climbed onto the pier railing, turning carefully to sit facing the skull with her feet dangling. When she reached down with her foot, she could almost touch the top of the racing skull—almost, but not quite.

She would just have to do her best. Hoping the polished bone wasn't as slippery as it looked, Maddy clamped her skateboard tightly under one arm and inched forward. Her toes brushed the top of the skull, and with a deep breath she slid off the railing. Her feet hit the top of the skull and, after a wobbly moment, she actually managed to find her balance. Grinning and proud of herself, she started to lower herself to sit . . . but apparently the skull thought she was ready and spun around, speeding out to sea.

Maddy lost her footing and slammed onto the top of the skull, her skateboard flying from her grasp. She cried out as she slid down the smooth bone, hands scrabbling for something to hold. As she fell past the eye socket, two blue-and-yellow tentacles shot forward from the dark opening. One of them caught her around the waist and she jerked to a stop just above the foaming sea, breath knocked out of her as though she had been punched in the stomach. The tentacle reeled her in like a fish, depositing her carefully in the eye socket, and a moment later the other tentacle drew in as well and dropped her skateboard at her feet. Shivering, Maddy scooped up her board and pushed herself deeper into the eye socket, as far from the opening as she could get.

Something tapped her shoulder.

Slowly, Maddy raised her eyes. A blue octopus with yellow spots was hanging from the top of the eye socket like a bouquet of tentacles. It climbed down, reached out, and straightened Maddy's shirt—which had gone askew in the fall—and then patted her on both cheeks. Its movements were slithery and low, like the world's strangest ice skater, and its skin rippled continuously, shifting both color and texture. Its pupils were horizontal slits, and a tube-like siphon opened and closed on the side of its head.

And then it began to tremble, its body stretching and morphing into something long and thin. What had been an octopus was now an exact replica of Maddy's skateboard, only with blue spots, sucker-y wheels, and a decidedly rubbery look.

"Wow," said Maddy. "That's, um . . . wow." She wasn't sure what else to say about an octopus that could turn into a skateboard. "Thank you for catching me. And my skateboard."

The octopus shuddered back to itself and tapped Maddy's chest with one tentacle. Somehow, she knew it was asking her name.

"Maddy," she said. She thought about shaking hands, but the math seemed too complicated. "What's yours?"

The octopus put one tentacle to its forehead in woe and collapsed onto the ground as though it were dead. Another tentacle morphed into a rose, which it placed on its chest. Then it peeked up at Maddy as though it were waiting for her to say something.

Maddy was terrible at charades, but she didn't want to let down the octopus who had just saved her.

"Your name is . . . Morgue?" she guessed.

The octopus shook its head and rose to stand on its tentacles, staggering about drunkenly, swooning and bumping into the walls of the eye socket.

"Klutz?" asked Maddy. "I'm sorry. I'm really, really bad at this."

With an annoyed squelch, the octopus dove out of the eye socket and plopped into the small pool of water gathered in the skull's jaw, sinking halfway into the churning foam that formed as the skull raced through the water. Then it turned a morbid shade of white, bloated itself to twice its size, and bobbed on the surface as though dead.

"Um . . . Driftwood?"

Just then Maddy's pirate skull pulled up next to Vanessa's,

and the muse glanced over and clapped her hands. "Oh, lovely," Vanessa called over the rush of the water. "You found Ophelia! She's the only mimic octopus I ever cried. All my other tears have been common octopuses, but Ophelia's from a particularly happy moment, so I think that's why. Ask her to mimic something! She's amazing!"

Maddy looked down at Ophelia, who had stopped trying to be a drowned Shakespearean character and was now clinging to the side of the skull. She couldn't think of a single thing to ask for. "Ophelia, what's your favorite?"

Ophelia turned a pleased purple and stretched across the skull's clattering teeth to form tall white letters.

"Cool," said Maddy, impressed. "The Hollywood Sign."

Ophelia squelched proudly and climbed back into the eye socket, plopping down on Maddy's skateboard and running her tentacles over the wheels as though trying to figure them out. Her whole body seemed to breathe.

"Do you like it?" asked Maddy. "It's really fun. I bet you've never been skateboarding, have you? If you want, I'll take you when we get back."

Ophelia cycled excitedly through several neon colors.

"It's a deal," said Maddy.

"Ahoy!" cried Vanessa. "Thar she blows!"

A three-mast sailing ship floated in the open sea ahead of them, with jade-green sails and a hull painted in blue and yellow circus stripes. Its name was stenciled in dark blue letters across the stern: *SHIP OF FOODS*—and then underneath it, in smaller letters: *The Galley of the Marvelous, proudly serving Il Circo delle Strade since 1905.* A wooden figurehead of a woman with long tendrils of hair and blue leg warmers extended from the bow.

"Is that you?" asked Maddy.

Vanessa turned a deep, sunburned red. "Yes, well, you know how it is," she said bashfully. "Muse and all. Part of the job."

The two racing skulls floated over to the Ship of Foods, which had clearly seen better days. The circus ship listed to one side, the letters were peeling and faded, and the deck looked like it could use a good scrubbing.

"You can leave your things in the skull," said Vanessa, tucking her skates into the eye socket and stepping gracefully onto the deck. "They'll wait for us while we eat."

Maddy went to slide her skateboard, with Ophelia still on it, deeper into the eye socket, but the octopus wrapped one tentacle questioningly around Maddy's ankle, turned a hopeful shade of lavender, and quivered like a puppy waiting to go on a walk. Maddy knew the octopus was asking if she could come with them.

"I'd love it," she said, and she held out one arm.

Ophelia flashed bright blue and scampered up Maddy's arm to perch on her shoulder like the world's most rubbery parrot. Maddy clambered off her skull and followed Vanessa down a short flight of stairs into the noisy ship's galley. The same dreamlike feeling of being here before washed over her, everything seeming vaguely familiar. That, along with having a mimic octopus riding on her shoulder, made it hard to stop smiling. But at the door to the circus café, the grin slipped off her face.

The room had gone quiet, everyone staring at her: a short, stout man in a spangled bathing suit with huge snakes wrapped around his arms and neck; a group of unicyclists with their unicycles propped up next to them; the troupe of Ichthyquilibrists looking up from a puzzle they had gathered around.

Maddy swallowed hard, and Ophelia turned an indignant stop-sign red.

"Everybody, this is Maddy," said Vanessa proudly. Somehow the ceilings, which didn't seem that tall, had stretched to accommodate Vanessa's full height. "Maddy, this is everybody. Or, at least, everybody who is here at the moment. There are a lot more everybodies who are other places right now."

The man with the snakes, who was sitting all by himself—possibly because the spangled gold bathing suit was all he was wearing, or possibly because his snakes were really quite large—spoke first. His face was round and his short, tightly curled black hair was oiled and shiny.

"You lit the marquee," he said, and even though his voice was soft and whispery, it carried clearly through the room.

"That was you?" cried someone who was juggling several plates, a saltshaker, and a very excited small dog. "I *thought* I felt the marquee light. But how can that be? Is the Ringmaster back?"

In the group of Ichthyquilibrists, Josi pushed her chair away from the table with a screech that sent shivers down Maddy's neck. Ophelia scrunched up to about half her usual size.

"We would know if he were back," said Josi, rising. "And he's not, so no one should be lighting the marquee. The marquee means a new show, and a new show goes against the decrees." She crossed her arms and stared at Maddy. "Are you going against our Ringmaster?"

"No one is going against anyone," said Vanessa in the soothing kind of voice you use to talk to an angry cat. "It's just . . . the marquee lit. It's exciting! Don't you think it's exciting? Maybe the circus is better!"

"The circus isn't better," said a voice near Maddy's ear. Maddy jumped and turned to see a woman covered in tattoos standing on the stairs behind them. Curly brown hair streaked with blue fell to her shoulders, multiple earrings shone from her ears, and a series of jeweled bracelets ran up each of her arms. She also had an orange chainsaw slung over her shoulder. "We would know if the circus was better. Excuse me, please," she added.

"So sorry, Adela," said Vanessa. "We're blocking the way. Come on, Maddy, let's get some food. Better to talk about this on a full stomach anyway."

"After you," said Adela, giving Maddy a faint smile. "And

Ophelia, mi corazón, good morning."

Ophelia blushed the same orange as Adela's chainsaw as they followed Vanessa into the room. Maddy swallowed hard. Years of being in group homes had made her used to walking into places where everyone stared, but she still didn't like it. The best thing to do was to keep your head up and pretend you didn't notice, unless someone smiled at you. Then it was okay to smile back.

No one smiled at her. Maddy felt her cheeks go hot and she fought to look straight ahead until they got to the buffet, which wound around the room.

"Eat up!" said Vanessa. "It's on me."

Maddy took a tray and eyed the buffet in front of her. Most of it didn't look like food at all. The first dish wobbled like gelatin but also kept changing size; the next looked like golf balls with spikes and made horrible high-pitched shrieking sounds. Something that looked like a living ice cube snapped at her and almost got her finger. Ophelia took some round patties that smelled like fish and tucked them under her tentacles. Vanessa went right to a pastry case filled with shards of glowing light that ricocheted around, leaving glowing smears on the glass. The muse caught a peach-colored shard and a crimson one, wrapped them in twine that hung by the side of the case, and dropped them onto her tray. Then she added a bowl of crunchy brown letters.

"Light, color, and letters!" sang Vanessa. Her voice still had that I'm-trying-not-to-worry sound. "My fav-o-rite!"

Maddy breathed a sigh of relief as she finally came to food she recognized. She passed by the slabs of raw steak, trying not to think about who those were for, and piled her tray with cheese pizza, mango slices, and chocolate pudding with whipped cream. She couldn't wait to eat.

"All set?" asked Vanessa. "Anyone want anything else? How about a nice frozen lemonade? Or, Ophelia, perhaps a saltwater bath to enjoy while you eat?"

Ophelia turned an affirmative yellow.

"Wonderful. Liquids are right behind you. Help yourself, and I'll ring us up."

At the end of the buffet sat an old-fashioned golden cash register with its money drawer open. No one seemed to be working it, and there was no money in the drawer. Vanessa pulled a shimmering strand of hair from her head and dropped it into the drawer, which instantly slammed shut. A moment later the register dinged and the drawer popped open again, empty.

"Just between you and me," whispered Vanessa as Ophelia used her tentacles to fill a trough with salt water, "there were probably at least ten good ideas in that strand of hair, far more than three lunches are worth. I do like to be generous, though. When the mood strikes, that is." She nodded to the man with the snakes. "Dov? May we join you?"

Dov gathered several snakes off a chair and gestured for them to sit.

"Dov is our resident snake charmer," said Vanessa. "He has the most amazing voice. He never has to speak loudly to be heard. And his snakes are the best I've ever seen! Sometimes they do this thing where they change colors and—"

"I do not charm them," interrupted Dov in his quiet voice. "I just make sure they are allowed to be what they are."

Vanessa leaned into Maddy. "He totally charms them," she said in a loud stage whisper. "It's just that they charm him, too."

Maddy smiled. She loved snakes. One of them, brown-and-green banded, slithered up and touched her arm with its thin tongue. Ophelia, though, didn't seem quite as sure; she dragged her saltwater bath as far from Dov and the snakes as possible before climbing in, tentacles draped over the sides.

"How did you know about the marquee lighting?" Maddy asked as the snake flowed over her arm and back to Dov.

"We feel the call to showtime when it lights," said Dov. "But it's been so long since we had a new show, none of us were really sure."

"A year," said Adela, setting a steaming mug of coffee on the table. "A very, very, *very* long year." She unslung the chainsaw from her shoulder and placed it carefully next to the coffee. She was all curves and muscles, her black tank top showing off the tattoos that rode up her arms and chest.

"No food, Adela?" asked Vanessa.

Adela sat, took a sip of her coffee, and shook her head. "I am tired of the same menu, day after day. Until the Ringmaster comes back to change our menus, I will find my food elsewhere."

"The Ringmaster does all the cooking?" Maddy asked. She had thought Ringmasters just announced the acts.

"The Ringmaster oversees everything," said Adela. "He doesn't cook, but he does set the menus. That way, we can be sure there is something here for everyone in the circus."

"I'm sure he would have left some other menus if he thought he would be gone this long," said Vanessa, unwrapping the peach light and taking a bite. Colored beams streamed out of her mouth.

Maddy stared at the chainsaw as she ate her pizza. Its handle was bright orange and its blade gleamed as though newly polished. As Maddy watched, a bendy arm grew out of the chainsaw's base, reached forward, and stole a piece of mango from Maddy's plate.

"Manners, Edith," chided Adela. "So sorry. She just loves anything orange." Edith the chainsaw whirled contritely and placed the mango slice, now dotted with machine oil, back on Maddy's plate. "So, Maddy. You lit the marquee, but the Ringmaster is not back. A call to a new show when new shows are not allowed . . . how can this be?"

Maddy could feel the other performers in the café pretending not to listen. "I don't know," she said. "It just lit. By itself."

From the back of the café, Josi snorted. "It doesn't just light by itself," she said. "The Ringmaster has to light it. Something isn't right. Vanessa, you shouldn't have brought her here."

"Vanessa can do whatever she likes," said Dov in his soft voice.

"*None* of us should be doing *anything* without the Ringmaster's permission!" snapped Josi. Everyone was listening openly now.

"Vanessa is our muse," said Adela firmly. "Muses don't need permission."

Josi cocked her head, and Maddy could feel the sand dancer's eyes boring into her. "She shouldn't be here," repeated Josi in a tone that meant you had better be careful.

Despite hating Extra Attention, a spark of anger knifed through Maddy. She set her jaw and stared back at Josi, forcing herself not to blink. After a moment, she saw a flash of something—irritation? respect?—in the sand dancer's eyes.

Adela, however, had risen from her seat. Three small piercings above her eyebrow caught the light. "What do you suggest we do, Josi? Sit and wait, as we have sat and waited for so long? I don't wish to leave the circus, but if things continue this way for much longer . . ." At this, Adela turned partway around so Maddy could see her back. There, high on her right shoulder, was a dark blue tattoo of a winged lion inside a circle, the same majestic lion Maddy had seen earlier on the pier. The lion's feathered wings were spread wide, their tips reaching outside the circle. The tattoo was gorgeous but it was starting to fade, and the ink looked old and weatherworn.

"The binding tattoo," Vanessa whispered to Maddy.

Adela nodded. "Yes. As you can see, my commitment is starting to waver. Edith here"—Adela turned back and laid a protective hand on the chainsaw, which quivered at her touch—"is bored." A collective gasp came from the café, but Adela kept speaking. "*I* am bored. Our audience, at least those who even realize we still exist, is bored."

"I'm kind of bored too, actually," called one of the Ichthyquilibrists from the back. Josi whipped her head around and glared, but the sand dancer who had spoken just tossed their hair over one scaled shoulder and said, "What? I am. We can't try anything new or even add anyone to our act. All we can do are the same acts over and over, with the same tricks and the same audience who's seen us a million times. What's fun about that?"

"But this is what I'm trying to tell you," said Vanessa, who had gone pale at the word *bored*. "Maddy offered to help find the Ringmaster and ask him to come back!"

"Finally!" called one of the unicyclists.

"Tell him we're all bored!" added the sand dancer. Maddy glanced at Vanessa, who seemed to become slightly sadder and more transparent with each mention of boredom.

"And hungry," added the juggler, winking at Adela. The small excited dog barked in agreement.

"What is *wrong* with all of you?" cried Josi, hands on hips. "You know we can't go look for him! You know the rules. He doesn't want us to find him, and as long as we choose to stay, we do what the Ringmaster says."

"But Maddy is not bound," pointed out Dov.

Maddy's hand went to her bracelet, and she glanced at Vanessa. Ever so slightly, Vanessa shook her head, as if to say, *No need to tell them. It's not one of ours.*

"And even if you do find him," Josi continued, swinging back around to glare at Maddy, "what then? So you ask him to come back. So what? Don't you think he *knows* we need him? If he wanted to come back, he would already *be* here."

Maddy opened her mouth, not even sure what she was going to say. But before she could speak, something shifted and hiccuped, a tiny tear in the fabric of time. Everyone seemed to feel it, and the whole café turned toward the door.

There, sitting on his haunches, was the winged lion.

Maddy drew in her breath as whispers flew through the room: *It's Kuma . . . the Ringmaster's lion . . . but . . . all alone? Without the Ringmaster?*

He was beautiful . . . and he was staring right at Maddy. She felt as though she had disconnected from the earth, as though all that existed were her and the chair that held her and the winged lion in the doorway. Slowly, she rose and took a tentative step toward the lion.

"If we needed a sign that this girl is here to help," said Adela, her face softening in a way that made her look much, much younger, "I believe it has just appeared."

Kuma unfurled his wings, spreading them as wide as they were on Adela's tattoo—and as he did, time stretched and paused, just enough to give a girl and a wild animal a moment alone. Everything and everyone else just *stopped*, frozen in an instant outside of the one she and the winged lion inhabited.

Maddy kept her eyes on the lion as she walked toward him. Up close, he was larger than she could have imagined, and his topaz eyes were the size of dinner plates.

"It's you," Maddy said. She ached to throw her arms around his neck but didn't think it would be welcome. "You brought me here, didn't you?"

Kuma flicked his tail. "I cannot tell you where he is," he said by way of no-answer. "For we are loyal, he and I."

"But you'll help." Maddy was certain of it. Suddenly, finding a Ringmaster who didn't want to be found seemed less impossible. "You're his lion, right? It's what they're all saying. You wouldn't be here if you didn't want to help."

Kuma's ears flattened against his head. "I am not *his*. We are each other's. He belongs to me as much as I belong to him. We have been together for a lifetime of catnip and wine, a universe of words and roars. Together we have run through the streets and slept in the sand. Together we have protected this city and this circus."

"Why are you crying?" asked Maddy. She reached out, thinking to wipe away the tear that ran down the lion's cheek, but then thought better of it and pulled back her hand.

"I'm not crying," said Kuma, even though he clearly was, and he made a show of licking his paw. "The place where the Ringmaster must stay is without sunshine, without open spaces. He is human and can survive there, albeit not happily. But I am feline and cannot, for it shatters my soul to be where I cannot run or bask or hunt. I stay by his side as much as I can, but I am nearing the end of my strength to live in such a place. Soon I will have to leave him for longer, and this I cannot bear."

Slowly, carefully, still not sure if it was okay, Maddy placed her hand on Kuma's head, between his ears where cats liked to be scratched. What would it be like to love someone so fully? What would it be like to have them love you back the same way? She could hardly imagine it, and her heart tore open with wanting. "Tell me what to do."

The lion let her hand rest on his head a moment before shaking it off, but Maddy thought he looked just the slightest bit pleased. "You are not bound to him, and yet you see us. Perhaps you can help him come home. To find him, you must ride the Race Thru the Clouds. It will bring you to him. And then, perhaps you will know what needs to be done, and perhaps you will be the one to do it." Kuma lifted his great head and sniffed the air, which now smelled to Maddy faintly of grasslands and freedom. "I cannot hold time for us any longer," he said. "It is a conundrum, this doorway of time. I can never decide whether to go in or stay out."

And before Maddy could even ask what the Race Thru the Clouds was, or how she was supposed to ride it, Kuma padded past her to the buffet, grabbed the largest piece of raw steak in his jaws, then turned and galloped up the stairway. Maddy raced up after him just in time to see him spread his copper wings and soar out to sea.

6

Time resumed.

Vanessa turned to Maddy, her turquoise eyes wide. "Did he stop time for you? Oh, he did, didn't he? Stopping time is his magic, it's how he talks to people when he's not with the Ringmaster. If he stopped time for you, then you *must* be someone who can help."

Maddy nodded, wishing she could hold the conversation close like a much-adored toy, but everyone was watching. She cleared her throat. "What's the Race Thru the Clouds?"

"Only the best roller coaster in the world!" The sand dancer who had said they were bored somersaulted over a table to get to Maddy. "Lucky you! I've always wanted to get chosen for it!"

"Calm down, Shishi," said Josi, rolling her eyes. "It's just a ride."

"It is not *just a ride*," exclaimed Shishi. "It's the fastest ride *ever*! And it's not only a roller coaster, it's also a *race*! Isn't that just the *best*?"

"Um . . ." said Maddy. Why did it have to be a roller coaster? She hated roller coasters, and she also hated racing. Going that fast made her feel as though she had lost herself somewhere along the way and was moving too quickly to even start a search party. Plus, she wasn't supposed to go on rides like that anymore, not with her new heart condition. And so she focused on something else that Shishi had said. "*You have to get chosen to ride?*"

"Here's the deal." Shishi jumped onto Maddy's table, slid into the splits, and leaned forward onto their elbows. Ophelia climbed out of her saltwater bath and spread all eight of her tentacles in a cephalopod version of the splits. "The Ballerina Clown has to okay you to race, and that creepy clown hardly ever okays *anybody*. But if you win, the race takes you wherever you want to go." Shishi sighed dreamily, eyes shining. "You're so lucky. Promise you'll come back and tell me all about it?"

Maddy was getting more and more confused. "I have to get permission from a *clown*?"

Vanessa stood up. "Yes," she said. "Although our Annie's more than just a clown. But if this is the plan, we'd best go now. The Race closes at sunset."

They said their goodbyes and boarded the skulls. Back in the eye socket with Ophelia, Maddy watched the sea as the skulls rushed back, thinking about races and roller coasters, about circus cafés and chainsaws. The skulls dropped them off just inside the surf zone, where it was shallow enough for Maddy to stand but not so shallow that the skulls risked getting stuck. Not a single person turned to look at them. The beach had grown crowded again, the storm long gone, and the late afternoon sun sent shadows dancing across the sand. Rollerskates draped over her shoulder, Vanessa leaped off her skull, ducked to avoid some low-flying pelicans, and then stepped easily over several surfers and three people playing catch, and still no one looked. Maddy slid off Eyepatch skull into cool, ankle-deep water— Ophelia on her shoulder and skateboard in hand—and bent down to unwrap a strand of seaweed from her foot. By the time she straightened up, Vanessa was clear across the beach. Maddy rushed to catch up.

"Whoops!" said Vanessa, stopping to wait for her. "I forgot you can't walk at muse speed. Here, take my hand. It'll go much faster."

Maddy slipped her hand into Vanessa's and they stepped forward, one single step that carried them all the way across the beach to a parking lot jammed with cars and people.

No one so much as blinked at a girl with an octopus on one shoulder or the tall, partially transparent woman wearing blue leg warmers. No one had seemed to notice the racing skulls, either. In the books Maddy read, there were plenty of stories about magical things made to look normal and everyday. It even had a name.

"Are we glamoured?" asked Maddy as they took another step that covered two city blocks.

Vanessa turned the color of blanched coral. "Heavens, no! What a dreadful idea. Why would you ask such a thing?"

Maddy shrugged, liking the cool weight of Ophelia on her shoulder. "No one seems to see us."

"Of course they don't. People see what they expect to see. Always have, always will. We don't need any special magic for that."

"Oh." Maddy had rather liked the idea of being glamoured.

"Glamoured," muttered Vanessa. "We're a street circus, thank you very much. It's grit that covers us, not glamour."

Maddy ducked her head to hide her smile as they took one more step to land on the corner of a busy intersection. There, mounted over the door of the building across from them, was a gigantic statue.

"Ta-da," said Vanessa proudly, gesturing to the statue. "Our very own Ballerina Clown!"

Maddy stared. The statue was at least three stories tall. The Ballerina Clown's white-gloved hands stretched gracefully to her sides, and one leg was raised in a frozen relevé. She wore a strapless blue leotard, a gray tutu, and red pointe shoes. Her face, though, was the face of a male hobo made up like a clown, complete with red clown nose, dark beard, floppy red hobo hat, and a single red tear trickling down the cheek. The wall behind her was purple and rippled and painted like a curtain illuminated by a spotlight.

Maddy loved her instantly.

"Clearance to the Race, please, Annie," Vanessa called out.

With a deafening crack, the Ballerina Clown detached herself from the side of the building and stepped down to the sidewalk, then walked on her toes over to them. She was taller than Vanessa by several feet. She bent over and patted Ophelia on the head with one giant white-gloved finger, and the mimic octopus turned a pleased shade of gray.

Then the Ballerina Clown raised her hands to the sky and spread her fingers wide.

"Jazz hands!" cried Vanessa, clapping. "I *love* jazz hands! I know it's retro of me," she whispered to Maddy, "but I can't help it."

Annie made a fist, drew it to her heart, took two little steps to the left, and fell to her knees like an overly dramatic rock star. Then she paused, as though waiting for an answer.

"She only speaks Interpretive Dance," Vanessa explained to Maddy, her features pinched into a mask of concentration. "Let me see . . . I think she said . . ." Her voice trailed off. "Hmmm. Manta rays like ice cream?"

The Ballerina Clown stood up, put her huge white-gloved fists on her hips, and swiveled her sad hobo head to glare at Vanessa.

"You don't have to get snippy with me," said Vanessa. "You know Interpretive Dance isn't my first language."

Maddy closed her eyes, tapping out the rhythm of the Ballerina Clown's dance with her foot: *TAP ta-ta TAP.* She could almost hear the question in the rhythm. And hadn't there been something a little bit why-ish about the hands, and a speedy, zoom-y kind of feeling in the two little hops?

"Can you say that again?" asked Maddy, opening her eyes. When the Ballerina Clown had finished, Maddy was sure she was right. She turned to Vanessa. "She wants to know why she should let me on the Race."

"You speak Interpretive Dance!" said Vanessa. "How marvelous!"

Maddy flushed, her face glowing with pride.

The Ballerina Clown tipped her hat at Maddy—although since the hat didn't come off, it was more like tipping her entire head. Then she did a series of dramatic flutter kicks, spun around with great meaning, and opened her eyes wide. Interpretive Dance was apparently *very* dramatic.

"I know, I know!" Vanessa raised her hand as though she were in school. "She said, 'Bicycle wheels should be tamed and well-fed.'"

Annie made a gesture toward Vanessa as if to say, *we never understand each other, but I love her anyway.*

"You want to know how I got here?" said Maddy to Annie.

Annie nodded and sank down to her knees, watching Maddy with painted-on eyes.

Maddy wasn't sure where to begin. She could usually tell which parts of her story grown-ups wanted to know by how they asked, but her Interpretive Dance wasn't good enough to catch the nuances. So she kept it as simple as she could. Ophelia tried to help, turning first into a small representation of the pier and then making her tentacles into sucker-y versions of Dov's snakes. When Maddy was finished, the Ballerina Clown rocked forward, pointed at Maddy, and reached one leg toward the sky.

Maddy looked down, tugging at her bracelet. "Vanessa asked me the same thing," she said quietly. "I'm just a kid. I'm not anyone special."

"Did she ask, *who are you?*" said Vanessa. The muse had sat down on the sidewalk to pull her skates back on, lacing them tightly as she spoke.

Maddy nodded. It seemed like such a simple question, and yet she still had no idea how to answer. "Can I go on the Race anyway?" she asked. "Even if I don't know?"

The Ballerina Clown went into a deep plié, sprang up en pointe, and then bent forward and touched Maddy gently on top of her head. Maddy smiled with relief.

"What did she say?" asked Vanessa, looking from Maddy to the Ballerina Clown.

"Yes," said Maddy, a bubbly, happy feeling rising inside her. "She said yes."

The Ballerina Clown started to grow. As she grew, she bent down and scooped up Maddy, Ophelia, and the skateboard in a hand that was now the size of a bed, then stood back up and kept growing until she was taller than the buildings, taller than the palm trees that lined the road. Maddy scooted to the side of Annie's hand to look down, and then scooted away again as she saw that Ophelia clearly didn't like being so close to the edge. The mimic octopus had covered her eyes with two tentacles and shriveled to the size of a tennis ball.

"Um . . . Vanessa?" Maddy called down from Annie's hand. The muse was a long way away. "Where are we going?"

"Don't worry!" Vanessa called back. "She's taking you to the Race! And you might need these." Vanessa pulled off her pale blue leg warmers, revealing another pair underneath them that were slightly lighter in color and less substantial, as though they had to grow into being. The muse rolled the leg warmers into a ball and threw them up to Maddy. "Catch!"

Maddy caught the leg warmer bundle, which was soft as kittens. "Thanks. But . . . why?"

"It's right in their name, dummy!" squawked a passing seagull. "Leg. Warmers. Duh!"

"They're filled with Muse Magic," called Vanessa, and the muse's voice sounded small and faraway. "You never know when that will come in handy."

"Plus, warm legs!" screeched the seagull.

Maddy slid on the leg warmers, pulling them all the way up to the bottom of her shorts just like Vanessa wore them. She knew she looked ridiculous and took a fierce pride in how much the other girls at the group home would tease her if they saw. Ophelia peeked through her tentacles, and then turned the bottom half of each tentacle a matching soft blue.

"One last thing," yelled Vanessa from below. "When you get to the Race, say what you mean and mean what you say. Ask carefully! Don't let the carny twist your words!"

"Don't let the what do what?" Maddy yelled back, but the Ballerina Clown had grown far too tall now and Vanessa didn't seem to hear. The muse waved merrily and skated off.

Maddy sat back, patted Ophelia—who had turned even more green and hidden her eyes again—and gazed out at the view. The ocean looked like a swash of teal-green paint on a canvas of sand, and the lowering sun cast a pinkish-gold tint over everything. Off in the distance, several racing skulls bobbed in the water, their heads shining with reflected sunlight.

And then Annie's fingers closed gently over Maddy and Ophelia, holding them safely in a sort-of cage, and the Ballerina Clown bent forward to lower them to the ground. She was so tall now that even with her feet planted where they had started, her torso stretched over several blocks. Maddy and Ophelia stepped out of Annie's hand onto a grassy roundabout at the intersection of five streets, right next to a bronze sculpture of a human torso. The Ballerina Clown patted them both on the head one more time, then drew her arm away and shrank back to size until Maddy couldn't see her anymore. Ophelia made a relieved *whoosh* through her siphon and uncovered her eyes, her color slowly returning to its original blue with yellow spots.

"I'm sorry," said Maddy. "I guess you don't like heights, right?"

The octopus shook her head vehemently.

"Let's try to keep you on the ground as much as possible, then."

Ophelia patted Maddy fondly on the cheek, then settled more comfortably on her shoulder. Maddy tucked her skateboard under her arm and turned in a slow circle. She didn't see anything that looked like a race or a roller coaster.

"What do you think?" she asked. "Which way?"

With a protesting metallic shriek, the bronze torso in the center of the roundabout swiveled on its base, tipped forward, and pointed toward an odd, curvy building painted in splashes of color.

Maddy shaded her eyes. "But that's just a building," she said.

Ophelia turned the sepia of an old-fashioned photograph, spiraled two of her tentacles into circles, and held them in front of Maddy's eyes like glasses. Suddenly, Maddy could hear an undercurrent of ghostly whispers from a long-ago amusement park: faded laughter, shrieks of joy, squeals of fear.

"Oh," said Maddy, her stomach doing an uncomfortable flip.

"Yeah. I see it now."

The odd curves and dips of the building had lengthened, twisting into an intricate roller coaster track of fast curves and steep drops and loops through the sky. In front of it all was a ticket booth with a blue-and-yellow striped awning, and at the booth sat a man. He wore an old-fashioned brown suit, a wide yellow tie knotted messily at his throat, and a brown tweed cap.

"Step right up, step right up," he called to them, and then grinned widely, showing a gold tooth. "The Race Thru the Clouds is open for business!"

7

"Come on now, whatcha waiting for?" The man at the ticket booth stood up and spread his arms wide. "Surely ya wanna ride the most spectacular, most wonderful, most thrilling coaster in the world! Step right up!"

Maddy loosened one of Ophelia's tentacles, which had wrapped around her windpipe as soon as the mimic octopus had seen how high the roller coaster went into the sky, and slowly crossed the street. Maddy didn't need the octopus glasses anymore. The coaster track that whirled and looped above them was now obvious—and terrifying.

The ticket taker watched them, grinning, and his outline seemed to shift for a moment. His face grew sallow, his eyes more shadowed, and his cap became frayed and dirty. "Step right up and take yer chances!" he called, his voice somehow sharper than it had been.

Maddy stopped walking abruptly, a knife of fear shooting through her.

"Ah," said the man. "I see, I see. You prefer the daylight, the friendly, the sparkle and shine? Very well, very well, I can accommodate that—at least for a while." His figure shifted back as though nothing had happened, although his grin still held a glint of something sinister. "Now then, lemme guess. You wanna find the Ringmaster, do you not?"

Maddy reached for Ophelia, who hooked a tentacle around Maddy's finger, and hesitantly approached the ticket booth. "How did you know?" she asked warily.

"Oh, I've seen plenty o' kids like you before, thinking you can make it big, wanting to ask the Ringmaster to take them in. So tell me . . . what's yer talent? Singer?"

Maddy hated it when people she had just met thought they knew her. She crossed her arms. On her shoulder, Ophelia crossed hers, too. "No," said Maddy.

"Wire walker?"

"No."

"Birdcalls? Make kelp grow? Do a backflip from where ya stand, right there?"

Maddy drew herself up taller. She wasn't going to tell him anything if she didn't have to. "The Ballerina Clown said I could ride. No one said I had to be able to *do* something. Are you going to let me on or not?"

"Oh, I see," said the ticket taker, sounding positively joyful. "Yer a no-talent."

Heat sprang to Maddy's face, and Ophelia turned a protesting shade of red.

"Aw, buck up! Plenty of room for no-talents around here. Besides, it's no never mind what I think. It's the Ringmaster what decides, it is. The Race Thru the Clouds ain't no ordinary coaster, see." The man stared up at the roller coaster with an expression of fondness. "She's the coaster of the future, the answer to yer every need. Just tell me where you want to go and she takes you there, lickety-split . . . *if* you win, of course."

Maddy looked up at the track. "Is it safe?" she asked. "It doesn't look safe."

The man let out a loud guffaw, and for a brief moment he was someone else again, someone sharp and dangerous. "This is Il Circo delle Strade, girly, not Disneyland. Sure, it's safe. Safe as life, that is. But then again, haven't you heard that you should never trust a carny?"

Maddy shifted slightly backward. "You're a carny?" she asked, remembering Vanessa's words. "What is that?"

"Newbie, are ya? *Carny* just means someone who works the rides, like me. We make this circus run, we do, and don't let nobody tell ya otherwise. Now, there's just the small matter of payment, and then we can get this show on the road."

Payment? Why hadn't anyone told her she had to pay to ride?

"I don't have any money," said Maddy.

The man laughed. "Money's not what gets you in, girly. Not here."

Maddy looked at Ophelia, who shrugged all of her tentacles. "What *does* get me in?"

"Whaddya got?"

All Maddy had was her skateboard, her clothes, and Vanessa's leg warmers—and she wasn't about to give any of that up. "Look," she said, "either tell me what it costs or don't. I don't need your stupid roller coaster. I don't even *like* roller coasters!" On her shoulder, Ophelia started dancing back and forth on six tentacles, her other two balled up like a prizefighter.

"Now we're talkin'," said the man happily. "I'll take *that* as payment."

"Take what?"

"Your righteous anger. That's *very* useful."

Ophelia turned a blistering orange and shook one tentacle at Maddy: *No-no-no.*

The man shrugged. "Well, then, offer up! Whatcha got? Hit me!"

Maddy bit her lower lip. What did she have to offer? She could feel her heart pounding, which gave her an idea. "I, um, I have this special condition—"

The man rolled his eyes. "Girly, you must think I'm as green as an unripe peach, as gullible as the dumbest mark who ever lived. Don't try to pawn yer half-rate illness off on me. Ya wanna ride, ya gotta give me something good." He looked pointedly at her bracelet.

"No!" Maddy's hand flew to her bracelet, but she tried to sound calm when she said, "I couldn't, anyway, even if I wanted to. It doesn't come off. See?"

"In that case," he said, looking suddenly and profoundly bored with the whole thing, "I'll take yer fondest wish."

"My what?"

"One fondest wish, take it or leave it. That's my final offer."

Maddy looked at Ophelia, who curled one tentacle into something that looked like a thumbs-up. "Um . . . okay, I guess. My fondest wish is . . . um, to find the Ringmaster."

"There ya go again, thinking I'm a new-and-fresh when I'm not neither." The man reached under the ticket counter and pulled out a blue-and-yellow striped wooden chest. In a flurry of movement, it unfolded into a very small blue-and-yellow striped stage. "Firstly, that's hardly yer fondest wish, and nextly, I'll choose the one I want, thank you very much. Now, step right up."

"Why can't I choose which one you take?"

"Them's the rules," said the man. "Take it or leave it."

Maddy's mouth had gone sawdust dry. She wasn't sure what her fondest wish was, not really. She had so many: a home, a family, a place to belong—and she didn't want to give any of those up, especially without being able to pick which one. Who would she be without the hope that held her together? What if this was a huge mistake?

Ophelia tentacled down Maddy's side and curled up like a cat at the base of the tiny stage.

"You think this is okay?" Maddy whispered to the octopus, who turned an *it's-the-best-we've-got* shade of blue.

Maddy tucked a stray piece of her hair behind her ear. She thought about the sadness of the winged lion, about a circus without its Ringmaster, about finally being able to talk to the magic. She didn't want to get on this ride, but she was going to anyway. She put her skateboard next to Ophelia and stepped up onto the platform.

"Okay," she said.

"About time!" The carny took his cap from his head and shook it once, hard. It turned into one of the white cartoon bunnies that had been on the mural.

"Bah," said the carny with disgust. "That sneaky magician told me he had cleaned out all the rabbits from this cap, he did. Magicians! Never trust 'em." He flipped the rabbit upside down, and it elongated into a thin purple scoop with a handle as long as Maddy's arm, like something a very tall person might use to serve ice cream. "That's more like it," he said. "Now, open wide!"

"You're sticking that thing down my *throat*?" Maddy cried, almost forgetting to be scared. "Uh-uh. No way."

"Girly, you are wearing on my very last nerve," said the

carny. "There's an easy way to do this, and there's a hard way. This here's the easy way. Wishes are drawn to troughs, see. They roll right in, so long as the scoop's the right color—and purple is *always* the right color."

Maddy chewed her lower lip. If she was going to do this, she had to do it. Squeezing her eyes shut, she opened her mouth.

Wish extraction felt a little like when you drank too much water and then tried to run with the water sloshing around in your insides, and a little like getting a corn chip caught in your throat.

"There's a right jumble in here, there is," said the carny as he poked around with the scoop.

A sudden crash of longing washed over Maddy, so intense she nearly crumpled.

"Whoa, Nelly!" said the carny. "Easy there. Didn't meant to loosen up so many at once! Hold up . . ."

Now it hurt, like the scoop was peeling off a scab deep in her belly. Maddy's legs wobbled and she almost fell over.

"Hold up hold up!" the carny yelled. "Don't move! Almost there . . . almost there . . . got it!"

The carny pulled the scoop out of her mouth and Maddy collapsed to her knees. Ophelia hurried over and wrapped Maddy in her tentacles.

"I'm okay," Maddy whispered, wiping her mouth with the back of her hand. She had an odd, background-y feeling, like walking into a room for a reason but then not having any idea what that reason was. She rose unsteadily to her feet as Ophelia climbed onto her shoulder.

The carny was rolling something that looked like a shriveled gray pea between his thumb and first finger.

"That's it?" Maddy asked. Shouldn't wishes be colorful and exciting? Hers seemed so small and forlorn. In her head, Maddy ran through an inventory of all the wishes she could remember. She still wanted to find the Ringmaster. She still wanted a family and home. She still longed for magic. If she remembered all that, then what was hidden in that ugly wrinkled thing? "That's my wish?"

"This one's a right secret, it is. It's the ones we don't even tell ourselves that turn hard and small like this."

He closed his fingers around her wish and gestured to Maddy to follow him to an open box under the ticket counter that was full of . . . well, Maddy wasn't quite sure *what* the things in the box were. They were all different sizes and all different metals, silver and copper and gold and brass. Some of them gleamed and winked while others were battered and tarnished. All of them seemed alive in a clockwork kind of way. One of them, a deep bronze, was crawling up the side of the box.

"Folks' fondest wishes," said the man proudly. "Ain't they something? There's them what will pay dearly for one of these, places in the circus where a box full o' wishes will get ya nigh whatever ya want. Ooh, lookie here, whydontcha!" The bronze wish had reached the top of the box, and now wings sprouted from its sides. "That's a sight you don't see every day. Look out!"

With a mechanical grinding sound, the wish soared into the air. It careened off the wall, knocked the man's cap clear off, and swooped so close to Maddy's head that its wingtips caught her hair. Then it burst out of the ticket booth and soared away.

"What was *that*?" gasped Maddy, patting her hair down. Ophelia turned into a hairbrush and tried to help, but the prongs were too rubbery and kept getting stuck.

"That, girly, was how ya get yer wish back. You got to call to it so fierce-like that it can't refuse. Lucky for me and my pocketbook, that's not so usual. Most folks're afraid to want that bad." The man tossed her small gray wish into the box, where it clattered down to the bottom, out of sight. It was so dull and small compared with the others. Maddy wanted to grab it back. "And now, yer all paid up."

A movement caught her eye. Maddy tore her gaze away from the box of wishes to look up. More of the roller coaster had materialized above them, more twists and turns, loops and drops. Ophelia turned a pale, uncertain green, and Maddy was fairly sure her own face was the same color.

"Let's go over the rest o' the rules." The man pulled a stained brown notebook from his pants pocket. "Rule number one: ya gotta have yer own ride."

"What?" cried Maddy, her attention snapping back.

"Ah, quit yer blubbering. Ya got some wheels right there," he said, pointing to her skateboard. "Hand it over and lemme take a look."

Maddy glanced uncertainly at Ophelia, who nodded. Reluctantly, Maddy passed her board to the man.

"I've seen better, but this'll do," he said, and he threw her skateboard into the air.

"Hey!" Maddy dashed forward to catch it—but instead of falling down the way things usually did when you threw them, her skateboard rose higher and began to stretch. When it was the size of a surfboard, it lowered down to the track, its wheels locking on with a loud click.

"Um . . ." Maddy's voice came out as a tiny squeak as she stared at her now-giant skateboard. "Doesn't it need a seat belt? Or a safety bar?"

"Did ya bring a seat belt or a safety bar?" asked the man.

"No, but—"

"Didn't think so."

Ophelia meeped and covered her eyes with her tentacles. Maddy felt like doing the same thing. She had found her skateboard in a dumpster when she was nine, and even back then its grip tape had been worn smooth and the nose of the board had a hairline fracture. Now, after three years of riding it everywhere, it had definitely seen better days. She wasn't even sure the wheels would hold up.

She turned to Ophelia. "You don't have to come," she said,

trying to sound brave. "I know you don't like heights."

Ophelia made an impatient *whooshing* sound through her siphon and then, with clear effort, turned back to her original blue with yellow spots. There was still a bit of a green undertone, but her meaning was clear. Maddy sighed with relief. If she had Ophelia with her, maybe she could do this. She squeezed one of Ophelia's tentacles, and the octopus squeezed back.

"What are the other rules?" she said to the carny.

"Rule number two, ya gotta say out loud where ya want to go before we start—but not yet!" he added as Maddy opened her mouth. "I'll tell ya when it's time. Rule number three, the Race chooses yer opponent. Rule number four, it starts as soon as your opponent appears and it finishes when one of youse crosses the finish line. Whoever crosses first is the winner."

Maddy looked up at the whirls and loops and sharp inclines of the coaster. "There's only one track," she said slowly. "So how can two people race?"

"Oh yeah. Yer gonna need this," said the man, and he held out a metal can.

"Spray paint?" asked Maddy as she took it. "What for?"

"To spray yerself a track," said the man. "Without a track, it's not such a smooth ride."

"Without a track?" Maddy repeated, trying not to panic any more than she already was.

The man grinned. "Oh, don't fuss so. We start ya off with a track. Ya only have to spray yer own once that one ends. Now, them's all the rules, and I been through them nice and proper like I'm supposed to. Let's get this show on the road!"

Maddy exhaled hard and looked at Ophelia. This was a terrible idea, but it seemed to be the only idea they had. "Well," she said, "I guess we're racing. Ready?"

Ophelia turned a determined hot pink and braced herself firmly on Maddy's shoulder.

"Okay then," said Maddy, more to herself than Ophelia. "Let's go."

Maddy got on her board, lying down on her stomach the way she had seen surfers do when they paddled out, and Ophelia scooted onto her back. Holding the front edge of the board with one hand and the spray paint can with the other, Maddy hooked her ankles around the board's tail. She patted her pocket to make sure she had her pills, her heartbeat already so strong she could feel it against the octopus's rubbery skin.

Breathe, she told herself. *Just breathe. You can do this.*

"*Now* ya can tell me," said the man. "If ya win, where do ya want the Race to take ya?"

Maddy tried very hard to do what Vanessa had said: to say what she meant and mean what she said. But her brain was clogged with fear. What if she had an episode in the middle of the ride, if her heart went wild and she couldn't see anymore? What then?

One hand at a time, she wiped her sweaty palms on her shorts.

"To the Ringmaster, please," she said, her voice a little shaky. "But the Ringmaster of Il Circo delle Strade. Not a different circus." She was very proud of herself for thinking to add this last part.

Unfortunately, there were other parts she didn't think to add. With a wolf-like grin, the carny started the ride.

8

Chikka chukka chikka-chikka chukka chikka chukka chikka-chikka chukka . . .

Why did all roller coasters make that horrid chugging sound when they went uphill? It was like the soundtrack in a shark movie: all it did was make everything scarier. Maddy tried to make it into a reassuring rhythm as she and her board climbed up the first incline, but her brain kept skipping from fear and she couldn't make anything stick. She hugged the board more tightly, every muscle in her body already aching, and pinned the spray paint can between her arm and the board so she could use both hands to hold on. Ophelia flattened herself onto Maddy's back like the world's most rubbery backpack and then shifted so all eight of her tentacles were wrapped around Maddy, strapping her firmly to the board.

"Thanks," Maddy said, the wind pulling the word from her mouth. She squinted up at the top of the climb. They were almost there . . . almost there . . . and then her board crested the hill. For a moment they teetered there, balanced. Maddy squeezed her eyes shut—but then thought better of it and opened them.

The nose of her board began to tip and now they were falling, hurtling down the first drop. Maddy started to scream but then clamped her teeth shut. They were going so fast it felt as though her stomach had vacated its normal spot in her body for somewhere else entirely, and the wind mashed the skin of her face against the bone and sent her hair flying into her eyes.

After what seemed like an eternity they hit the end of the drop, where the track took a sharp turn to the right. But Maddy's skateboard didn't. In a scene right from her nightmares, her board flew straight off the track into nothingness.

Now Maddy *did* scream, and the spray paint can rolled out from beneath her and tumbled off the side of the board. At the same time, a whoop of joy came from above as a boy on a skateboard dropped out of the sky, crouching and holding a can of gold spray paint. He was tall and thin and skater-boy cool, and red and gold sparks shot from the tail of his board as he sped through the air. It was Skeeter Chen, the boy from the drum circle.

"Help!" screamed Maddy.

Skeeter looked down and a look of shock crossed his face.

"Pull up!" he yelled. "Hurry!"

Maddy yanked hard on the nose of her board. To her surprise it responded, angling away from the ground. She let out a strangled cry of relief.

"Seagull!" Skeeter cried. "Look out!"

Maddy threw her body weight to the side to avoid the seagull that was flying straight at her, flipping into a barrel roll that made her stomach crash against her throat.

"Learn to drive, moron!" screeched the gull as she tumbled away.

Maddy righted her board, her fingers slippery with sweat. She could feel Ophelia trembling against her. "Sorry!" she yelled, both to the gull and the octopus. Her board was bucking and shaking now, like a horse trying to throw her off.

"What do I do?" she shouted to Skeeter. "I dropped my spray paint can!"

Skeeter's eyes widened. Quickly, he shook his can of paint and sprayed a line of shimmering gold into the air, where it hardened into a golden track. He dropped onto it, his wheels clicking in. "Use my track!" he yelled. "Lock in behind me!"

Fighting against her board, Maddy pulled up and aimed for the golden track. When she was just above it, she straightened her arms like a push-up—Ophelia stretched to give her room—and then let herself slam back onto the board, sending it straight down onto Skeeter's track. Her wheels clicked in with a jolt that rattled her teeth. Red and gold sparks from Skeeter's board washed over her, causing Ophelia to morph into a fireproof vest across Maddy's back.

"You okay?" Skeeter called over his shoulder.

Maddy spit hair out of her mouth. Her ride was better, but not much. "I think so."

"Just hold on," said Skeeter. "It's my track, not yours, so your ride won't be as smooth, but just hold on and you'll be fine. You'll have to forfeit, though."

"Forfeit?" cried Maddy. Not after all that! Not after giving up her fondest wish and coming all the way here just to help! No. They were not forfeiting. She was here to race.

Skeeter lifted one shoulder. Even his shrugs were cool. "You can't race without a track."

The fireproof vest that was Ophelia released itself from Maddy's back and became something hard and cylindrical. It rolled down the board, bumped into her side, and wrapped one faintly green tentacle around Maddy's arm. Maddy glanced over. A blue-and-yellow spray paint can, covered with suckers, was holding tightly to her arm with one tentacle.

"Ophelia, you're brilliant!" cried Maddy. Carefully, she let go of the board with one hand and picked up the can, which instantly glommed onto Maddy's palm. A moment later, a stream of yellow-spotted blue ink shot from the siphon on the side of the paint can, the ink hardening into a track.

"Yes!" Maddy yelled. She pulled her board from Skeeter's track and aimed it for Ophelia's blue-and-yellow one. Her wheels connected and her ride smoothed out.

Skeeter's smile cut dimples into both cheeks. "Octopus ink? That is a most excellent trick! *Now* we can race!" He jumped to face her so he was riding backward on his board, spreading his arms wide with a flourish. *"Theydies and gentlethems, elders and wee ones, and especially those between and betwixt and more than the sum of their parts! Now, above the sea and below the sky, the daring Race Thru the Clouds commences! Racer one, on the Golden Express powered by Magical Shooting Stars, is Skeeter Chen—that's me, by the way—the Fastest Boy on Wheels! Racer two, riding a board of dubious origin but with eight-tentacled power, is Octogirl, Queen of the Skateboard Cephalopods! Riders, set your boards!"*

Even though she was terrified, even though the ground rushed by beneath her in a blur and the wind made her eyes water, even though she was scared about how hard her heart was pounding, Maddy couldn't help but smile a little. Octogirl was the best nickname she had ever heard.

Skeeter bowed. Then he did three perfect spins and a loop that was so fast Maddy could barely follow it with her eyes. "See you at the finish line, Octogirl!"

And he took off, whooping with joy.

"Go, Ophelia!" shouted Maddy, suddenly determined to win at all costs. "GO!"

Ophelia sprayed more track and their board raced forward. Still, Skeeter pulled out easily in front of them, twirling and spinning and leaping, shouting happily every time he landed another trick.

"Is this race graded on difficulty?" Maddy yelled. "I can't do any tricks!"

"Nah," Skeeter yelled back. He was pulling farther ahead with each trick he did. "I just like doing stuff."

Skeeter seemed able to speed and slow at will—he was doing it now as he leaped off his board and did a full twist in the air before landing again—but Maddy's board stayed at the same steady rate. Was there some control she was missing? Gingerly, she let go with one hand and ran it along the edges and bottom of the board where she could reach, feeling for a lever or a button, but found nothing. How did she make it go faster?

Just then, Ophelia sprayed a sharp turn that brought them around to face the ocean—and Maddy momentarily forgot they were racing. It was just about sunset, Maddy's favorite time of day, and the view made her gasp. The sea had gone a deep, steely blue while the sky glowed soft lavender, pinks and oranges tinging the clouds. Long cantaloupe-colored shadows stretched from the people walking along the shore, some of them alone, some hand in hand, some in groups. A laughing little boy chased waves as they withdrew from the shore, and his footsteps in the wet sand shone as though lit up by spotlights. Maddy inhaled deeply, breathing in the smells of salt and picnics as she soared over the sea and the sky and the circus itself. A wild joy filled her and chills flew up her arms.

With an unexpected jolt, her board picked up speed.

"Whoa!" Maddy grabbed on more tightly. What was *that*? She squinted, eyes watering from the wind, as Ophelia aimed her ink so their track hovered above the bike path that stretched along the coastline. Even with the setting sun, scores of people still skated or biked below. None of them even looked up to see a girl and an octopus flying through the air on a giant skateboard just over their heads.

The thought of it made Maddy laugh out loud.

Her board went faster.

An impossibly tall, partially transparent woman skated on the path below Maddy, passing right through other people and ruffling their clothes and hair like a gentle sea breeze. The lightning bolts on her skates glowed white in the waning light.

"Vanessa!" yelled Maddy.

Vanessa looked up. "Oh, lovely!" she called back. "You're racing Skeeter!"

An odd giddiness bounced around inside of Maddy, unlike anything she had ever felt before. Her board went faster. How was that happening? Now they were right on Skeeter's tail! Just one more burst of speed might do it, if she could only figure out *how*.

Below her, the sand began to roil and rise, glinting like sequins in the sunset-streaked sky. Seven sand dancers formed one by one, the long rays of the sun sending their shadows flying long and thin over the beach. Their silvery-blue scales glistened as they flipped up to balance one on top of the other, the top dancer kicking into a splits handstand to unfurl a sign held between his feet: *Go, Racers!*

It felt like hot fudge and vanilla ice cream, like long summer days in the pool, like discovering that the world was far more shining than you had ever dared to hope. Maddy wanted to save that feeling, to wrap it up like a gift she could open whenever she wanted. She wanted to shout it to the whole world.

Her board went faster.

And in a flash, she understood. Delight! Her board went on delight! She let out a sharp laugh, startling Ophelia so much that the spray paint can momentarily became a puffer fish.

"Sorry, sorry!" cried Maddy, as Ophelia made a disgruntled sound and shifted back into the spray paint can. "But I figured it out! Hurry, Ophelia, more track!"

Now that she knew what to look for, it was easy. After all, this *was* a street circus, and delight was everywhere. They swooped over a limo painted to look like purple leopard skin. On its hood sat a Chihuahua wearing an embarrassingly matching sweater. Maddy risked letting go with one hand to wave as they passed, causing the dog to bark so frantically that its owner, also dressed in purple leopard print, got out of the car to soothe it.

Maddy's board went faster.

For the first time ever, racing was *fun*.

Skeeter whooped, spraying his track over the boardwalk, Maddy just a half-second behind him. They whizzed by a mural of a man in a gas mask rappelling down the side of a building, and as they passed the man turned his head to watch. Almost side by side, Maddy and Skeeter flew over the street with the cartoon bunnies, who had come out of their mural and were bouncing two-dimensionally around the grassy meridian.

"Hi, cute bunnies!" Maddy yelled, and her board went faster.

But so did Skeeter's. He sprayed his track into a loop and Ophelia did the same. Maddy's board screeched in protest as she willed it forward with her delight, its nose almost touching Skeeter's heels. Both boards made a fast turn, and now they were flying over blocks and blocks of streets made of water instead of asphalt, canals that were wide and shallow and lined with a mix of mansions and weatherworn beach shacks. Some of the homes even had small docks, rowboats and canoes tied to them with loose rope. In each block, wooden footbridges crossed from one side of the canal to the other. It looked like the pictures Maddy had seen of Venice, Italy, and suddenly it all made sense. Venice, California, was built to look like Venice, Italy!

And her board went faster.

Ophelia sprayed a clever twist in the track and they banked over what looked to be the main canal. Something big splashed in the water as they flew overhead, and Maddy turned her head just in time to see a large, iridescent fishtail attached to a woman with dark skin and short black hair disappear into the water.

And her board went faster.

Maddy was almost close enough to reach out and touch the tail of Skeeter's board. In the sky in front of them, a beam of light from the sunset twisted itself into glowing letters that scrolled across the canal:

Finito ~ To Go Where You Have Asked

"Come on, Ophelia!" cried Maddy. "Come *on!*"

The paint can Ophelia made an almost-empty-sounding wheeze, forcing a last bit of octopus ink into the air. A rush of love filled Maddy. Who would have ever thought she would be someone who had an octopus for a friend? It was about the best thing she could imagine.

And with that, her board put on a terrific burst of speed. It hurtled past Skeeter and right through the words in the sky, tearing the ribbon into golden pieces. In the distance, a conch shell blew. Gasping with joy, Maddy held on as her board slowed and then stopped, hovering above the canals. Ophelia let out a tired *poof,* morphed back into her octopus shape, and collapsed in Maddy's hand, snoring tiny octopus snores.

Skeeter skidded to a stop next to her, face shining with sweat. He looked as happy as if he had been the one to win. "Nice job, Octogirl!"

Shakily, Maddy pushed herself up to sit, being careful not to wake Ophelia. "Is it over?" she asked.

"Yup." Skeeter used the bottom of his shirt to wipe sweat from his eyes. "You won. That was a great race."

Maddy grinned so wide it hurt. "Ophelia," she whispered to the sleeping octopus, "we did it! *You* did it! You were amazing!"

In her sleep, Ophelia let out a quiet, contented meep.

Maddy looked back at Skeeter and then away, suddenly too embarrassed to meet his gaze. "Thank you for helping me in the beginning," she said, watching their reflection in the canal below. "That's why I won."

"Nah." Skeeter's eyes were shining, his long eyelashes sending shadows onto his cheeks. He looked as though he laughed a lot. Maddy liked that. "You did it all on your own. Well, you and that octopus, anyway."

Maddy placed Ophelia carefully on the board and flexed her fingers. A light breeze ruffled her hair and sent a shiver over her. "What happens now?"

The smile slipped from Skeeter's face, but was back so fast Maddy thought maybe she had imagined it. "You won, so the Race should take you where you asked to go."

Maddy's heart clenched. It had never occurred to her that Skeeter must have been racing to go somewhere, too. Had she taken something important from him? She shifted uncomfortably. "How?" she asked.

"Like this," said the disembodied voice of the carny, and with no warning her board dropped out of the sky. Maddy shrieked and scooped up Ophelia with one hand, tucking herself around the sleeping octopus to protect her as they fell. She heard Skeeter yell something, and a second later her board gave a hard jolt. Skeeter had grabbed the tail of her board and was skidding across the sky behind them as he tried to slow her down. But it was no use. Maddy's board slammed into the canal, the impact sending Skeeter somersaulting away as her board bounced like a jet ski over the water's surface, knocking the breath from her. And then the board gave a particularly hard bounce, and Maddy and Ophelia went tumbling into the murky green water.

9

The canals were warm, the warm of water that didn't move enough.

Ophelia had jetted out of Maddy's arms the moment they hit the water. Eyes squeezed shut as she sank, Maddy reminded herself that the mimic octopus was all right—was, in fact, perfectly at home here, and that she, Maddy, would be all right, too. She was still sinking, but she had seen how shallow the canals were when she flew over them, shallow enough for her to stand up in. All she had to do was reach down with her feet and the bottom would be there . . . she just had to reach . . . reach more . . . just a little more . . .

Where was the bottom?

Maddy was a good swimmer. Until her heart condition had gotten worse, she had spent every summer at the public pools.

But now, her feet found nothing but water. She kicked hard toward what she thought was the surface but it didn't seem to matter; she was still sinking and her lungs were starting to hurt. She tried not to panic. At least Ophelia had come back, although now the octopus was climbing up her legs and then her torso, squeezing Maddy's already taxed lungs. Maddy reached down to loosen the octopus's grip, but instead of rubbery tentacles there was only soft, wet wool. For a moment Maddy's brain couldn't register what it was. Then she realized that Vanessa's leg warmers were rising up around her body, choking off her air.

Now she panicked for real. Maddy thrashed around, tearing frantically at the soaked fabric as the leg warmers rose up over her face. But no matter how hard she pulled, the leg warmers snapped back against her mouth and nose, molding to the shape of her face. Falling through the water, chest burning, throat on fire, Maddy couldn't hold her breath any longer. Against her will, she opened her mouth and took a great, sobbing gasp . . .

. . . and doubled over, coughing violently as she sucked in air. Cool, real air! Her hands flew to her face, feeling every piece of yarn that covered her mouth and nose as she took another half-crying, half-laughing, all-miraculous breath.

She could breathe underwater! It must be Muse Magic! The leg warmers had even grown holes for her arms so she could swim. Flushed with relief, Maddy sent a silent but fervent *thank you* to Vanessa as the leg warmers rose up to cover her eyes.

Maybe Muse Magic would let her see underwater, too? She slit her eyes open. Sure enough, the murky green water snapped into focus, the pattern of the weave marring her vision like looking through a screen door. Pieces of seaweed and plastic drifted past, along with schools of small silver fish that darted out of her way.

Almost giddy, Maddy tried to get her bearings. Her bubbles were rising, so she aimed herself in that direction and tried to follow them to the surface. The leg warmers stretched down over her bare feet—her flip-flops had come off in the fall and were probably long gone—to form fins. Maddy kicked toward the surface, but the leg warmers had a different idea. Rather than helping her swim up, they spun her around and propelled her straight down. Maddy fought against them, struggling to turn back around, but the leg warmers were too strong. Finally, though, she stopped fighting. Muse Magic clearly wanted her to sink, so that's what she would do. As long as she could breathe, she would be okay. Vanessa's leg warmers wouldn't take her somewhere dangerous . . . right?

In the distance, yellow polka dots became visible through the murk, swimming toward her.

"Ophelia!" cried Maddy, sending happy bubbles into the water. The mimic octopus turned a joyous purple and grabbed on to her shoulder. Sinking was much better with Ophelia there.

Below them, the bottom of the canal came into focus and

Maddy blinked. Was that a hole at the bottom of the canal? It was! There was a hole below them, big enough for a bus to drive through, and there was light shining through it as though there were sky on the other side. The fins propelled them toward the hole and then right through it, and suddenly they were indeed no longer in water but falling through sky.

Immediately, the leg warmers peeled away from Maddy's face and feet and re-formed as glider wings on either side of her. A gust of air propelled Maddy and Ophelia through a twilit sky, the mimic octopus meeping unhappily. Maddy shook her head to get her wet hair out of her eyes, and now she could see they were soaring toward an enclosed bridge made of white stone, a bridge floating in the air with stairs on either side of it connecting it to a canal that was also suspended in the sky.

In a flash Maddy understood. The Race had sent her here, so this must be where she would find the Ringmaster. But the bridge didn't feel right. It felt menacing. It was completely closed in by its walls and roof, making it look like a prison. There were even bars over the small square windows that ran along the top of the walls, and water tracks streaked down the stone as though the bridge itself had been crying. The whole thing looked ancient and foreboding.

Maddy's stomach clenched. She didn't want to go there. She tried to steer away, but the leg warmers wouldn't let her change course. Instead, they folded into pleats, slowing her down. And then the leg warmers tucked back into themselves, dropping

Maddy and Ophelia right onto the roof of the bridge—which opened up and sucked them inside as though it were quicksand.

They landed on the hard stone floor of the bridge. It was freezing and musty, and the stone walls shone with moisture. Ophelia had slipped halfway down Maddy's arm and was flashing an alarmed ochre.

"I don't know why we're here, either," said Maddy, turning around slowly as Ophelia righted herself and climbed back onto Maddy's shoulder. An uncomfortable stillness sat over everything, a stillness like the moment right after you've said something terribly wrong. Dim light filtered through the high, small windows.

And then, from the far side of the bridge, something moved.

Maddy tensed, goose bumps prickling her skin. Surely that couldn't be the Ringmaster . . . could it? Whatever it was, it was coming toward them, pushing damp air in front of it. The air itself felt like a real thing, with weight and substance, and it smelled like rotting trash. Ophelia pulsed bright and frantic.

"I agree," said Maddy, backing up. "Let's get out of here." But before she could take another step, a crush of loneliness slammed into her. Maddy cried out and stumbled; it felt as though the loneliness were seeping inside of her, moving through her skin and into her veins.

And then the loneliness spoke.

Unwanted. Unloved. No one wants you. No one has ever wanted you.

Run! shouted every part of Maddy, but she couldn't seem to get her legs to work.

You will never have a family, said the voice. *You will always be unwanted and friendless.*

Maddy tried calling to Ophelia, but loneliness squeezed the breath out of her and she doubled over, crumpling to the ground. It felt as though the entire bridge had fallen on top of her.

From somewhere far away, tentacles pulled at her.

Maddy curled into a ball. The voice was right; she was nothing. She was no longer three-dimensional; she was flattened, smashed, and there was no room in her two-dimensional self for hope or love or magic. Why had she ever thought otherwise? She was nothing, had always been nothing, would always be nothing. Her future had been decided from the moment her parents had left her on the doorstep of strangers.

On the cold floor of the stone bridge, she covered her face with her hands and sobbed.

She could feel Ophelia let go of her—of course, because Maddy wasn't worth saving, wasn't worth having as a friend, wasn't worth anything. And then a very determined, sucker-y sled scooped her up, skidded her off the bridge and down the stone stairs, and plopped them both into the freezing water of the floating canal.

Maddy came up sputtering and choking, Ophelia on her shoulder. Her memory was fuzzy. What had just happened? Hadn't she been crying? Before she could ask anything, though, a hand wrapped around her ankle and a woman's voice said—distinctly and with great irritation— "Non ancora!"

Then the hand pulled them under.

Maddy jackknifed in the water, trying to unwrap the fingers from her ankle. Luckily, the leg warmers were already doing their job, rising up over Maddy's mouth and nose.

"Stai fermo!" the woman's voice said, sounding even more exasperated. "Be still!"

The leg warmers rose high enough for Maddy to see . . . and she stopped struggling. The hand on Maddy's leg belonged to a woman with cropped black hair, deep olive skin, and a beautiful, iridescent fish tail that was currently pumping up and down with great force, sending currents whooshing past Maddy's ears and almost blocking out the mermaid's angry muttering.

"Brainless carny" . . . pump . . . "ruining my waterways" . . . pump . . . "And you, Ophelia! I am *disappointed*. The Ponte dei Sospiri, *honestly!*" . . . pump . . . "What were you *thinking?*"

"Um . . . hi," began Maddy, not sure if the leg warmers would make her understandable underwater. Apparently, they did, because the mermaid came to an abrupt halt—which sent Ophelia tumbling over Maddy's shoulder—and flashed Maddy a look of extreme annoyance.

"Silenzio!" The mermaid's hair was styled around her hairline in stiff, lacquered curls that were so perfect they looked as though they had been painted onto her head. She pointed one long, webbed finger at Maddy. "Do not speak. Do not say a word. Do not even think."

Maddy blinked as Ophelia climbed back onto her shoulder.

"Ben fatto," said the mermaid with grim satisfaction, and she turned away again and pulled Maddy and Ophelia deeper down. Strangely, though, the water grew lighter and lighter, until—even though Maddy was sure they had been sinking—they popped up at the surface of the same canal Maddy had crashed into earlier. Twilight streaked the sky and water. Four ducks paddled past, making soft, gossipy quacks that somehow Maddy understood: *There's a girl in the canals. With Isabette! There goes the neighborhood. Hey, look, bread crumbs!*

The mermaid was already firing off a rapid stream of Italian words that Maddy was pretty sure weren't very nice, switching to barely accented English halfway through.

"Barton!" she yelled, still tugging Maddy by her ankle. Maddy struggled to keep her head above water and Ophelia turned into a floatie and wrapped herself around Maddy's arm. "Barton, you fool! Show yourself!"

There was the flicker of a cigarette lighter and then the carny stepped forward, a lit cigar in his mouth. "Nice night, ain't it, Isabette?" he said, and blew three perfect smoke rings.

"What is the meaning of *this*?" Isabette punctuated the word with a sharp jab to Maddy's ribs.

"Ow!" said Maddy.

"Silenzio!" roared the mermaid.

Maddy frowned. She would have thought mermaids would be more magical and less like group home leaders.

The carny grinned at Maddy. "Good on ya for winning," he said.

"Is Skeeter okay?" asked Maddy.

Isabette made a snorting sound of disgust. "The Chen boy? I should have known he was involved."

"Skeets can take care of himself," said Barton, blowing another smoke ring.

"What about my skateboard?" Maddy asked, not sure she wanted to hear the answer. It was only a skateboard, but they had been through a lot together.

"Dunno. Prob'ly washed out to sea if you didn't hold on to it—hey!"

Isabette had slapped her tail on the water with a crack, drenching both Barton and his cigar, which went out. "Enough chitchat. Explain yourself!"

Barton wiped water off his face. Then he pulled a small pair of scissors from his vest pocket, clipped off the end of his cigar, and relit it. Maddy could feel Isabette fuming as she waited.

"Wanted to see the Ringmaster, did she not?" said Barton finally. "And she won. So the Race took her there."

Maddy was so surprised that she stopped trying to hold herself up, and the half of her that wasn't supported by an octopus floatie dipped under the water.

"But," she sputtered, "the Ringmaster wasn't there! The Race didn't take me to him at all, it just sent me to that bridge! What *was* that, anyway?"

Isabette's eyebrows rose into perfect arcs and her dark eyes went from Maddy to the carny and back again. "But . . . the Ponte dei Sospiri . . ." Isabette broke off, looking at Maddy appraisingly. "Ah," she said.

"Is the Race broken?" asked Maddy.

"Broken?" said the carny, looking positively delighted. "Not a chance, girly. So, the Race sent ya to the Bridge of Sighs, did it? Now ain't that just somethin'!"

Tug, went Maddy's heart.

Maddy frowned. That was odd, her heart tugging when she

was already right in the middle of magic. Usually that only happened when it was calling her *to* magic.

"That was not *some bridge*," said Isabette, but her tone was less angry and more thoughtful. "That was the Ponte dei Sospiri, the Bridge of Sighs, where all the waterways lead." The mermaid turned back to Barton. "*My* waterways, might I add. That *I* am responsible for. That *I* look after. And that I don't appreciate having littered with unexpected company."

"You may be in charge of all the waterways," said Barton, "but you ain't in charge of the circus. And just because the Ringmaster defers to you—"

"The Ringmaster understands the importance of the canals," cut in Isabette. "And you'd do well to remember that the next time you decide to send someone plummeting into them."

Tug, went Maddy's heart, a little stronger.

"This one is not ready for the Ponte dei Sospiri," Isabette continued. "Even if the Race did send her."

"Why would the Race take me to—" Maddy began, but then something entirely new happened. Her *bracelet* gave a clear, distinct tug on her arm, as though she were holding the hand of a little kid who wanted to go a different direction. Maddy stared as her bracelet yanked again, with force this time, as though the little kid had turned into a circus strongman. It felt as though her shoulder might come right out of its socket.

This wasn't at all like the tug of her heart, which was more like a yearning than an actual tug. This was a *real* tug, a physical one, and it pulled Maddy backward and away from the mermaid until she was stretched out on the surface of the canal. Only Isabette's hand on her ankle was keeping her from being dragged away. The Ophelia floatie hugged her arm tighter.

Tug, went Maddy's heart and bracelet in unison. *Tug. TUG.*

Maddy had always loved it when her heart pulled her somewhere. But her *bracelet* pulling as well? If her bracelet was a binding, and if that binding was pulling her somewhere in sync with her heart . . . then that might mean . . .

Hollowness scraped at Maddy's insides. She didn't even want to think about the possibility that the pull of her own heart didn't even belong to her.

TUG, went her bracelet.

This time, it yanked so hard it pulled Isabette as well. The mermaid turned to Maddy, about to yell, but then her eyes traveled down to Maddy's wrist.

Tug, went the bracelet and her heart. *TUG TUG TUG.*

Several small creases appeared on Isabette's forehead.

"I don't know what it's doing," said Maddy worriedly. "This has never happened before."

Isabette said nothing.

TUG! TUG TUG TUG!

Slowly and deliberately, Isabette let go of Maddy's ankle.

TUG!

Pulled by her bracelet, Maddy went speeding backward across the canal. Water pried four of Ophelia's tentacles loose, but Maddy grabbed the octopus and held on tightly as they went skimming across the surface of the water, faster and faster. Houses, bridges, and canals blurred together in Maddy's vision as they sped past, her bracelet pulling them here and there, back and forth, until she was totally lost. And then with one last, hard yank, her bracelet pulled them right out of the water into a room that solidified around them, a room that smelled of stale popcorn. Maddy lost her grip on Ophelia, who went tumbling away. Her own limbs flailing, Maddy skidded across the floor, slammed against something solid, and bounced off to land on her hands and knees on a soft blue-and-yellow striped rug. By her side, Ophelia had returned to her original blue and yellow, coordinating nicely.

Coughing canal water out of her lungs, Maddy wiped salt from her eyes . . . and froze. In front of her was a pair of glossy dress shoes the rich, ghostly purple of the sky at dusk, attached to a pair of legs clad in beautifully tailored pants.

Slowly, Maddy raised her eyes. Ophelia sprang to her tentacles like she was tap dancing and turned a stunning shade of sunset red.

"Now that," said the man standing above them, "was quite an impressive entrance. But do get up, dear girl—and you, too, dear Ophelia. You're dripping all over the carpet."

11

There, leaning somewhat theatrically on a long black cane topped with a large seashell, was the man who had to be the Ringmaster.

Like his cane, the Ringmaster was long and thin. He had proud, hooded eyes and a proud, hooked nose, and his skin was a similar brown to Maddy's. Dark hair flopped over his forehead and his tuxedo swirled with all the colors of a city by the sea: turquoise and concrete, seafoam and palm tree green, all shot through with the sheen of oil on water. His top hat and vest were the color of midnight; the carnation tucked through a buttonhole was the same vivid sunset red that Ophelia had become.

Maddy scrambled to her feet, made more difficult by the fact that the floor kept lurching beneath her, and looked down at herself. Her tank top and shorts had been ratty even before they were drenched and spotted with green muck from the canals. Now they were frankly embarrassing. Murky water ran from her in rivulets and pooled on the carpet.

"I'm sorry," she said. "Um . . . do you have a towel?"

"A towel? My dear girl, surely we can do better than that." The Ringmaster removed his top hat with a flourish and flicked it sharply. Ophelia jumped out of the way at the last moment as beach sand flew from the brim of the hat, settling over Maddy and drying her and her clothing instantly. "Towels are so mundane."

Maddy brushed sand from her arms and legs, doing her best not to stare at the Ringmaster and failing miserably. She couldn't help it. He was perfect, even better than she'd expected.

The Ringmaster swept the remaining sand from the brim of his hat and replaced it at a jaunty angle on his head. Then he snapped his fingers and a beach ball rolled forward, exploded in a shower of confetti, and disgorged a pair of yellow flip-flops that marched of their own accord to Maddy's side.

"We have quite an extensive lost and found," said the Ringmaster as the flip-flops collapsed in front of her. Ophelia poked them with a tentacle, then nodded her approval. "Shoes are one of the most common things people leave behind—we are a beach circus, after all. Please, take them. Yellow is not my color. It makes my feet look jaundiced."

The flip-flops were warm, as though they had been sitting

in the noonday sun, and they fit perfectly. "Thank you," said Maddy, wiggling her toes with pleasure. Ophelia climbed up Maddy's side, settling on her shoulder. "You're the Ringmaster, right?"

The Ringmaster made a sweeping bow. "The Eminent Signor Zavala, at your service."

Maddy started to introduce herself.

"No!" the Ringmaster interrupted, holding one hand out in a grand gesture. "Don't tell me, for I can read your mind. Think your name, loud and clear in your head . . . think . . . think . . ." He furrowed his brow and closed his eyes.

Maddy grinned. *Maddy,* she thought as hard as she could. Ophelia helped by rubbing Maddy's temples with two tentacles. *Maddy. Maddy Maddy Maddy Maddy.*

The Ringmaster opened his eyes and gazed thoughtfully at the ceiling.

Maddy. Maddy Maddy Maddy!

The Ringmaster shook his head. "Alas," he said, lifting an eyebrow in a mischievous way that told Maddy he had never actually thought the mind reading would work. "The spirits are against me today. I'm afraid you'll just have to tell me."

"I'm Maddy." Somehow that didn't seem quite enough, so she added, "Madeline Adriana."

"It is my great good pleasure to make your acquaintance, Madeline Adriana," said the Ringmaster. "And, Ophelia, it's charming to see you again. I haven't had an audience . . . I mean *company* . . . in quite some time. Won't you both come in?" He made a curling gesture with one hand and lights blazed on all around them.

Maddy's smile grew as Ophelia clapped her tentacles. It was exactly what the backstage of a circus should look like, only more so. The large room overflowed with shelves and was studded with at least a dozen brightly painted doors that seemed to promise adventure behind each one. Trunks marked with names such as *FACE PAINTS* and *JUGGLING PINS* balanced in tottering stacks that were taller than Maddy. One box was tipped over, shimmering fabrics spilling from its open top. Another kept bursting into flame and then dousing itself with a floating bucket of water. On the shelves, hats of differing colors and trims vied for space with sequined costumes. Seashells filled an entire cabinet; ropes and other props Maddy couldn't identify filled another.

The only wall without shelves was made of an aquarium that reached from floor to ceiling, full of colorful corals and glittering small fish. As the floor lurched and shook, the water in the tank sloshed softly. Ophelia turned a pleased pink and tentacled down Maddy's side, across the floor, and up the side of the tank, somehow managing to make herself small enough to ooze in through a tiny filter near the ceiling. The mimic octopus dropped to the bottom of the tank and settled down—causing several small crabs to scuttle hurriedly out of the way—and waved happily at Maddy.

Maddy waved back, then turned her attention to the room. It was so grand it took her a few moments to notice that, as Kuma had said, there were no windows, no natural light, and certainly no space to run. On top of one of the shelves, a small, sad-looking plastic bottle pumped out clouds of vapor. Maddy stepped closer and inhaled: imitation buttered popcorn and fake taffy.

"I miss the smells of my circus," explained the Ringmaster. "This was the best I could do under the circumstances."

"It's not bad," lied Maddy.

The Ringmaster raised an eyebrow. "Surely you have better taste than that, my dear girl."

Maddy smiled shyly. "I guess," she said. "Um . . . where are we?"

"We are, in a manner of speaking, inside Il Circo delle Strade. My current home, as it were," he added ruefully.

"You're trying to save the circus," said Maddy. "Vanessa told me."

At the sound of the muse's name, the Ringmaster made a pained face. "Vanessa. She's quite angry with me, I suppose? I never meant to be gone this long."

"She's not angry," said Maddy. "She's worried." She took a deep breath and then dove right in. "I'm here to ask you to come back. To the outside, I mean. To Venice."

"Vanessa sent you, did she?"

"No," said Maddy. "I offered. I, um . . . Vanessa said I lit the marquee."

The Ringmaster's gaze sharpened on her. "Indeed?" he said. "And how did you do that?"

"I don't know," said Maddy, looking away from what suddenly felt like Extra Attention. "When Vanessa told me what was happening, I asked if I could help, and then I rode the Race Thru the Clouds against Skeeter and I won, but the Race didn't send me here, it sent me to some bridge instead, and then I met Isabette, and then—"

"Stop," yelled the Ringmaster, putting his hands over his ears. "My lord! That is a *terrible* way to tell a story. How will you ever put on a good show if you can't tell a proper story?"

Irritation bubbled up in Maddy. She didn't want to put on a show. All she wanted was to explain what had happened so far. She rubbed her bracelet against her shorts, thinking of the fastest, most direct way to say what she had to say. "Sorry. It's just that . . . well . . . can you come back?"

The Ringmaster dropped his hands from his ears. "Completely out of the question."

"Are you sure?" asked Maddy, a little desperately.

"Quite sure. It is not going well, this rescue mission of mine. Not at all. You have, I assume, noticed that shaking around us?"

Maddy nodded.

"Listen closely, and answer if you can: What is it?"

Maddy listened. The rhythm vibrated in her chest and down her limbs; she could make it out more clearly now:

Tha thump. Thadda thump. Tha-tha thump. Thadda thump.

It rattled the props and the walls and shook the water in the aquarium. And not only that . . .

Her bracelet. Maddy wrapped her hand around it, feeling it pulse softly in time with the beat of the room.

Tha thump. Thadda thump. Tha-tha thump. Thadda thump.

Maddy hated guessing games. She always felt silly and slow when she guessed wrong. But this time, she was pretty sure she was right.

"It's a heartbeat," she began, then paused. There was something off about the rhythm, as though the beat itself couldn't quite decide which way to go. "But there's something wrong with it."

The Ringmaster looked pleased. "Very good, very good indeed. Yes, it is a heartbeat, and yes, there is something wrong with it. And that, my dear girl, is why I cannot return."

"I don't understand," said Maddy. The wrongness of the rhythm worried at her, like the buzz of a mosquito. She itched to make it right.

"Of course you don't, for I haven't explained much yet. After all, for a story to work, you must banter to build anticipation and then drop a few intriguing hints." The Ringmaster raised one eyebrow. "Revealing too much too soon spoils the magic."

"I don't think there's time to do all that, what you just said." Maddy tried not to sound as impatient as she felt. "Vanessa . . . well, she's disappearing. Everyone is frightened—and, um, bored. They said to tell you they're bored."

The Ringmaster made a strangled sound.

"Can't you just come back?" asked Maddy.

A shadow passed over the Ringmaster's face. He looked down at his hands, dark and weathered by sun and salt. "My dear girl," he said quietly. "There is nothing I would like more than to return to the stage of my beloved circus. I do not belong behind the curtain for this long. But I am sworn to protect Il Circo delle Strade. I cannot return until the circus is healed."

Maddy shuffled uncomfortably. "Oh. Then, could you . . . I don't know . . . maybe let them come here and talk to *you*?"

"Surely you have met my performers?" asked the Ringmaster. When Maddy nodded, he said, "Then you'll know what an opinionated bunch they are. That makes for a wonderful show but is not at all helpful for making decisions. If they found me, I'd never be free of their ideas and their arguments and their helpful suggestions. There is, you know, a reason for having only one Ringmaster."

Maddy fiddled with her bracelet. Josi had been right. What had Maddy planned to do, really, once she found the Ringmaster? She looked around the room, at all the bright circus things just sitting there.

"But they need you," she said finally.

The Ringmaster sighed, loudly and dramatically. "Of *course* they need me. I am their Ringmaster. You speak as though I don't care what happens in my circus, when there is nothing that I care about more."

Maddy didn't know what to say. She looked around at the walls that shook, at the shelves packed with circus supplies no one was using, at the sad puffs of phony scents coming from the plastic bottle. "Do you know what's wrong?" she asked. "With the circus?"

"Ah!" said the Ringmaster happily. "A perfect opening for a small yet dramatic story. It's been so very long since I had someone to perform for—sorry, I mean someone to talk to."

Maddy frowned. "But don't you think—"

"Of course! You are exactly right!" exclaimed the Ringmaster. He spun around so his suit tails went flying, a swash of seafoam tracing his movement. "We need props."

"I didn't mean—" Maddy began.

"Props!" cried the Ringmaster grandly. He pointed his cane at the shelf filled with seashells, and a rust-colored shell rolled off the shelf, landed with a soft thud on the carpet, and turned into a rust-colored beanbag chair. The chair slid up behind Maddy, bumping the backs of her knees and making her sit. It was surprisingly comfortable, if a bit hard. Then the Ringmaster removed his hat, turned it so she could see there was nothing inside, reached in, and pulled out a handful of candies wrapped in colored paper.

"Circus treats!" he said, presenting them to her with a bow.

Maddy hadn't eaten since lunch at the circus café, and now

her stomach growled. She unwrapped a candy from its waxed paper, popped it into her mouth . . . then immediately gagged and spit it out.

A guffaw of laughter came from the Ringmaster. "Apologies, dear girl, for the old circus trick. We take our saltwater taffy quite literally here. Perhaps you'd prefer a real supper, with some beignets for dessert?"

Maddy used the wrapper to wipe the disgusting ball of salt off her palm and tried to unpucker her mouth. "Yes, please."

The Ringmaster reached again into his top hat. This time, he pulled out a metal tray filled with a dish of macaroni and cheese, a pile of hot roasted almonds, and five perfectly fried pillows of dough coated in cinnamon sugar. A midnight-blue wooden fork and a blue-and-yellow striped cloth napkin were tucked neatly into one side.

"More to your liking, I do hope?" asked the Ringmaster as he handed it to her. Maddy settled the tray on her lap and took a hesitant bite of the macaroni and cheese. It was delicious, and totally normal. Relieved, she wolfed it down. Then she ate a beignet, which turned out to be a fancy doughnut.

As she ate, the Ringmaster stepped away from her and placed both of his sun-weathered hands on his cane.

"Consider this a master class in storytelling," he said, tipping his top hat over his eyes at a rakish angle. Then he lifted his cane and twirled it like a propeller. In its wake appeared an image of a small boy with a hobo bag over his shoulder. Ophelia swam to the front of the tank and pressed herself against the glass to watch.

"Once upon a time," said the Ringmaster, "I was a street child."

Maddy sat up straighter. Up until now she hadn't been sure how people joined the circus. She thought maybe you had to be born into it. But here was the Ringmaster himself, saying he had started out just like her. Maybe he had even been in a group home and escaped!

"I had no home, but I was clever and I soon found the places where people might give a hungry boy an apple or a dime for standing on his hands or throwing his voice."

The boy in the image tossed away his hobo bag and began to cartwheel and flip. An audience gathered around him, throwing coins at his feet.

"Of all the places, Venice was my favorite. It had a magic that anyone could feel. But there was a deeper magic as well, something more powerful, something that only those of us who truly loved the city were able to see. *That* is the magic of Il Circo delle Strade. Il Circo *is* Venice, and Venice *is* Il Circo, but this deeper magic is visible only to those of us who love this place enough to see what it actually is: the most fabulous circus of them all."

The Ringmaster made a gesture and the sound of the heartbeat around them rose as though amplified. It rattled the doors on their hinges and sloshed the water in the fish tank, making Ophelia sway back and forth.

Tha thump. Thadda thump. Tha-tha thump. Thadda thump.

The wrongness of rhythm made Maddy feel a little ill. "So that heartbeat . . . are you saying that's the deeper magic? Like, um . . . the heartbeat of the circus?"

The Ringmaster sighed loudly and dropped his hands to his sides, causing the heartbeat to go back to a quieter volume. "My dear girl, please do not rush the storyteller. Everything must unfold at exactly the right pace or your show will not work."

"But—"

The Ringmaster zipped his finger across his lips.

Maddy closed her mouth, barely able to sit still. She pulled Vanessa's leg warmers up her legs and then scrunched them down again, practically bouncing with impatience.

The Ringmaster cleared his throat, leisurely brushed off his lapels, and continued. "Those of us who loved Venice and could feel its deeper magic were drawn to each other. One by one, we chose to be part of Il Circo. There was nothing we wouldn't try, no act too daring! Those who could see only the surface of the city looked at this place as merely an entertaining way to spend an afternoon. But those of us who could see it for what it is . . . well, we know what is real. And what is real . . ." And here, the Ringmaster paused and drew his hand through the air. A miniature wave formed behind it, spray touching Maddy's cheeks as it crested. ". . . is magic."

The wave in the air crashed, breaking into dozens of glimmering, floating bubbles, their surfaces sheened with color.

One of them bumped against Maddy and popped, letting out a faintly fishy scent and a small burst of applause. Ophelia climbed quickly up the side of the tank and poked a single tentacle out of the filter to pop another bubble, sending more applause through the room.

"Oh my, thank you," said the Ringmaster, bowing. "Really, you're too kind. Thank you, thank you! Now, where was I? Ah, yes. What a glorious time that was, with Venice and the circus so very alive! But things began to change. All but one of the piers burned down. The canals failed and grew stagnant. And for the first time, we needed a leader—someone to protect us through the changing times. Someone to ensure that the heart of Il Circo delle Strade would always beat true and strong."

Maddy stared at the Ringmaster, an uncomfortable pressure building behind her eyelids. She couldn't help but notice that the Ringmaster's eyes were so much like hers, the same width, the same almost-black.

"Ahem," stage-whispered the Ringmaster. "Now is the time in the story for audience participation, which is a vital part of the storytelling process. It makes the audience feel involved."

"Oh," said Maddy. "Sorry. Um . . . I guess that's when you became the Ringmaster?"

The Ringmaster threw his cane into the air, where it shrank into a matching baton, which he caught with a flair. "Indeed it was! We asked Vanessa, the Muse of Venice, to select a Ringmaster based on popular vote. I was honored to be chosen. I swore to protect Il Circo with all my being, all my magic, all my everything, and by request I designed our binding tattoo. Vanessa infused the tattoo with Muse Magic so it would appear when someone committed their loyalty to the circus, and vanish if they chose to leave." In one smooth gesture, the Ringmaster swept up his shirt cuff so Maddy could see the tattoo on the back of his wrist—the same as Adela's—and then slid the sleeve down again. "And ever since then, I have done what I promised, what I was born to do. I have protected my circus and made sure Il Circo remains as it was meant to be."

The Ringmaster took a low, deep bow, staying there a surprisingly long time. Finally, he raised his eyes. "Applause," he hissed through his teeth.

"Oh!" Maddy applauded dutifully as the Ringmaster smiled and bowed and smiled and bowed. Inside the tank, Ophelia clapped as well. "But . . . there's more, right? Like, why the circus is sick?"

The Ringmaster straightened. "Patience, my dear girl! To tell a story well, you must give your audience time to revel in the happy ending before moving on to harder times. Otherwise, there's no pow to your punch, no razzle to your dazzle. Think splash! Think sparkle! Think drama!"

Maddy bit her lip. The Ringmaster's hair was thick and dark and wavy like hers. And hadn't she heard his voice somewhere before? She stared at her hands, willing away the unexpected question that flashed into her mind as a bubble popped against her arm, sending forth another staccato burst of applause. The Ringmaster took another deep bow.

"I'm not very good at sparkle," she said as the Ringmaster straightened up.

"Clearly," said the Ringmaster dryly. "Ah well. When you're starved for an audience . . . forgive me again, I mean *company* . . . you make do with what you have. Now, as you suspected, the heartbeat that shakes these walls is the heartbeat of the circus. Like all living things, the circus has a heart—the Heart at the End of the World—which beats the true rhythm of the circus. But a while ago, perhaps a year or so, the Heart began to lose itself, its rhythm slipping further from what it was. This, my dear girl, is why the circus is sick. I came here to help the Heart find its way back to its proper rhythm, but it has not gone quite as planned. You asked, before, where we are. The answer is that we are almost—but not quite—at the Heart at the End of the World. We are at its front door, so to speak. And for some reason I can no longer walk through that door into the Heart itself. The path I have always used will not let me pass. So I am stuck out here, standing in the foyer and doing what I can, while the real show is inside."

The ache in Maddy's head was now throbbing in time with the heartbeat. "How come the path to the Heart won't let you in?"

"That, I do not know."

Even the way the Ringmaster stood reminded Maddy of . . .

something. Or someone. "But can't you come back, just for a little while? To see everyone?"

"Alas, I cannot," said the Ringmaster. "And here is why."

He made a broad gesture with one hand and the wall behind him grew transparent, becoming a window that looked into the depth of a golden sea. In the middle of the sea sat an enormous human heart. It was as wide as a schoolyard and as tall as a castle—and it was wrapped with lengths and lengths of thick black rope. Looking at it made Maddy's whole body hurt. With a jolt, she realized it was a Ringmaster's whip, pressing so tightly into the Heart at the End of the World that glistening muscle oozed between the strands. The whip was squeezing the Heart with one rhythm while the Heart itself was beating another. That was why the rhythm was so off, so wrong.

In the tank, Ophelia turned a worried gray.

"It isn't pretty, but I'm afraid it *is* necessary," said the Ringmaster. "Bindings are one of my specialties. My whip and my will are binding the heartbeat steady, trying to help the Heart return to its original rhythm. This is the best I can do until I can find my way in, for—as with any heart—true and lasting rhythms can only be set from the inside. This particular type of binding will not work if I am not nearby. Were I to leave, even for a short time, my whip would release its grip on the Heart and come find me, leaving the Heart with no guidance at all. I shudder to think what might happen then."

And the Ringmaster *did* shudder, violently and dramatically, and the wall grew opaque again—but the image of the Heart, sick and swollen and forcibly contained, stayed imprinted on Maddy's mind. She opened her mouth to ask how she could help, but to her dismay something else rushed out instead.

"Are you my father?" her mouth asked without her.

The Ringmaster stared at her, clearly astonished. Then he did the most awful thing possible.

He began to laugh.

Heat flushed up the back of Maddy's neck. She jumped to her feet and went over to the aquarium, where Ophelia stared at her with big, worried eyes. Maddy looked away, making a show of watching two colorful clownfish chase each other around a miniature big top, but Ophelia wasn't fooled. The octopus climbed out of the filter and down the side of the aquarium onto Maddy's shoulder, and Maddy's eyes blurred as she tried not to cry. The worst of it was, she knew better. Of course she did. It was the first thing every group home kid learned backward and forward: No one is coming to save you. You aren't royalty in disguise. This is your life, like it or not. These are the cards you were dealt.

Ophelia patted her cheek, leaving behind a cool saltwater tang. Maddy reached up and gently squeezed one tentacle.

"Oh, my dear girl, I *am* sorry." The Ringmaster, no longer laughing, came up behind them. "I didn't mean to be rude, but this circus is my work, my family, my whole life. It is quite enough progeny for me." The Ringmaster turned Maddy to face him and lifted her chin with one hand. "Come now. Imagine what a terrible father I would make, all dazzle and flash? While that may sound fun, I am told that children need rules and boundaries as well."

"You have rules," said Maddy, a little more sulkily than she had intended. "Vanessa told me. No New Acts and No New Audience."

The Ringmaster smiled a little sadly and released her chin as a few more soap bubbles floated past. "You are correct. I do indeed have rules. But what I most certainly do not have are children."

Maddy ducked her head in hopes the Ringmaster wouldn't see the tears that stung at her eyes. He cleared his throat and looked away, poking bubble after bubble with his baton until the sound of applause covered Maddy's sniffs. Ophelia turned into a box of tissues but couldn't seem to replicate the tissues themselves, so she morphed back to herself and meeped apologetically.

"I'm okay," Maddy whispered as the applause around them died down. She swiped one last time at the wet on her cheeks. On her wrist, her bracelet pulsed gently.

The Ringmaster turned back to her. He seemed about to speak, but then his eyes traveled down to her bracelet.

"My dear girl," he said slowly. "Wherever did you get that?"

"From my parents," said Maddy—and then, for the first time ever, added, "I think."

"May I?" asked the Ringmaster, reaching for it.

Maddy held out her arm.

The Ringmaster wrapped two fingers around her wrist as though taking her pulse, turning her arm this way and that as he studied her bracelet. "Interesting," he murmured. "Interesting indeed."

"What's interesting?" asked Maddy.

The Ringmaster released her arm. "What is interesting," he said, and his gaze on Maddy was as warm as a sun-drenched sea, "is that you appear to be bound to the Heart at the End of the World."

12

"I've never even *heard* of Il Circo delle Strade before today!" said Maddy. "How could I be bound to the heart of something I've never heard of?"

But a strange light was flaring inside of her, catching at her with a wild, nameless hope. For didn't the whole circus seem strangely familiar, as though she had been here before? As though she had . . .

. . . perhaps . . .

. . . been *born* here?

"Oh!" she said, her voice louder than she had intended, making Ophelia jump. Excitement ricocheted inside of her like a trapped sparrow. "They were part of the circus, weren't they? They had to be, and that means you know them, right? You must have! Please, tell me who they are!"

"My dear girl, whatever are you talking about?"

"My parents! They gave me this bracelet, and this bracelet binds me to the heart of Il Circo, so they had to be part of it . . . right?" Maddy could hardly stand still. She showed Ophelia the silver band, then showed it to the Ringmaster again, as though that were proof enough. "And if they were part of the circus, you must know who they are!"

The Ringmaster frowned. "It is true that I know everyone in Il Circo. It is also true that no one in the circus has ever had a child they gave up, or even a child now unaccounted for. I am sorry, Madeline Adriana. I do not know your parents."

"But you must have!" she pressed. "They had to be here, they just had to!"

This time when the Ringmaster spoke, his voice had an undercurrent of steel. "Do not forget that I was an orphan myself. I know how it feels. Had I known your parents, had either of them been bound to Il Circo, I would have found a home for you. Not with me, mind you, but somewhere. No child becomes parentless on my watch."

Maddy could hear the truth of it in his voice, and the sparrow of excitement within her became a flurry of beaks and talons ripping at her insides. The pure joy of thinking she might find her parents had made her forget the simple, basic fact of her existence: Her parents didn't want her. They had given her up. If they were even still alive, they probably didn't want to be found. Maddy imagined opening a door in her ribs and letting the angry sparrow fly away so it couldn't tear her apart anymore. Without it, her chest felt surprisingly small and cold. She reached up and hooked her finger around one of Ophelia's tentacles, trying to force any sign of sadness from her face. It must not have worked, though, as the Ringmaster put one gnarled hand on her shoulder. They stood there for a long moment, until Maddy looked up and nodded.

The Ringmaster took his hand back, studying Maddy. "You said you wished to help save Il Circo, did you not?"

Maddy gave another tiny nod, not yet ready to speak. Maybe she could still belong somewhere. Maybe, even without parents, she could have a real home.

"Come," said the Ringmaster, and he led them to one of the doors, this one painted a rich gold that matched the color of the sea outside. He pulled a large, ornate key from his pocket, fitted it into the lock, and swung the door open. The heartbeat around them grew louder.

Tha thump. Thadda thump. Tha-tha thump. Thadda thump.

Behind the door was a tunnel with odd, curved walls that were rough and striated and glistening pink and red. Maddy could only see down the first few feet, for after that the tunnel twisted away into darkness. Ophelia hid in Maddy's hair as moist, dank air blew from the doorway.

The Ringmaster took off his top hat and bowed deeply. "Watch," he instructed, and then he went to step through the doorway. As though an invisible trampoline covered the entrance, his foot bounced back. He tried several more times, from different angles and directions, once even running at full speed, but each time the doorway bounced him away. Finally, he bowed again and set the top hat back on his head. Thin, tired lines that Maddy hadn't noticed before radiated from the corners of his eyes.

"As you see, I cannot go through—even though this is the same path I have traveled many, many times before." The Ringmaster flicked his fingers and a copper lantern popped into his hand, blazing light. He passed the lantern to Maddy, who held it well away from Ophelia. "But you are bound to the Heart, so perhaps it will let you step through the door. This is just the pathway there, mind you, not the Heart itself, but it is straight and true and should lead you inside."

Maddy nodded. Her stomach, while still churning, had settled down enough for her to talk without her voice breaking. She looked at Ophelia.

"Okay?" she asked.

Ophelia unwrapped her tentacle from Maddy's finger and made a walking motion down Maddy's arm. Then she tipped her head forward in a *yes*.

"Okay," Maddy repeated, mostly to herself. She still felt small and empty, but this was something she could do. "I should just . . . step through the door?"

The Ringmaster nodded. "If you can," he said.

Lantern in hand, octopus on shoulder, Maddy tentatively

stepped over the threshold. It was like walking through any other doorway, with nothing pushing back at her or bouncing her away. The Ringmaster let out a great breath of air, sagging as though he had just set down something heavy.

Illuminated by her lantern, the inside of the hallway looked disturbingly like human muscle. Ophelia's skin turned a matching, striated red.

"It's not a *real* heart, is it?" Maddy asked, a little nervously.

"All hearts are real," said the Ringmaster.

Tha thump. Thadda thump. Tha-tha thump. Thadda thump.

Deep inside her, Maddy felt her own heart respond, skittering and straining, trying to match the rhythm around her. And as it did, a thought bounced just out of reach. She paused, struggling to capture it.

It was something about her heart condition, the one no doctor could diagnose.

Something about how it had started about a year ago . . . around the same time the Ringmaster had said that the Heart at the End of the World began to lose its rhythm.

Something about her bracelet binding her to that very Heart.

Maddy's hand flew to her mouth, making the lantern in her other hand sway and bounce, sending wild shadows jumping across the muscled walls. She felt faint with understanding.

"Is this why I'm sick?" The question came out as a whisper. "It is, isn't it?"

The Ringmaster lifted an eyebrow quizzically.

"I . . . um, I have a heart condition." Maddy paused and swallowed hard. She glanced at her bracelet and then back at the Ringmaster. "No one knows what it is. I haven't been sick for very long, though. Only about a year. Like the Heart at the End of the World."

"I see," said the Ringmaster. His eyes, too, flicked to the bracelet on her wrist.

"If I'm sick because the Heart at the End of the World is sick," Maddy said, hardly daring to hope, "does that mean that when it's better, I will be too? Since I'm, um, bound to it?"

"Bindings are tricky things," said the Ringmaster. "They can be unpredictable. I did not create yours, and so I cannot say for sure . . . but had I to guess, the answer would be yes."

Maddy didn't know where to look. She could be healthy again, like she used to be. She could have a life without being sick, without worrying about doctors and lying down and Extra Attention. The beating of the walls seeped into her bones.

She held out her braceleted arm to the Ringmaster. "What if I don't want to be bound?" she asked. "Can you take this off me?"

The Ringmaster took her wrist, once again studying her bracelet. "No," he said finally. "It appears that only you can do that."

"I can't," said Maddy firmly. "I've tried."

The Ringmaster looked at her, his dark eyes unreadable. "Bindings rarely break the way we think they should," he said.

"I cannot tell exactly how this one works, but I can see the magic for its removal by the wearer threaded through it. If you truly want it off, you will discover how to do it."

Maddy tightened her hold on the lantern as Ophelia rearranged herself on Maddy's shoulder. *Did* she truly want her bracelet off? Even now, even knowing what she thought she might know, she wasn't sure. There was no denying that it made her feel special, made her feel like she had something all her own. If she could help the Ringmaster get the Heart at the End of the World back to its rhythm, and if that meant she wouldn't be sick anymore, maybe then her bracelet would just feel magical again. She nodded once, at no one in particular.

"What do I do when I get inside the Heart?" she asked.

The Ringmaster grasped the seashell at the end of his baton. The shell had shrunk to the size of a silver dollar, and now the Ringmaster twisted it off and offered it to her. "Once you are inside the Heart, smash this shell. It will call me to you, and from there I will be able to lead the Heart back to its rhythm. Only then can I return to my beloved circus."

Maddy reached out through the doorway the Ringmaster could not pass and took the shell, slipping it into her shirt pocket with her pills. Ophelia used a tentacle to tuck the shell deeper into the pocket.

"Just follow the path," said the Ringmaster. "And perhaps you do not need me to say it, but break a leg."

"It's not a show," said Maddy quietly. On her shoulder,

Ophelia flashed bright white and became, for a moment, a shining marquee.

"My dear girl," said the Ringmaster gravely, *everything* is a show."

13

THA THUMP. THADDA THUMP. THA-THA THUMP.
THADDA THUMP.

The heartbeat here sounded as though someone had turned
the bass all the way up on the hugest speakers possible, and
Maddy's own heart vibrated in time like a tuning fork. She
could see only as far as the lantern illuminated, and each step
took her full concentration so as not to slip on the wet muscle.
On her shoulder, Ophelia shifted with her as they tried to keep
each other balanced.

"This is okay, right?" asked Maddy as she followed the tunnel deeper in. "We won't get stuck in here or anything, will
we?"

Ophelia turned a green-means-go kind of color. It looked

somewhat sickly in the red tunnel, but it was enough for Maddy to feel better. But then the pathway opened up into a fork.

Maddy stopped and stared. The path on the right was sunk in darkness, while the one on the left flickered with dim, inviting sunlight. She chewed on her lip as she and Ophelia glanced from one side the other. Why hadn't the Ringmaster told them which way to go?

"What do you think?" she asked.

The mimic octopus shrugged all eight tentacles.

"Yeah," said Maddy. "I agree."

Maddy waited a few moments to see whether her bracelet or her heart would tug or pull, but neither one did. It figured that now, when she actually needed direction, they were silent.

"Left," she said finally. She was tired of the dark, tired of the unknown. Besides, surely a circus heart would be lit up and shiny. Ophelia nodded her agreement, and they turned to the left.

THA THUMP. THADDA THUMP. THA-THA THUMP. THADDA THUMP.

Maddy's own heart was starting to pound with the same uneven rhythm, her chest aching with each beat while her breath stabbed into her ribs. If this was what it was like when she was still outside the Heart, how bad would it be once she was inside of it? She wasn't sure she could take it. She glanced at Ophelia, who cooed soothingly.

"I'll be all right," said Maddy, and she clamped her teeth together.

THA THUMP. THADDA THUMP. THA-THA THUMP. THADDA THUMP.

The next time the tunnel split, Maddy looked at Ophelia and Ophelia looked at Maddy.

"Let's just keep going toward the sun," said Maddy. Her jaw was starting to ache. "Sound okay?"

Ophelia flashed green. Maddy tried to walk quickly, not wanting to keep them in this tunnel one second longer than she had to, not with her own heart so wild. At the next split in the path, she thought she heard the sound of the ocean coming from the brighter path.

Tha thump. Thadda thump. Tha-tha thump. Thadda thump.

"That way!" said Maddy, thinking of the sea of golden liquid around the Heart. "It has to be, right?"

With every step, the sound of the waves grew stronger. And so Maddy wasn't really surprised when the tunnel began to slosh with salt water, although the water was clear rather than golden. She wasn't really surprised when the muscle beneath them gave way entirely to ocean, the leg warmers rising to cover her face as Ophelia let go of her shoulder to swim alongside her and the lantern vanished into the current. She wasn't even that surprised when Isabette swam up, exhaled sharply through her nose—Maddy could tell because of all the bubbles—and grabbed Maddy's arm to pull her through the water. And she *definitely* wasn't surprised that Isabette looked highly irritated.

But she *was* a little surprised when they surfaced not inside the Heart, but right back in the same Venice canal. Ophelia popped up next to them as the leg warmers slid back from Maddy's face and rearranged themselves around her calves like wet, woolen ankle weights. The nighttime air felt cool against her wet skin.

"Out," commanded Isabette, pointing sternly to a floating wooden platform moored to the side of the canal. Maddy clambered onto it—she couldn't wait to get out of the water, honestly—and sat, shivering, on the edge with her knees pulled to her chest. She could feel her pill bottle and the Ringmaster's shell in her pocket as her knees pressed against them. The wood of the dock beneath her was warm from earlier in the day, and a beautiful crescent moon hung high in the sky.

In the water, Ophelia became a fancy serving platter and looked at Maddy hungrily.

"Of course," said Maddy. "Have a good dinner. I'll see you soon."

Ophelia made a relieved *whoosh* and jetted away, leaving a small puff of blue-and-yellow ink in the water.

As soon as the octopus was gone, Isabette slapped her own arms—a little forcefully, Maddy thought—onto the platform to hold herself up in the water, and then took the kind of inhale that group home leaders take before they yell at you for a very, very long time.

Maddy flopped onto her back and steeled herself for a lecture, her mind racing. Why was she back here instead of inside the Heart at the End of the World? Was this where the Heart was? And most of all—was she really bound to it?

"What were you thinking—" began Isabette sternly. But before she could continue, another voice cut her off.

"Octogirl! Yo, Octogirl!"

Maddy jumped up. "Skeeter!" she cried happily.

Skeeter was running over a footbridge toward them, a skateboard under each arm and his hair sticking up as though he had towel-dried it with electricity. He jumped lightly onto the floating dock, right over Isabette's folded arms.

"Oh, hey, Isabette," he said without even looking at her. Isabette huffed like a bull about to charge. "Octogirl, you okay? You hit the canal so hard after the Race, I thought . . . well, never mind what I thought. I've been looking for you forever, and I just saw your octopus friend, and, well . . . you're okay, right?"

Even in the dark, Skeeter looked exhausted, with puffy circles under his eyes. Maddy nodded, too overcome to speak. Surely Skeeter couldn't mean that he had been walking through the canals since she crashed . . . could he? That was hours ago!

"Good," said Skeeter. "Man, I'm sorry. I should have caught you. At least I caught *this*, though . . . and you're okay . . . so . . ."

He handed over her skateboard.

Maddy didn't feel cold anymore, not with Skeeter smiling at her and giving her back the skateboard she never thought she'd see again. "I can't believe you have this!" she said, hugging her board. "Thank you! But . . . Skeeter? How long have you been looking for me?"

"Since your board dumped you," said Skeeter. "I figured you'd come up in the same place, or at least I hoped you would, and—"

"Enough!" Isabette slammed her fish tail onto the canal's surface. Murky water doused them both, but Maddy didn't care. She had never had someone her own age come looking for her before, someone who maybe, actually, even wanted to spend time with her. The thought made her cheeks flush with happiness.

"That's the nicest thing anyone's ever done for me," she whispered to Skeeter—but quietly, hoping Isabette couldn't hear.

"Aw, shucks," Skeeter whispered back, his dimples deepening. "It was nothing. By the way, that was a sweet crash you did into the water. When you bring the Ringmaster back, maybe that can be a new act. We could call it *Octogirl's Spectacular Fall from the Sky.*"

"Silenzio!" Isabette yelled. "Skeeter Chen, this is partly your fault! You and your breaking of our rules, trying to join the circus when you're not of age! And what has come of it? More rules broken, and my waterways dirtied with crashing girls.

And *you*"—she turned to Maddy—"trying to enter the Heart! You are not ready. You are not even *close* to ready!"

"The Ringmaster thought I was," Maddy shot back. She was tired of people telling her what she was and wasn't ready for. She held up her braceleted wrist. "Did you know about this?" she demanded. "About me being bound?"

Skeeter's eyes grew wide. "Whoa," he said. "What's *that*?"

"Apparently," said Maddy, still staring at Isabette, "it's a binding."

Isabette's lips pressed into a thin line, and then softened. "Va bene," she admitted. "Yes. I knew."

"How did you get that?" Skeeter broke in excitedly. "Aren't you too young, like me? And why is it different from the other bindings? They're all tattoos. Why isn't yours a tattoo?"

Maddy let her arm drop. She was suddenly exhausted, and even holding up her hand seemed like far too much work. "Because it's not the same kind," she said wearily. "It isn't one the Ringmaster designed, and I didn't ask for it like you asked for yours. It binds me to the Heart at the End of the World."

"You're bound to the heart of the circus?" Skeeter didn't look at all sleepy anymore. "Octogirl, that is *so cool*!"

"Is it?" asked Maddy. "But what if I don't *want* to be bound? To anything?"

"There is always a choice," said Isabette.

Maddy swung to face the mermaid. "Everyone keeps saying that," she cried, and she yanked hard at her bracelet. "But it isn't true! Look! It doesn't come off, so how can there be a choice? I thought this was a gift from my parents, something that let me see magic, but now I don't even know what it is. I don't even know who *I* am!"

"You're Octogirl," said Skeeter, like this was the easiest, most obvious thing in the world. "That's who you are."

Maddy tried to force a smile. *Octogirl* was fine—no, it was great. But it wasn't enough. It didn't tell her anything about her bracelet, or her parents, or herself before now. Not really.

Isabette sighed. When she spoke, her tone was slightly softer. "You are not ready for the Heart at the End of the World. It will not let you in if you choose only the bright parts that feel safe."

"I went the wrong way, you mean," said Maddy bitterly. After all that. After racing and winning and finding the Ringmaster when no one else could, she was back where she started. She sat down on the wooden dock and dropped her head into her hands, wishing Ophelia was on her shoulder. Skeeter sat down next to her.

The mermaid sighed again. "You could not have known which way to go," she said. "The Ringmaster sent you through *his* door, *his* way into the Heart. That doorway could never work for anyone but him. He should have known it would not work for you."

Maddy lifted her head. "He seemed awfully sure it was the right way."

"It *was*—for him, and only for him," said Isabette. "And only for the person he was when that doorway first formed, not for who he is now. The way in is different for everyone, and even then, no one's path stays the same for an entire lifetime."

Maddy looked over the side of the floating dock, at the rippled reflection of the crescent moon on the dark water. "What's *my* way, then?" she asked.

"I cannot know," said Isabette. "No one can but you. But what I do know is this: You must be prepared to accept all of the Heart or it will not let you in. You must accept all of Il Circo."

Next to her, Skeeter sat up taller, suddenly alert.

"But I *do*," said Maddy, a little wounded at the accusation. Hadn't she offered to help? Hadn't she loved all of it?

With one powerful push from her tail, Isabette propelled herself out of the canal and onto the dock, sliding across the wet wood until she was only inches from Maddy. Skeeter jumped up and out of the way, grabbing his board, but Maddy sat very, very still. Her heart pounded and skittered as she and Isabette stared at each other.

"Do you?" Isabette asked, her voice low. Her lashes were black and thick and she smelled of salt and wildness. "Do you really? You cannot keep walking only toward the brightness and expect to understand this circus enough for its Heart to let you in. Il Circo delle Strade is so much more than sunshine on the boardwalk and the sparkle of daytime tricks. It is also danger and sharpness and the things we give up. Be very clear about this."

Skeeter whistled low through his teeth. "The nighttime circus," he said.

"Yes," said the mermaid, her eyes on Maddy. "You must accept all of Il Circo if you wish to enter the Heart. You must go to the nighttime circus and see it for what it is, see *all* of Il Circo for what it is. And then you must accept it all."

Skeeter shuffled uncertainly from one foot to the other, skateboard dangling by his side. "I don't know, Octogirl," he said. "Kids aren't allowed. It's too . . ." He paused, searching for the word. "Too much," he finally finished.

"No one will stop you, not in the nighttime," said Isabette. She flashed Skeeter a look. "How is it that you, who cares nothing for our rules, have not yet stepped into the night?"

"I don't mind rules," Skeeter shot back. "Except for the one that says I'm too young to join the circus. That rule is dumb." He paused for a moment and then shrugged uncomfortably. "With the nighttime circus . . . it's just . . . I've heard things."

Maddy wasn't sure she could face something that made Skeeter sound frightened. "What kinds of things?" she asked.

"Just . . . things," said Skeeter. "The crowds, for one. They're different at night. It's not like the daytime, where the circus is spread through the whole city. At nighttime, the performers and the audience . . . they're all mixed together. There's no space."

"The nighttime circus does not allow for space," said Isabette. She tilted her head as if listening, and then added, "It has already begun. If you wish to get inside the Heart, you must go. That is the first step."

Maddy was tired. She was so, so tired. "Does it have to be

tonight?" she asked. All she wanted to do was lie down. "Can I go another time?"

Something in Isabette's face shifted, making her seem somehow more far away. "Of course," said the mermaid. "Do whatever you want. Perhaps you would rather return?"

"Return?" asked Maddy. "Return where?"

"To your life before. The group home will take you in without question. The magic can do that, should you wish. It can make it easy for you to return without any fuss, as though you had never been gone at all. You always have a choice."

"Octogirl?" said Skeeter. "You don't want to go back . . . do you?"

Maddy stared at the wooden slats of the dock, so tired she felt light-headed. She didn't want to go to the nighttime circus, not really. But going back to the group home? Back to talking to another version of Waterfall T and pretending she didn't see things that others couldn't, pretending her bracelet was just another piece of jewelry? She could never choose that. For she was no longer a girl who let others lead her away from the magic that she knew was there. No, she was a girl who had raced through the sky on a giant skateboard. She was a girl who had talked to a mermaid and a lion with wings. She was a girl with an octopus for a friend.

She was fairly certain she would never be the other kind of girl again.

"If I do this," said Maddy slowly, "if I go to the nighttime circus, then the Heart will let me in?"

"No," said Isabette, and an unexpected look of sympathy softened her features. "The nighttime circus is only the first step. You must face it and see it for what it is, yes. But then you must face *yourself* as well. To do that, you must return to the Ponte dei Sospiri, the Bridge of Sighs, and make it across. Then and only then will the Heart let you in, for no one may enter the Heart without first crossing the Bridge of Sighs."

A shiver ran up the backs of Maddy's legs. She knew something had happened on that bridge, something terrible, but she couldn't remember exactly what.

"What's the Bridge of Sighs?" asked Skeeter.

"It is the last step to entering the Heart," Isabette said.

"Well, that's not cryptic or anything," said Skeeter, but under his breath so Isabette wouldn't hear.

"I was there," said Maddy slowly. "But I don't remember much about it. Just that it was cold and dark and . . . awful." Out of long habit, Maddy spun her bracelet around her wrist, staring at the shiny silver band, at her name carved in curvy letters. She could feel both Skeeter and Isabette watching her.

"Okay," she said finally, taking a deep breath. "The nighttime circus and then the Bridge of Sighs. I'm ready. Um . . . is there any way I can dry my clothing first? It's really cold."

"Of course," said Isabette, and without moving any other part of herself, she flicked her mermaid tail up until the very tip of it was touching Maddy's shirt. As soon as it did, water ran out of Maddy's clothing and across Isabette's tail like a tiny river. Soon Maddy's tank top and shorts were completely dry. Only a fine film of white salt over the fabric even hinted at the fact that Maddy had ever been drenched.

"Whoa," said Skeeter, and his voice sounded almost normal again, almost confident and brash. "Nice trick."

"*Trick?*" Isabette's brows pulled together in distaste. "I am sure you don't intend to compare control over the waterways to a mere circus trick. What I have is a *responsibility*, not a trick."

Isabette had a dangerous look on her face. Maddy stood up hastily, before things got out of hand.

"I should go," she said, almost adding, *before I change my mind.*

Skeeter cleared his throat. "Well, then," he said, and he ran one hand through his spiky hair, making it stand up even more. "Let's do it. *Up next in the daring adventures of Octogirl, Queen of the Skateboard Cephalopods, and Skeeter Chen, the Fastest Boy on Wheels: our intrepid heroes brave the Nighttime Circus. Chills! Thrills! Danger! Will they survive?*"

The word *survive* hovered in the night air, leaving behind a trace of uncertainty. But all Maddy heard was one thing, and suddenly she wasn't so tired after all.

"You're coming with me?" she asked.

"Wouldn't miss it for the world," said Skeeter, flashing a halfway-convincing grin.

Maddy gripped her skateboard, gratitude welling up in her,

and then turned to Isabette. "I should tell Ophelia. Do you know where she went?"

"Do not worry about the octopus," said the mermaid. "She will be fine, and the nighttime circus is not a place she needs to go. I will tell her where you are, and she will find you when you finish with what needs to be done."

Maddy didn't like the sound of that at all. She glanced at Skeeter, who wasn't even trying to smile anymore.

"The nighttime is gathered now at the mouth of the pier," Isabette continued, and she pushed off the side of the dock into the water as a shadowy bird soared by, its dark green wings shining black in the nighttime. "Go there and see truly. Then decide what you will do."

Isabette turned to leave.

"Wait!" called Maddy.

The mermaid paused, one slender hand on the dock. Her olive skin glowed.

Maddy almost wasn't sure why she was still asking, but the question burned inside her. "Did you know my parents?"

Isabette smiled an odd, soft smile. "Ciao, bambina," she said, and slid silently under the water, her tail catching a silvery spark of moonlight.

The nighttime air was cool and still as Maddy and Skeeter
made their way through the canals toward the main street, the
only illumination coming from the few porchlights that were
still on. Noises that in the daytime were soft and happy—wind
chimes, ducks, water lapping at the edges of the canal—sounded
eerie and frightening, and in the background was a crashing
so thunderous and constant that it took Maddy a moment to
realize it was the sound of the sea. She had never heard waves
roar like that before. She had also never been out this late at
night before. But because Skeeter was with her, she didn't jump
at every sound, or startle when the wind made shadows dance
across the walkway.

Near the end of the canal, Maddy could just make out the
silhouette of the large bird that had soared by. It was standing

ankle-deep in the shallow water, so still that it could have been a sculpture. Its body was thick and stocky, and a light-colored plume curved from the back of its head. She wondered what it was.

"Night heron," said a soft voice from behind. "They come to the canals to hunt, but only at night."

Maddy gave a small shriek as she and Skeeter both jumped. Behind them stood a man with snakes coiled around his arms and neck.

"Dov," said Skeeter, blowing out a hard exhale and half-laughing. "Dude. You nearly gave us a heart attack."

"I don't think that's Dov," whispered Maddy, her stomach twisting in on itself.

The person behind them looked like Dov, with the same round face and tightly curled hair, the same spangled bathing suit. But something wasn't right in the way he was holding himself, and his face had taken on a rough, hungry look. The snakes, too, looked more dangerous somehow. One of them wove toward Maddy, unblinking, and she drew back as its tongue flicked over her hand, her arm, her shoulder.

"Sure it is," said Skeeter, but he sounded uncertain. "Dov? That's you, right?"

"The nighttime circus is beginning," said Dov-who-was-not-Dov, and he moved past them. Maddy and Skeeter pressed back into the bushes, out of his way, his snakes hissing as he turned and headed toward the pier.

And then the drumming started, a sound like a hundred drummers hitting their drums over and over again in unison.

BAM. BAM. BAM. BAM.

This was no daytime rhythm made to accompany glittery acrobats and muses with lightning bolt skates. This was something altogether different, and it clawed at Maddy's insides and made her skin itch and burn.

"I don't like this, Octogirl," said Skeeter quietly.

"Me either," said Maddy. "But we're still going, right?"

Skeeter nodded slowly. "I guess. I'm as ready as I'm going to be."

"Me too," said Maddy, and together they stepped out of the canal and turned toward the nighttime circus.

The crowd was taking shape. Unlike the daytime circus, which had seemed to show up in sparks of magic here and there throughout the city, the nighttime circus was gathered in one place, a dense, roiling mass of people. Maddy caught flashes of white-painted clown faces with leering red lips and people in grotesque wooden masks. Torches lined the street, their smoke throwing everything into distortion like fun-house mirrors, and loud, strange laughter pierced the air alongside the sound of the drums.

BAM. BAM. BAM. BAM.

Maddy didn't realize she had stopped walking until Skeeter ran right into her.

"Sorry," she managed to say. Skeeter's face was pale, his

mouth set in a tight line. Maddy surprised herself and reached for his hand.

"It's just Il Circo," she whispered, as much to herself as to him. Her heart was beginning to race. "Right?"

Skeeter's lips tried to do something resembling a smile, but then gave up. "Right-e-o," he said. "Let's just . . . let's not get separated, okay?"

"Deal," said Maddy.

Holding hands, they walked forward.

Maddy had never been anywhere so crowded in her entire life—it was like stepping inside a ferocious, living animal. She had no idea there were this many audience members for Il Circo. In the daytime they must all be spread out, here and there across the boardwalk and the beaches and the canals. She liked that so much better, and she tightened her grip on Skeeter's hand as they were jostled from every side by people twice her size.

"Look out!" cried Skeeter, pulling her out of the way as someone with red hair gelled into horns on either side of his head raced past on a unicycle. Maddy teetered and crashed into someone else; when she turned to apologize, the words froze in her mouth. It was a gnarled, human tree, reaching out branches to grab her. Skeeter yanked her out of the tree's grasp, but now they were right in the path of a group of tumblers wearing skeleton masks who were cartwheeling and flipping through the crowd, knocking over anyone who didn't move fast enough.

Maddy's heart slammed against her ribs and her breath came

short and sharp. Isabette had said she had to accept the night-time circus, but how could she ever do that? This was nothing like the daytime. This was awful, too much like a group home where if you looked away for even a second someone would steal your things or tell a lie to get you into trouble. Why couldn't she just stay in the daytime, in the part of the circus that was welcoming and fun? Surely the Heart understood that the day-time was better! Surely it didn't want her to be scared . . .

. . . did it?

As the crowd roared around them, Maddy patted her pocket, the shape of the pill bottle next to the Ringmaster's shell a com-forting reminder of safety. If she had to, she could always take a pill. They calmed her heart, but they also made her sleepy and slow. She didn't want to take one, not here, not in the mid-dle of *this*, where she needed to stay alert. Instead, she tried to breathe more deeply. When she had been little and scared of the dark, an older girl at one of the homes had taught her a calm-ing breath, breathing in and out to the count of five. She did that now, counting under her breath as she and Skeeter tried to find a path through the crowd. With a jolt, Maddy realized that the older girl, who had seemed so very grown-up at the time, had been the same age that she was now. The thought gave her courage as they cut behind a booth selling nightmares—and almost slammed into someone selling fondest wishes.

Maddy skidded to a halt, but Skeeter didn't.

"There's more space over there," he said, pointing to the

side of the street where no one was gathered. A building stood there, the sidewalk below it clean and empty. On the side of the building was a sweeping, weathered mural of an impossibly long, lean woman diving sideways, her arms stretched forward to clasp hold of one of the building's circular windows. She had no discernible facial features, as though the artist had forgotten to paint them, and her dark hair stretched behind her the entire length of the wall.

"Just one second," said Maddy. She wanted to get out of the crowd, too, but she had to at least ask about her wish. "Is that okay?"

When Skeeter nodded, Maddy backed up a few steps, pulling Skeeter with her. The carny stood with his box of fondest wishes taped closed at his feet, the top of it bulging as though the things inside wanted to get out.

"Well, well, well," said the carny. There was no sign here of the friendly barker, no jolly and boisterous ticket taker. "Up late tonight, ain't we, girly? Yo, Skeets."

"Hey, Barton," Skeeter replied, glancing around uneasily.

"You two here for the nighttime circus? Kids ain't allowed, ya know. It's no never mind to me, of course. Long as you ain't asking if it's *safe*." He grinned then, and his grin reminded Maddy of the coyotes that used to roam the hills near one of her group homes. Living there had been so sad—the coyotes had been thin and menacing, and people's pets always disappeared.

Maybe stopping had been a mistake.

But she was here now, so she may as well ask what she wanted to ask. Maddy backed up, out of Barton's reach, just in case.

"Is my wish in there?" she asked.

"Lemme see," said the carny, pulling one hand from a pocket to rub his chin in an exaggerated movement. "Which one was yours, again? Oh, right, that puny hard one. Nah, the ones that ain't developed, they don't sell."

Maddy counted her inhale and exhale, then did it again. Next to her, she could hear Skeeter breathing hard as well. "Can I have it back, then?" she asked.

"Not my call to make, girly. Ya want it back bad enough, it'll come all on its own. But think good and hard before ya call back a wish. I been in this business a long time, and lemme tell ya, sometimes losing yer fondest wish makes you lost. But other times . . ."

BAM. BAM. BAM. BAM.

The carny's voice trailed off as the drums grew louder.

"What happens other times?" asked Maddy, raising her voice to be heard.

The carny looked over their heads at whatever was happening behind them, and then swept up his sign and box in one practiced movement. "Other times, girly? Well, other times, it frees ya. Have fun, kiddies. Be careful . . . or don't. Either way, gotta run!"

Within seconds, Barton was lost in the crowd. At the same time, an act had started up right near them, two women in demon masks flinging knives at each other with such force that Maddy could hear the blades whistling as they flew past. The cheering, hooting crowd pressed closer and someone bumped into Skeeter. He stumbled into Maddy, grasping her shoulder for balance.

"Octogirl," said Skeeter, his voice low and urgent. "I have to get out of here. The crowds . . . I can't . . ."

Maddy turned to look at her friend. He didn't look right at all. "Come on," she said, but now they were trapped, bodies pressing in from all sides. The knife throwers were moving through the crowds, tossing their blades back and forth as they went. One of them brushed by Maddy, close enough that she could see knife-shaped scars running up one arm.

Maddy spun around but another act had started, blocking the way. It was Dov, covered in snakes and standing on top of a rickety aluminum ladder. He had snakes in each hand and draped over his neck, snakes slithering up his arms and around his torso. Nothing showed but his eyes. He looked like a seething mass of snakes.

BAM. BAM. BAM. BAM.

Someone with a tusked mask ran out of the crowd and lunged at her; Maddy screamed and jumped away, pulling Skeeter with her. The person in the mask laughed and then spun and jumped at someone else. Maddy's chest burned as though it might explode and she could hear Skeeter's breath in her ear, loud and labored. They swung around and turned back-to-back, still holding hands, circling and looking for any opening in the crowd.

On the pier the flick of fire sounded, another act blazing to life. And now the drummers came into view, dozens and dozens of them all playing the same beat.

BAM! BAM! BAM! BAM!

The sound pounded in Maddy's skull, in her whole body, relentless and loud. Everyone shrieked and surged forward, once again pushing Maddy and Skeeter along with them into a rush of smoke that billowed into the air. An army of figures dancing on stilts came from behind the drummers, each of them twirling fireballs on strings. Firelight glinted off their scaled skin, silhouetted their muscular forms, and sent menacing shadows flickering over their faces.

"Don't let go of my hand!" yelled Maddy as they were buffeted along with the crowd, but she didn't have to worry. Skeeter was squeezing her so hard she thought her fingers might break.

More and more people were pressing past them, crushing them from every side. Maddy could feel the pulse in her throat too hard, too fast, and Skeeter's hand in hers was slick with sweat. They had to get away from the drums and the smoke and the wrongness of this circus.

"There!" she yelled, pointing to a gap in the crowd. She rushed forward, dragging Skeeter with her, darting to the sidewalk under the mural of the faceless woman. Skeeter pulled his hand from hers and leaned against the wall, doubling over.

"Can't . . . breathe," he said, sliding down to sit. "All the peo-ple . . . pushing."

Maddy leaned against the wall as well, letting her head drop. Tiredness soaked through every part of her.

She didn't understand what she was supposed to be doing here. See the nighttime circus for what it was? That seemed obvious: it was awful. And accept it? How? And more import-ant, *why*? *Why* did she have to accept things that were scary and mean? She wanted to go back to the daylight, where things were nicer. Let everyone else have the nighttime circus. She would take the day.

Maddy glanced at Skeeter, who was cradling his head with his hands and gasping for air, and guilt welled up in her. It was her fault he was here. She had to get them out. She looked past the pier, where the empty beach shone like pale bone in the moonlight. Maybe they could cut across the beach to get free of everyone, and then double back to the canals. Maybe they could try again another night, when she was ready.

But even as she planned their escape, Maddy knew she wasn't going anywhere. She couldn't. Isabette had already told her that to get into the Heart at the End of the World she had to accept the nighttime circus, and to help the daytime circus she had to get into the Heart. So that meant she had to stay. Maddy stared at the beach without really seeing it, thoughts spinning in her mind. There were things in her life she didn't like but had accepted anyway, weren't there? Things like living in group homes or not having parents? Accepting something didn't have to mean she liked it. It just meant . . .

Oh.

It just meant she saw what was real.

Maybe she could do the same here.

"I can do this," she whispered to herself, to the night air, to the faceless mural above them. And as soon as she did, an odd sensation of warmth on her skin sparked and burned. It seemed to come from the mural, from the woman diving across the wall, and with it came another thought: Maybe accepting the nighttime circus was more about being willing to even try than it was about anything else. Maddy paused for a moment, feeling the rightness of that as the magic brushed against her. Then she pushed away from the wall.

Isabette had told her to see it for what it was. And so, Maddy looked.

The stilt dancers were moving toward her, the fire lighting them all a deep orange. Now she recognized Josi, the dancer's shark teeth bared as she tossed fireballs into the air. As each fireball rose, it split apart and grew tails of flame until Josi was spinning four fireballs, then eight, then sixteen.

"Hey!" yelled Josi, her voice loud through the spinning fire as she stared right at Maddy. "Girl who could see us! What do you see now?"

The other stilt dancers began to twist themselves into shapes, terrifying and gorgeous, fire flying all around them.

Maddy drew in a breath. She knew these dancers, knew them from the daytime—but, like Dov, they were different here, unrestrained and wild. She took in the rows and rows of pointed teeth, the hair that looked like living whips, the noses that had elongated and broadened into shark snouts. Their scaled skin glowed reddish with fire, and the red mixed with the silvery-water of their daytime skin, two opposing forces battling it out as though each dancer might pull themselves apart.

Maddy looked closer. What *did* she see? Some of the dancers had singed hair; one had a burn on her shoulder. Their act was dangerous, yes, and frightening . . . but it was also something else. Wasn't the focus in their eyes more than just recklessness? Wasn't there also determination and fervor and—perhaps— even a fierce kind of love? And now, within each of the stilt dancers, Maddy could see it: the spark of the same people who grew out of glittering, sun-drenched sand. She could see them flash between their two selves, daytime and nighttime, like two photographs that had been combined to make something rich and full and entirely whole. It was still terrifying . . . but also, in its own way, beautiful. Not daytime beautiful, but something entirely different—an untamed, feral beauty all its own.

Her whole body tingling, Maddy rose onto her tiptoes to see better, finding Dov above the crowds. She could see it in him, too, and in the snakes that covered him—the beauty and the wildness, the daytime and the night. Dov opened his mouth to speak, and even though he was far away from her, his whispery voice carried over the roar of the crowd as it had in the circus café.

"Without the nighttime," he said, "we cannot have the day, and without the day there is no nighttime. We need the freedom of all of it."

And now Maddy could see that the masked people trying to scare everyone were laughing with pleasure, that they were in fact having fun—and so were many of the people being scared. The knife-throwers had paused in their act and were showing the human tree—who was actually someone wearing an amazingly lifelike tree costume—how to toss a knife the right way. A group of people with terrifying, painted-on clown faces wandered past, talking about where they should go eat when the circus was over. Back and forth, daytime and night, everywhere she could see. Maddy felt as though she had never looked at anything so closely before.

"Oh," said Maddy wonderingly. "It isn't one or the other. It's both. It's always both. It's just two sides of the same thing."

Standing on stilts above Maddy, Josi caught her fireballs one after the other, somehow not getting burned, and then crouched down to get closer to Maddy's height.

"Yes," said Josi. "And now that you see it for what it is, you can choose. Accept it or don't, but know what it is."

"Why are you helping me?" Maddy asked. "I thought you didn't like me."

"I don't," said Josi. "I think we should do what the Ringmaster wants and not ask questions. But I love this circus. If you can save it, I want it saved. Some things are bigger than any of us. But now that you see, you can decide."

To Maddy's surprise, her decision seemed obvious—and completely different from what she had thought.

"But that's easy," she said, a smile growing as she looked at Josi and then at Skeeter, who gave her an uncertain smile in return. She understood! She knew now what Isabette had meant by accepting it all. She spread her arms wide, taking in the whole of the nighttime circus. "I don't just accept it. I *love* it! All of it, the daytime and the nighttime, the whole circus! It's . . ." She paused, nodding to herself, knowing this was right. "It's Something Perfect."

For a moment nothing happened. And then, all at once, the overpowering scent of magic thickened the air. With a sound like the whistling wind, the woman in the mural stepped out of the wall.

15

The faceless woman from the mural moved like oil, fluid and wavy, her form as elongated in life as she was on the wall. A ripple of quiet spread through the nighttime circus as the woman sank to one knee in front of Maddy and Skeeter and raised the circular window from the building in front of her like a shield, dark hair streaming for yards behind her. Power emanated from her every movement.

Maddy couldn't pull her eyes away, and Skeeter scrambled to his feet.

"I AM THE NIGHTTIME FACE OF THE MUSE," said the woman, her voice deep and booming and coming from her mouthless face.

"Vanessa?" asked Maddy hesitantly. This woman looked nothing like the sun-kissed muse of the daytime.

"I ANSWER TO NO NAME AND EVERY NAME. I PROTECT ALL WHO TRULY WISH TO SEE."

Maddy nodded, everything clicking into place like the perfect counterbeat. "You're both, too, just like the circus. Daytime and nighttime."

"MANY FACES, ONE SELF."

Josi cleared her throat, the sound loud in the silence, and rose to her full height on her stilts. "All right, revelers," she called. "Nothing left to see here; let's get a move on." With a last nod to Maddy, Josi turned away, walking on stilts back down the pier. One by one, all the members of the nighttime circus followed her. The end of the pier glowed red and then blue, swirling around the people and melting them away into smoke and mist until the street was empty and still. Only Maddy, Skeeter, and the nighttime muse remained.

The nighttime muse rose, hovering above the pavement without quite touching it. "SEEING THINGS FOR WHAT THEY ARE UNLOCKS THEIR BEAUTY," she said. "COME."

The nighttime muse walk-floated toward the beach, a light breeze making her outline shimmer. Maddy and Skeeter ran after her, pausing only to kick off their shoes at the sand. They all stopped at the water's edge, where the cold, wet sand shifted under Maddy's feet and between her toes. The crescent moon hung low in the horizon like the left-behind smile of the Cheshire Cat. The nighttime muse turned her eyeless face to them, dark hair billowing. She looked as though she were beginning to dissolve.

"YOU ARE SAFE HERE," she said. "REST." And the nighttime muse drifted apart into a million particles of color that wafted out to sea and disappeared.

For a long moment Maddy and Skeeter stood silently, side by side. Neither spoke.

"Whoa," Skeeter said finally. His color had returned and he looked more like himself.

"Yeah," agreed Maddy.

They started to laugh. Soon they were both laughing so hard they collapsed onto the wet sand, which made them laugh even more. Maddy wasn't sure why, exactly, just that it was such a relief. They had walked through the nighttime circus and they were still here, together, safe and sound. Moonlight caught the inside of the waves that rolled into shore, turning the water a glassy green.

Finally, their laughter trailed off. Skeeter flopped onto his back in the sand and threw one arm over his eyes. Still smiling, Maddy watched the moonlight sparkle on the water.

"I am *wiped*," said Skeeter.

"Me too," said Maddy—but she wasn't, not really. She wasn't sure she had ever felt more awake.

"Octogirl?" asked Skeeter sleepily.

"Yeah?" answered Maddy.

"What's your real name, anyway?"

Maddy flicked some sand at Skeeter, who was half asleep. "It's Maddy. I can't believe you didn't know that!"

There was a long pause, where she thought maybe Skeeter had fallen asleep for real. Then he said, "Huh."

"What?"

"I like Octogirl better."

"Yeah," Maddy said, smiling. Moonlight danced on the water like spilled treasure. "Me too."

A quiet snore answered her. Maddy pulled her knees to her chest and wrapped her arms around them. She felt warm and loose, separate from her body, as though she had no skin holding her together. She felt free.

She watched the light on the water, listening to the sound of the waves. After some time—she wasn't sure how long—a movement caught her eye. Was it her imagination, or was the moonlight actually floating *above* the water? Maddy stood quietly, so as not to wake Skeeter, and stepped into the surf. Waves lapped at her ankles, sending goose bumps swirling over her, and now she was sure of it: The moonlight was moving toward her like a living thing, a ribbon of quicksilver. Maddy held her breath with wonder as the silvery light encircled her.

Hello, little one, it said. Its voice was rich as midnight, deep as promises.

A breeze lifted Maddy's hair, brushing it across her face. "Hello," she whispered. "Who are you?"

I am Moonlight-on-the-Water. I live where there is water and there is moonlight.

Another shiver ran down the backs of Maddy's legs and then up her neck. "Are you part of the nighttime circus?"

I am part of everything and nothing. I am light and shadow. I help all little ones.

"I'm not that little," said Maddy with some indignation. "I'm twelve."

All humans are little. Little is not the same as insignificant.

Maddy watched the moonlight travel down her arm and glint off her bracelet. "You're beautiful."

I am only I, ever-shifting yet selfsame. I wax and wane. Some use me to reassure themselves that magic exists, others to reassure themselves that it does not. It is I who remind sailors at sea that they are so small and the world is so large. It is I who remind lovers on distant shores that they are so large and the world is so small. I am hidden and seen, like wishes and fears, and I light the nighttime faces of the world. Do you wish to see?

"Oh yes," said Maddy. "Yes, please."

Moonlight-on-the-Water stretched taut, then split lengthwise. One ribbon settled back on the water, making it ripple with light, but the other rose into the air, crackling and alive. A smell like burnt wire sizzled in Maddy's nose as one end of the floating ribbon struck the crest of a wave . . . and it was as though someone had flipped on the switch for the entire world.

The ocean came to life with glowing flecks of green that

spangled the waves, racing up and over as the water crashed to shore. Seafoam lapped at Maddy's feet and coated her legs with luminous dots. When the water receded, constellations of sparkling green stayed behind, dotting the beach. Almost breathless, Maddy scooped up a handful of sand that was filled with countless small plants, each alight and pulsing.

Look up, said Moonlight-on-the-Water.

Maddy lifted her head and gasped, letting the sand run through her fingers. The stars were moving, rearranging themselves in the night sky. She had always thought of stars as white, but now she could clearly see all the colors: reds and blues, yellows and greens. She backed out of the water and lay down in the sand so she could see better, spreading out her arms. Next to her, Skeeter snored softly.

One set of stars, perhaps a small galaxy, began to move independently from the rest to form the outline of a human figure in the sky. The figure rose, shimmering and wavering with starlight, and reached up to touch another galaxy, which took shape into a long bar, rings dangling from chains like a heavenly gymnastics set. With great deliberateness, the figure opened one starry hand and caught hold of an ice-blue ring.

For a moment, the figure hung one-armed from the ring, twirling in place, leaving trails of stardust in its wake. A great humming filled Maddy's ears, the sound so familiar and yet so haunting she thought perhaps she had always known it but had somehow and impossibly forgotten. It felt as though her heart were exploding out of her, as though she could actually feel the slow, spinning movement of the Earth. She thought she might be falling into the sky.

It felt like infinity.

The starry figure pushed off and reached to catch a ring of fiery red, swinging an impossible distance between rings and twirling as it went. It moved with a lovely slowness, as though time meant nothing, as though it existed on a scale so vastly different from worrying about group homes and pills and sicknesses that, suddenly, Maddy understood what it meant to be a little one.

When it reached the last ring, a filmy spiral of stars lined up beneath the figure, forming a giant net, and the spinning figure released the ring and drifted languidly on its back, falling in slow motion and trailing stardust. It touched onto the net of stars, which gave beneath its weight, and slowly rebounded, rising into the air and tucking into a triple somersault as the net transformed itself into a trampoline, catching the figure with ease.

And now other figures were forming, all of them humanlike, all of them made of stars. In slow motion, in the motion of the night sky, of a scale so large it hurt to even imagine, the figures cartwheeled and flipped and dove. Over and under each other they moved, bouncing from trampoline to rings and back again, stars shifting and sliding.

As the starry figures whirled and spun, as the sand cradled

her, as the universe sang, Maddy felt giddy with happiness. The crescent moon sank toward the horizon. And then slowly, so slowly Maddy thought she might already have fallen asleep, one of the figures reached toward her with its starry hand. Slowly, so slowly, Maddy lifted her own hand in return, barely breathing as starry fingers closed around her own. It felt like light, like space dust, like music come to life. A million thoughts and things to say swirled through Maddy's sleepy mind, but then the starry hand squeezed hers lightly and let go, drawing back into the sky. Next to her, Skeeter smiled in his sleep.

The bottom edge of the crescent moon dipped beneath the horizon. In the sky, the figures began to float apart, stars and galaxies breaking away and swirling back into place.

I am only I, said Moonlight-on-the-Water, its voice distant and dim. *I am everywhere that there is water and there is moonlight. I will always help all little ones.*

The last of the moon disappeared as it set. At the same time, something squelched out of the waves to Maddy's side.

"Ophelia!" cried Maddy.

Ophelia tapped a fond·hello on Maddy's arm, then stretched into a blue blanket festooned with yellow dots. The octopus blanket inched over Maddy and Skeeter like a caterpillar, gently suckering around them to tuck them in.

"I missed you, too, Ophelia," Maddy whispered happily, and she sank into a deep, dreamless sleep.

16

"Yo, Octogirl!"

Maddy woke with a start, her confused brain wondering why this group home had no roof and why there was so much sand in the bed. Then everything came rushing back. She turned to find Skeeter was no longer next to her and sat up quickly. The octopus blanket that had been wrapped around the two of them fell to the sand in a disheveled heap that shimmered into an equally disheveled Ophelia, who stretched her tentacles, patted Maddy's arm, and jetted into the next wave to rehydrate.

Skeeter was running across the sand toward Maddy, holding a paper bag. "You're up!" he said as he reached her. "What a night, right? What about that nighttime circus? I'm glad you ended up loving it, but man . . . let's never do that again." He sank down cross-legged and took a pastry from the bag. "I got us breakfast, funnel cakes with raspberry jam. They're an Il Circo specialty!"

"Oh, yum!" said Maddy, taking the pastry. She was starving. "Thanks!"

Skeeter pulled another funnel cake from the bag. The glassy sea was just starting to glow with sunlight, early morning surfers bobbing in the water and fishermen on the pier yelling in a good-morning sort of way to each other in several different languages. Everyone seemed to know Skeeter, waving and calling hellos. It made Maddy feel like she was part of something, sitting here with him. The beach itself, the whole world, looked different from yesterday, like a more real version of itself. Maddy stared hard at all of it, trying to see the nighttime in the day the way she had seen the daytime in the night.

She was so wrapped up in her thoughts that she didn't realize Skeeter had been talking to her until he poked her arm and said, "Earth to Octogirl!"

"Sorry!" she said, starting. "What?"

"First, I asked if you want another funnel cake, and next, I was wondering what else happened with the Ringmaster."

"Um . . . yes to the funnel cake, and kind of a lot with the Ringmaster," said Maddy. She took another pastry, and as she ate she told Skeeter everything that had happened. He listened so carefully she didn't once worry about not being able to tell a good story.

When she was done, Skeeter took a bite, chewed thoughtfully, and then said, "So now we need to figure out a way to get you back to that Bridge of Sighs so you can get inside the Heart. Since I don't really have a binding—I only have a sort-of one—I should be able to—"

"You don't have a binding?" interrupted Maddy. "I thought everyone who was part of Il Circo had one."

"Everyone who's part of the circus does," said Skeeter, wiping powdered sugar from his face. "But I'm not actually part of the circus. Not officially, anyway."

Maddy stared in astonishment. "How is that possible? You have a flying skateboard! You do tricks *in the sky!*"

"You know how Isabette said I don't like rules? She's right. I was only seven when I met the Ringmaster and fell in love with Il Circo. He told me that I could stay, but that I was too young to join full-out. Isabette thought he should have sent me away, but he didn't. And then the circus got sick and the Ringmaster set the decrees and left . . . but I stayed."

"How old do you have to be to join the circus?" asked Maddy.

"Fourteen," said Skeeter. "I'm thirteen now, so one more year to go."

"We're almost the same age," said Maddy. Out in the water, Ophelia had started to body surf. "I'm twelve."

Skeeter gave her a sheepish look and lowered his voice. "Don't tell anyone, but . . . yeah, I'm actually twelve, too. When the Ringmaster found me, I was six . . . although I tried to get him to believe I was ten so I could get an act sooner. He didn't fall for it, so I went with seven and that seemed to work."

The image of scrappy little Skeeter pretending to be ten made Maddy giggle. He was pretty scrawny now. She could only imagine him as a little kid.

"Hey!" protested Skeeter. "I can pass for older. Watch me!" And he made a serious, somber expression, which only made her laugh more.

"Yeah, you look, like, twenty or something," said Maddy, trying to keep a straight face. "I won't tell anyone you're only twelve."

"Sweet," said Skeeter, and he took a giant bite of pastry and puffed out his cheeks, which made them both start laughing again.

"I can't believe you're not part of the circus," said Maddy after she caught her breath. "Your tricks are amazing! You must practice all the time."

"Aw, shucks," said Skeeter, his face pinkening. "They're all kind of old now. I have a ton of new ones worked out in my head, but I can't actually try them because of the decrees." He fell quiet, watching the surfers bobbing in the water. "I really want Il Circo to start up again. My sort-of binding won't let me help find the Ringmaster, but I bet it'd let me help you find that Bridge."

"What, exactly, is a sort-of binding?" Maddy asked.

Skeeter looked pleased with himself. "It's another reason

Isabette is mad at me. The Ringmaster said no, but I kept bugging him." He waggled his eyebrows. "I'm *very* persuasive."

"Can I see it?"

Skeeter made a show of checking to make sure no one could see them, and then angled away from her and pulled up the back of his T-shirt. Tattooed on his right shoulder blade was the same image of Kuma in a circle, but it was dark green instead of blue. Other than the color, it was just like the ones Maddy had already seen.

"It's kind of a kids' version," said Skeeter, letting his shirt fall. "The Ringmaster made this special ink that isn't permanent. Which is another thing . . . he needs to be here to redo it every year. It's starting to fade, and not because I'm thinking of leaving. If he doesn't come back soon, well . . ." Skeeter paused for a long moment. "Without him here, I'm a little afraid I'll get kicked out because I'm too young. It's silly, I guess. I know most people don't care. But that's why I kept asking the Ringmaster to make this for me. I wanted to feel like, I don't know. Like I belonged here."

Maddy nodded. She knew that feeling all too well. "Skeeter . . ." she began.

"Yeah?"

Maddy poked her fingers in the sand, making little holes. "Did you ask the Race to take you somewhere? Or did you just race for fun?"

"Both. I mean, I always love to race. But I did ask to go

somewhere. The same place as you, actually."

This wasn't what Maddy had expected. "To see the Ringmaster?"

"It probably wouldn't have worked, because of my sort-of binding, but it's so faded I thought it might be okay. Besides, I didn't want to find him to bring him back to the circus. I just wanted to ask him, um, if he would teach me to announce the acts. Like an apprentice." Skeeter's face turned a deep red. "I thought, maybe, if I could learn, he might let me help him sometimes."

"You'd be perfect!" said Maddy, a little in awe the way she always was when someone actually liked Extra Attention.

Skeeter shrugged again, but his dimples had come back.

"So . . ." Maddy said slowly, not sure whether she wanted to know the answer. "What happens if you try to do something the Ringmaster doesn't want you to do?"

"Nothing bad, really," said Skeeter. He stared up into the sky. "It's more like you just forget you were even thinking about that thing in the first place. I have all these new tricks in my head, right? But the Ringmaster said no new acts. So every time I get on my board, I don't remember that's what I wanted to do. And by the time I *do* remember, I'm already going to sleep or nowhere near my skateboard or something like that. Happens every time. Not that I've been trying that, of course!" Skeeter grinned at her and then shrugged. "Honestly, it's more annoying than anything. But I still remember I want to help you find the Bridge of Sighs, so that must be okay." He looked into the paper bag that had held the funnel cakes, turned it upside down, and shook it. A few crumbs fell onto the sand. "Empty," he said sadly.

"Are you still hungry?" Maddy asked. "Do you want to go home and grab some more food?"

Skeeter licked his fingers. "I am home," he said.

"I mean *home*-home. To your house."

Skeeter gave Maddy a long look. "Octogirl, I *am* home. I live here."

It took Maddy a moment to understand, and then she flushed. "You mean, you sleep here and everything? On the beach, like last night?"

"Not on the beach, exactly," he said. "But yeah. I live here."

"With your parents?" asked Maddy, although she thought she already knew the answer.

"Nope," said Skeeter. "Just me."

Maddy took a deep breath. Out in the sea, Ophelia popped to the surface, rode a wave into shore, and tentacled over to Maddy. Maddy put an arm around the mimic octopus, who snuggled against her. "I don't have parents either," she said. "I've been in group homes my whole life."

Ophelia turned a sad white.

"I'm sorry, Octogirl. That sounds awful." Skeeter picked up a broken shell and used it to make a tic-tac-toe board in the sand. "I *do* have parents. At least, I have a mom. I just . . . I don't see her. I got moved into the foster system when I was three, and man, I hated it. Skateboarding was the only time I felt, I don't know. Like things made sense. I met the Ringmaster at the skate park back there." He used the shell to draw an X on the tic-tac-toe board and then handed the shell to Maddy.

"I never met my parents," Maddy said. She put an O in the corner of the tic-tac-toe board and passed the shell back to Skeeter. "But . . . well . . . I always thought they'd come back for me."

Skeeter snorted, drew another X, and then tossed the shell onto the sand instead of handing it back to her. "Trust me," he said shortly. "You're probably better off they didn't."

Ophelia wrapped a tentacle around the shell, pulled it to her, and began to draw in the sand. Maddy turned her head sideways and squinted at the picture. "Is that . . . octopus eggs hatching?" Maddy waited while Ophelia sketched a rough octopus with Xs for eyes. "Oh. Wow. Octopus moms die when their kids are born? That's, um, that's too bad. But Vanessa is kind of your mom, right?"

Ophelia drew some more.

"Oh," said Maddy as the picture became clearer. "I'm glad octopuses don't care about parents. That's probably good."

Ophelia turned a happy yellow in agreement and handed the shell to Maddy. Maddy wrapped her hand around it, squeezing it just hard enough for the pain to make asking the next question possible. Even so, she couldn't look at Skeeter as she spoke. Instead, she stared at the surfers in the water as they paddled to catch waves.

"Is it enough?" she asked quietly. "The circus, I mean?"

"Enough?" Skeeter asked. "Enough what?"

Maddy looked down. Her bracelet shone in the morning sun. "Enough to make up for not having a family."

Skeeter's dimples deepened in his cheeks. Ophelia draped herself over Maddy's lap.

"Yeah, Octogirl," said Skeeter. "Oh, yeah. It most definitely is."

Maddy stared at the ocean, her eyes blurring.

"Hey," said Skeeter, standing and brushing sand off his shorts. "Let's go look for that annoying mermaid and see if she can tell us how to get to the Bridge. Race you to the canals!"

Maddy nodded gratefully and grabbed their skateboards, handing Skeeter his as she rose to stand. She wiped her eyes as Ophelia scampered up her shoulder.

"You know I hate racing, though, right?" she said with a half-smile.

A dimple flashed in Skeeter's cheek as they made their way across the sand to the bike path. "Yup," he said. "Good thing, too, or I'd never win again!"

They jumped on their boards and headed to the canals.

17

Isabette did not want to be found.

After an hour of searching the canals, Maddy and Skeeter finally gave up and sat on one of the tiny wooden docks in front of someone's home, their skateboards crisscrossed between them. Ophelia climbed over the edge of the dock and splashed into the canal.

"Maybe I should fall into the canal again, too," said Maddy, watching Ophelia. She was only half kidding. "Maybe then Isabette would appear."

"Won't help," said Skeeter, as Ophelia settled on the bottom of the canal in a puff of silt and made herself look like a particularly nondescript rock. "She's probably off patrolling some other waterways right now—" Skeeter broke off.

Maddy glanced away from Ophelia to see why Skeeter had stopped talking, then jumped to her feet. Time had shivered and stopped, freezing Skeeter mid-sentence. Excitement flaring inside her, Maddy spun around. There in the canal was the winged lion. He stood ankle-deep in the water, tail flicking. Lightning-fast, he darted his paw into the water and tossed several of the small fish into the air, making a satisfied purring-type sound as they splashed back down. Then he waded to Maddy's side, taking care not to step on Ophelia.

"Have you news?" he asked.

Words rushed out of Maddy as though they were leaping from a starting gate. "Oh, Kuma, I found the Ringmaster and I tried to get him to come back, but he can't, not yet, and then I tried to get into the Heart, but that didn't work either because I have to find my own way and not use his. I'm doing my best to bring him back, I promise! I just have to find the Bridge of Sighs and cross it, although I don't know where it is or how to do that . . . and oh, so much has happened! Do you know how to get to the Bridge of Sighs?"

Kuma flicked his tail. "I do not," he said. "I am feline. We are already quite satisfied with all of what we are, and therefore the Ponte dei Sospiri holds nothing for my kind. What I do know is that the bridge reveals itself only to those who seek it. If you want to find it, you must look."

"I *am* looking!" cried Maddy.

"Then you will find it."

Time shuddered. A ripple of annoyance crossed Kuma's features.

"The door of time continues to taunt me," said Kuma. "I must go. I came to tell you that when you enter the Heart and break the shell to call the Ringmaster to you, I, too, will come. By his side, I can speak without stopping time. We can talk freely then." He spread his wings. "Let us meet again soon."

Maddy watched Kuma fly away until all she could see of him was a gleam of sunlight on copper wings. Skeeter shifted behind her.

"Am I dreaming?" Skeeter asked, yawning. "Or was that the Ringmaster's lion?"

"Yes, but he doesn't belong to the Ringmaster," said Maddy as Ophelia tentacled up onto the dock. "They belong to each other."

"Sweet," said Skeeter. "What did he say?"

"That the way we find the Bridge of Sighs is that we just keep searching."

Skeeter stood up and stretched. "That sounds exactly like something Vanessa would say. One of the first things she ever told me was that if I wanted to be in the circus, I couldn't just sit around waiting for inspiration because sometimes you just have to go looking for it. Maybe she knows how to get to the Bridge. Let's go see if she's awake!"

Like her nighttime self, Vanessa lived in a mural, although hers was filled with sunlight and daytime. It was painted on the side of a youth hostel overlooking the alley behind the board-walk, the flags from different countries placed all across its roof rippling in the ocean breeze. The mural stood two stories high, an artist's rendition of the boardwalk with pieces of Il Circo in the background: Annie the Ballerina Clown, a skateboard, a gondola, and an orange chainsaw that looked very much like Edith. Painted in the foreground of it all, as though she were standing watch over the whole thing, was Vanessa.

Even though it was still early morning, the alley bustled with life. Shopkeepers setting up for the day pulled carts filled with sarongs and jewelry and crystals. Cyclists dressed in tight-fitting, brightly colored clothing whizzed past, talking loudly to one another. Cars honked and swerved.

"How can you tell if she's awake?" asked Maddy, even though it seemed impossible to sleep through so much noise. The Muse of Venice, though, was probably used to it. On Maddy's shoulder, Ophelia became a rubbery gong that made a soft, squishy sound, way too quiet to wake anyone.

"Nice one!" said Skeeter. Ophelia morphed back into herself and turned a pleased, giggly kind of magenta. "Maybe a little louder, though. Like this." Skeeter waited for a car to pass, then hopped on his skateboard, executed a perfect 360 with his arms wide, and called out, "Oh great and wondrous muse of Il Circo delle Strade, please grace us with your presence!"

Nothing happened.

Skeeter jumped off his board, flipped it into the air, caught it, and then tucked it under one arm. "Or, like this," he said, grinning and cupping his hands around his mouth. "Yo, Vanessa! You up?"

The sound of wind chimes tinkled briefly in the air, and Vanessa shimmered and stepped out of the wall, leaving a paler version of herself behind.

"Good morning!" she said, shrinking to basketball-player height. "How perfectly lovely to see you all. Are you in need of some inspiration?"

"Not exactly," said Maddy. "We were wondering if you could tell us—"

A car screeched to a halt and honked at Skeeter, who jumped out of the way.

"Tell you what?" asked Vanessa.

"If you could tell us how to find—" Maddy began again.

"Look out, you kids!" yelled the leader of a pack of bicyclists, swerving so close around Maddy that she could feel the wind.

"Maybe we could go somewhere else to talk?" yelled the muse over the laughter of the cyclists. "Skeeter, how about your place?"

Maddy turned to Skeeter. "You have a place? I thought . . . I thought you didn't have anywhere to go."

"I said I lived *here* when we were on the beach," said Skeeter with a grin. "I didn't say I didn't have a place."

Skeeter led them to a spot on the sand next to the skate park, where three short concrete walls, each a little taller than

Maddy and about as long as a school bus, and several very strange, giant concrete cones, shaped like the pointy part of a wizard's hat, stuck out of the sand. It looked as though someone had dropped house parts on the beach and then forgotten about them.

"You live *here*?" asked Maddy.

Each of the walls and cones was completely covered in graffiti art that lapped over itself in a riot of color and shape. Maddy walked up to one of the walls and ran her fingers over the word *VENICE* written in bright bubble letters, a painted surfer riding the crest of the *C*. Did Skeeter have a roof to sleep under, or did he just curl up by these walls? Where did he go when it rained?

"Yeah," said Skeeter proudly. "Pretty great, right?"

"Watching the artists paint is one of my favorite things in the whole circus," declared Vanessa. "Now, what is it you need?"

"Um," Maddy said, trying not to worry about Skeeter. Ophelia laid one tentacle against the wall, instantly matching the color and texture perfectly. "Right. The Bridge of Sighs. I have to go, but I don't know how to find it again. Can you help me get there?"

"The Bridge of Sighs?" A small, worried crease appeared between Vanessa's eyebrows. "Are you sure? You're awfully young. Most grown-ups can't even do it."

"Everyone keeps telling me I'm not ready," said Maddy with exasperation, "but no one will tell me what I actually have to *do*."

"You'll have to do the same thing everyone who crosses the Ponte dei Sospiri has to do, of course," said Vanessa. "You'll have to face the most frightening thing you can imagine."

Maddy swallowed hard. No wonder people didn't like to talk about the Bridge. "Which is . . . what?" she asked, not sure she wanted to hear the answer.

"I can't say," said Vanessa. "It's *your* imagination."

"I can imagine some pretty frightening things," said Skeeter, his voice low.

Maddy chewed her lip. So could she.

"Can it kill you?" she asked after a long moment.

Vanessa's face changed slightly, and for the first time Maddy could see the shadow of the nighttime muse in the contours of her cheeks and the hollows of her eyes. "Yes," Vanessa said kindly. "Of course."

Maddy wrapped her arms around herself. Her skin felt raw and shivery.

"I'm going with you," said Skeeter, and Ophelia pointed at herself with one tentacle and nodded vigorously.

"Thank you," Maddy said. "I wish you both could, I really, really do. But, um, I don't think that's allowed. I think it's for only one person at a time. I think it's personal."

Skeeter crossed his arms. "Then I'll go, and you stay here. Octogirl, you shouldn't have to do this. You barely know any of us."

"But that's not true," Maddy said, and even with the thought of facing the most frightening thing she could imagine, a warmth flowed through her. "I know *all* of you. I know the circus somehow, even though I just got here. And I'm the one who's bound to the Heart at the End of the World but not to the Ringmaster." She looked at Vanessa. "It has to be me, doesn't it? And I have to go alone."

It wasn't a question. Maddy already knew the answer.

"Yes," said Vanessa, tearing up. She waved her hand in front of her eyes. "Oh dear. I can't cry here. We're way too far from water for my baby octopus tears to make it alive. They can't breathe on land the way Ophelia can. Excuse me." With one giant step, she was gone.

Maddy looked at Skeeter. His arms were still crossed, his jaw set.

"Skeeter," she began.

"I don't like this," he interrupted, kicking at some sand. "But if it's what you have to do, then I'll help you any way I can."

Ophelia turned a definitive, me-too kind of yellow.

Maddy smiled gratefully. "Thanks," she said. "Um . . . is Vanessa coming back? She didn't tell me how to get there."

"Probably not," said Skeeter. "She doesn't remember things unless they're right in front of her. And I don't think she knows or she would have said so right away. But I know someone else we can ask." Skeeter leaned back against the graffiti wall and patted the spot next to him. "Come lean."

"Is this more mural magic?" Maddy asked as she leaned next

to him. Ophelia put a tentacle against the wall, again shifting her color to match the art underneath it. The graffiti wall was warm from the morning sun and felt almost sticky, as though the layers of paint had never quite dried. Maddy closed her eyes, liking how it felt.

"I can tell you history," whispered a voice.

Maddy's eyes flew open. "Whoa! Who is that?"

"I knew it!" said Skeeter. "It's the art. I knew you'd be able to hear it! Not everyone does."

"I can tell you deeper history," said another voice, more distant than the first.

"You're too old to remember anything," said a third voice. "She'd do better talking to us."

"We know the foundation on which your history rests, newcomer." The distant voice sounded angry. "This was our turf first."

"This is amazing!" said Maddy.

Skeeter grinned. "Graffiti artists have been painting these walls forever, covering what's here with newer stuff. One guy painted me a sweet bed a while back, two or three layers deep. That's where I sleep."

"You sleep inside graffiti art? I don't care what anyone says, you are *totally* part of this circus." Maddy turned and pressed her hand against the painted surfer.

"Back off, dude!" said a muffled voice beneath her fingers. "This is *my* wave."

"She don't want your wave, man," said another voice. "She wants to know how to find the Ponte dei Sospiri and get to the Heart at the End of the World."

"They know how to find the bridge!" cried Maddy "Skeeter, you're *brilliant*!"

Skeeter's face turned pink. "I just know that the art's been here a long time and knows a lot. And some of it loves to talk. Like, *really* loves to talk. But remember, Octogirl . . . it's art, so it's not always . . . uh . . . literal."

"We have been here since the beginning," said another voice, and this one was the oldest of all, ancient and cracked. "We can tell you stories, if you but come to visit."

Maddy ran her hands over the wall. "How do we get in?"

"Dude," said the painted surfer, and the edges of the world began to blur like watercolors in the rain. "You just gotta ask."

18

Maddy tumbled through a waterfall of thick, sticky color, the sharp tang of spray paint stinging her eyes and nose. Skeeter swam by, doing an easy backstroke through the paint, and Ophelia jetted alongside him, her skin shifting to match whatever color she was near.

"Where are we?" Maddy asked, but instead of her words being audible, they appeared over her head in a graffiti talk bubble, one colorful letter at a time.

"In the art," said Skeeter, his words scrolling out of his mouth like text. "I don't know exactly where, though. The art never takes you the same way twice, but if you follow its lead you'll get where you need to go. It's the same with my bed—the art always takes me a different way to get there. Pretty cool, right?"

As soon as Skeeter finished talking, a charcoal-drawn staircase rose in front of them, and Maddy stepped onto it. Ophelia clambered up to her shoulder and Maddy gasped; the mimic octopus had become an animated drawing, all moving lines and colors.

"The art likes to change you." Skeeter, who was now a line-drawn cartoon, stepped onto the staircase behind her, his words bright and colorful and very heavily punctuated. He looked down at himself and did a little dance. "Sweet!! I'm a comic book!!!"

Maddy looked at her own arms. She, too, was no longer flesh and blood, but rendered in sweeps of richly colored paint: burnished skin, thick black hair, metallic silver bracelet. She smiled as she touched her arm and her hand came back covered in shimmering, oily brown.

"Pretty great, right?" Skeeter asked in comic book lettering, patches of scribbled pink appearing on his cheeks. "Lead on, Octogirl! You're the one the art invited, so you're the one it will talk to."

Maddy led them up the charcoal staircase, rainbows of color beading off them as they climbed. Halfway up, the whole staircase flipped upside down so they were hanging from their feet, blood rushing to Maddy's head as ground became sky. She grabbed hold of Ophelia to make sure the octopus didn't fall. At the top of the staircase—or the bottom, Maddy wasn't sure—the world righted itself, and the three of them stepped into a field of vertical black lines almost as tall as Maddy that were rustling like grass in a warm, acetone-scented breeze.

Tug, went her heart.

"This way," said Maddy, pushing the black lines out of the way to clear a path. Skeeter followed a few steps behind, so it wasn't until Ophelia tapped her on the shoulder and pointed up that Maddy realized he had said something. Cartoon letters spelling LOOK OUT floated by just in time for Maddy to jump out of the way of a gigantic cartoon skateboarder with an oversized head. As he whizzed by, he reached out, grabbed them all, and swung them onto the back of his board. Maddy held on to one of the skateboarder's white high-tops, her hair and several of Ophelia's tentacles whipping behind them, as Skeeter balanced with his arms out to his sides, the words HA! HA! HA! scrolling out of his mouth.

They whizzed out of the black-and-white landscape into a painted sunset, where vivid pink and orange drips melted from the sky and dangled in long, runny vines.

Tug.

Maddy tapped Skeeter and pointed. When he nodded, she held Ophelia on her shoulder with one hand and jumped for the paint vines, grabbing onto a yellow-orange one with her free hand. Behind her, Skeeter caught a pinkish-red vine as the graffiti skateboarder zoomed out of the frame. They dangled above a moving sidewalk, painted images flashing past as years of graffiti art unrolled beneath them and moved them further and further into the past.

A trio of words loped toward them:

LIVE LOVE LAUGH

Tug.

"Now!" Maddy cried, the letters flowing out of her mouth in purple calligraphy. She let go of her yellow-orange strand and dropped onto the back of the word *LIVE*, Ophelia with her. Skeeter missed the second word but caught the third, grabbing the horns of *LAUGH* as it picked up speed.

"Yeehaw!" he hollered, one arm in the air, his words like a lasso.

They galloped through the art, paint rushing by in torrents that coated Maddy's face and hands and turned Ophelia into a wash of color. They rode over a painted boardwalk onto a painted shoreline where their steeds came to a halt. Maddy and Skeeter climbed off and patted their words, which galloped away. On the painted beach, neon-blue waves lapped the shore and deposited thousands of small blue arrows onto the sand, all pointing in the same direction. Matching blue arrows flowed over Ophelia's skin like a billboard.

This one was easy: they followed the arrows. Suddenly they were no longer on the beach, but were instead walking down an acid-green trail, Ophelia swimming next to them in the painted air.

And then, the deep and dusty voice spoke, its words audible and not written.

"I was here when it all began," intoned the voice. "The circus, the art, the Ringmaster."

Maddy, Ophelia, and Skeeter spun around. In front of them loomed a massive painted face, its eyes shut. It was ancient and cracked, deep indigo blue save for two sweeps of black for its eyes and two sweeps of magenta for its lips. Bits of paint flaked from its cheeks and nose.

The magenta lips moved as it spoke, the rest of the face staying motionless. "The Ringmaster made us this home. We, the arte delle strade, are forever grateful to him."

"The art of the streets," Maddy said, her words coming out in fancy script. She was proud of herself for being able to translate.

"These walls have housed us, layer upon layer," the indigo face continued as though Maddy hadn't spoken. "We are grateful for remembrance, for never being sandblasted away. We elders hold the history; our newer brethren hold the now. All is important. All is needed. You must warn the Ringmaster."

"Warn him?" asked Maddy. "About what?"

"The Ringmaster has forgotten," said the face. "But we never do."

Maddy glanced at Skeeter, who gave a cartoon shrug.

"See what I mean about art?" his words wrote in the air.

"I have to cross the Bridge of Sighs," Maddy said to the face.

"Please, can you tell me how to get there?"

"We cannot tell you exactly," said the ancient voice of the indigo face. "We can only suggest. The interpretation is always up to you."

"But you said you could help," said Maddy. She tried not to sound frustrated, but the words scrolling out of her mouth were a little more frayed and spikey than before. "Can't you just tell me—"

"Oh, for heaven's sake!" boomed a deep male voice, making Maddy jump. "Stop being so free-form! Here, pass me the girl."

Something picked Maddy up by the back of her shirt, lifted her high, and then dropped her lightly onto a springy bed of pavement-colored paint. Ophelia swam after her and perched gently on her shoulder, but Skeeter and the blue-painted face stayed far below.

"I'm over here," said the deep male voice. "Here. No, not down there. *Here!*"

Maddy spun around. On a brick wall in front of her was a larger-than-life painting of a gray-haired man. He wore a suit of a long-ago era with an elegant gold pocket watch looped from his buttonhole, and his short white beard matched his thick mustache, which turned up slightly at the edges. He was gazing at her expectantly.

When she didn't say anything, he said, rather grandly, "It is I!"

"Um . . . hello," said Maddy. Below her, Skeeter was jumping up and down and shouting something, but he was too far away for her to read his words. "I'm sorry. Who are you, exactly?"

The man in the mural pointed to something painted on the building.

"Abbot Kinney, 1850–1920," Maddy read. "Oh. Hi."

The mural waited. When Maddy didn't say anything else, it said, its deep voice a bit exasperated, "I am Abbot Kinney. I created Venice of America, as it used to be called, and therefore Il Circo delle Strade. Or, rather, the me who was alive did. Abbot's Folly, they called it. They said it could never work. They said I was crazy. I showed them, didn't I? And since I built the whole thing—or, rather, the me who was alive did—I suspect I can answer most of your questions. You wish to find the Bridge of Sighs?"

"Yes! Can you tell me how to get there?"

"Indeed I can. You must think in terms of ends and beginnings," said the mural. "The Bridge of Sighs leads to the Heart, does it not?"

Maddy and Ophelia both nodded.

"And the Heart is at the End of the World. Correct?"

"Ye-es," said Maddy slowly. Ophelia kept nodding.

"Then the way there is simple!"

Ophelia stopped nodding.

"It is?" asked Maddy.

"Goodness, yes," said the mural. "Everything has an end, and everything has a beginning. But with a little sleight of hand, a dash of circus magic, the end becomes the beginning and it all starts again. Find the beginning and you find the end. Find the end and you find the beginning. Clear as paint!"

"Paint isn't clear," Maddy pointed out.

"A petty detail," said the mural. "Most things are both an end and a beginning, an exit as well as an entrance. Submerge yourself in the End of the World and you will find the beginning of the Bridge."

"Do you mean I should go back to the Ringmaster?" Maddy was trying very hard to understand. "He's at the End of the World."

"Correction; the Ringmaster is on the *surface* of the End of the World. To find the Bridge, you must go underneath. You must submerge."

This piece of art didn't seem any less free-form to Maddy. "But . . . if I could submerge myself in the End of the World, wouldn't that mean I was *already* inside the Heart?"

"Why are you making this so difficult?" said the mural of Abbot Kinney. "Everything is one uninterrupted circle, just like your bracelet. A fine gift, by the way."

Maddy's hand flew to her bracelet, forgetting it was a metallic swath of paint now and not a solid thing, so her palm came back coated with silver. "You know about my bracelet? Does that mean you know my parents? Were they in the circus?"

"An interesting question," said the mural. "One I am afraid I cannot answer. But what I *can* answer is how to find the Bridge of Sighs. Submerge yourself in the End of the World. That will lead you to the Bridge, which will lead you to the beginning, which will lead you to the end, which will lead you to the beginning, which will lead you to the end, which will . . ." The mural of Abbot Kinney seemed to be stuck, the words scrolling out of its mouth in one continuous loop of ticker tape that flowed over the side of the wall and snaked its way to Maddy, rising up her legs and body. Ophelia picked up a section of words and wrapped it around herself like a scarf, end-to-beginning-to-end.

"Please," cried Maddy as she fought to free herself. "I don't understand!"

The never-ending ticker tape words, ends leading to beginnings leading to ends leading to beginnings, formed an open doorway marked *EXIT* and began to propel her toward it. Clearly the art was done with her. With a sigh, Maddy wrapped one arm around Ophelia and stepped through the door.

"That didn't even make any sense!" Maddy was pacing in the sand, glaring at the graffiti art for good measure, Ophelia watching from atop the wall. Were all circuses like this, all spark and magic with no common sense? "If I could find the End of the World in the first place, I would already be there and I wouldn't have to get to the Bridge."

"Maddy," said Skeeter.

Maddy kept pacing. ". . . and I think he knew my parents, but he wouldn't tell me, no one will tell me, and—"

"Maddy."

"—maybe we should go talk to Vanessa again—"

Skeeter jumped in front of her, hands extended like stop signs. "Octogirl!" he yelled. "Stop!"

Maddy broke off and blinked. "What?"

Skeeter pointed toward the beach. "Just my humble opinion, but aren't we *at* the end of the world? I mean, kind of? Or the end of the continent, anyway, and the beginning of the ocean? End and beginning, same-y same, just like Abbot Kinney said?"

Ophelia stood up on four of her tentacles, pointed at the sea with her other four, and nodded vigorously.

Maddy frowned at the water. "That seems too easy."

"I've lived with the art a long time," said Skeeter, "and if I say so myself, I'm pretty good at figuring it out. So why don't we just dive in and see? Worst thing that happens is that we go for a morning swim, which is pretty sweet, right? What do you think?"

Ophelia shimmied a little, her whole body plumping up.

Maddy shaded her eyes and stared at the waves. Much as she hated to admit it, ocean swimming looked a little scary, nothing like the public pools where she spent her summers. But Skeeter looked so proud of himself, and it wasn't as though Maddy had any better ideas. Plus, she did have Vanessa's leg warmers. At least she wouldn't drown.

"Okay," she said.

Skeeter whooped and pumped his fist in the air. "Excellent! Got a bathing suit?"

Maddy looked down at herself. Her shorts, tank top, and leg warmers were so stiff with salt and sand that they were practically a Maddy-shaped suit of armor. If she stepped out of them, they would probably stand up by themselves. She started to laugh. "Um . . . seriously?"

Skeeter grinned. "Low maintenance," he said approvingly. "Makes for an excellent circus girl."

Maddy felt her face grow warm and looked away to hide the blush. In the water, three girls about her age dove under a wave together and popped up on the other side, laughing and splashing. Maddy wondered if they were sisters or friends, but for the first time she could remember, the wondering wasn't painful. For the first time in her life, *she* had real friends, too, and magic ones at that.

This friend thing was pretty great.

"Come on! Race you!" Skeeter cried, and took off down the beach.

"Hey, no fair!" cried Maddy. She held out her arm, waited for Ophelia to jump onto her shoulder, and then ran after him. They stopped at the water's edge, Maddy panting and Skeeter very annoyingly not out of breath at all. Ophelia tentacled down Maddy's side into the surf zone, turning the exact same color and texture as the waves that washed over her.

"So, just one thing." Maddy gestured toward the ocean and the surfers and the people playing in the waves. "I don't know how to do that."

"Do what?" asked Skeeter, kicking off his shoes.

"That," said Maddy, pointing at the girls diving under another wave. She slipped her flip-flops off and put them next to Skeeter's. "Swim in the ocean." She didn't mention that she wasn't supposed to swim at all anymore, not with her heart condition. Surreptitiously she patted her pocket, hoping the waterproofing for her pill bottle was still working. She could feel the Ringmaster's shell nestled up against the bottle, safe and sound.

"Octogirl!" Skeeter opened his eyes wide in pretend shock and then whipped off his shirt in one fast motion and tossed it on top of their shoes. "Don't tell me you've never been in the ocean before? Not even once? How have you lived? Are you sure you're okay? Do you need to lie down?"

Maddy rolled her eyes and swatted his arm.

"Ow! Nice right hook!" Skeeter said, fake wincing. "Really, though, swimming through the waves is pretty much the best thing ever, other than skateboarding. I bet you're a total natural. Anyway, you're gonna love it; it's swell. Get it? *Swell?*"

Maddy groaned. Skeeter took a bow.

"But seriously, folks," said Skeeter, straightening, "the main thing is, don't ever turn your back on the ocean and you'll be fine. Come on, I'll show you!"

They waded out, Ophelia jetting ahead of them. Water pushed at Maddy's legs as the surf rushed in and then pulled as it rushed out, making it harder to move than she had expected. When she was in as far as her knees, she bent over and scrunched the soaked leg warmers down around her ankles.

Her bracelet started to pulse.

Maddy yanked her hand out of the water and stared. Water

dripped down her arm as her bracelet squeezed her wrist—and suddenly, everything clicked into place.

"Skeeter!" she yelled, eyes still on her bracelet. "I think I figured it out! I think it's salt water!"

Skeeter shaded his eyes. *"Octogirl Figures Out the Ocean,"* he announced in a booming voice. *"Come one, come all!"*

Maddy was too busy staring at her bracelet to even roll her eyes. "No, I mean my *bracelet*! You know how I said it never pulled me before, or pulsed? And then it started to, in the canal? It's doing it again! It has to be the salt water! I've only ever put my *feet* in the ocean before this, never my arms, even when I rode the skulls to the circus café. And until yesterday I only ever swam in swimming pools." Suddenly, the idea that the sea might be the End of the World seemed much more likely.

"Cool!" said Skeeter. "So now what? Do we go out farther or stay here?"

"Let's see," said Maddy, and she dunked her arm back into the water. Her bracelet took on a definite rhythm . . . and then, faint and far away, she heard the same rhythm echoed back to her.

Tha thump. Tha-tha thump. Tha thump. Thadda thump.

"The Heart!" Maddy cried. "I can hear it! Skeeter, you were right, this is it!"

Maddy raced forward, hurrying to get far enough out so she could go all the way under and submerge, the way Abbot Kinney said, but the rolling swells pushed back. They threw her off balance and peppered her legs with sand and slimy bits of seaweed. She pushed harder, dragging herself through the water, waiting for her bracelet to tell her where to go.

"Octogirl!" Skeeter's voice sounded strangely far away. Maddy looked back. How had she gotten so far ahead of him? "Look out!"

Maddy snapped her head up to see a huge wave building in front of her. Her body went cold. "What do I do?" she yelled.

"Keep your eyes on the wave," he shouted back, "and dive under it when it crests! If you dive under, it will push you back up on the other side!"

Out of the corner of her eye, Maddy could see the three girls waiting for the same wave. They didn't look scared at all. The wave reached the other girls first, and as it did, all three of them dove underneath as one and came up on the other side. None of them seemed to drown.

And now the wave was on her. She could do this. Holding her nose, she dove forward and down, right through the breaking wave. Cold water covered her and her hands brushed the silty bottom as the wave crashed above her, thumping in that weird, underwater way sound traveled. And through the sound of the wave . . .

Tha thump. Tha-tha thump. Tha thump. Thadda thump.

The wave pounded past. Maddy could feel what Skeeter had meant, an upward swell lifting her, wanting to push her back up to the surface on the far side of the wave. But there was another pull: her bracelet, yanking her downward. This time, though, Maddy didn't panic. This time, she knew what to expect. She screwed her eyes shut and held her breath until Vanessa's leg warmers rose up to cover her face, formed fins at her feet, and propelled her down through the water and right through a hole at the bottom of the sea.

20

Maddy dropped into a purpled, twilit sky, the leg warmers becoming glider wings that once again sent her soaring toward the Bridge of Sighs. It still looked like a fortress, especially in the waning light.

She bit her lip. She had thought she was ready to be on the Bridge again, but she wasn't. Not quite. Not yet. And so, even though she didn't think it would work, she tipped to one side. To her surprise, the leg warmers didn't fight her but let her steer, and relief washed over her. She landed on the bank of the floating canal, right next to the white stone steps that led up to the Bridge. The leg warmers drew back from her face and body, pooling wet around her ankles and bare feet.

Maddy sat down on the bottom step, her back to the Bridge above her, purposely not looking at it. She didn't want to go up.

She wished she wasn't soaking wet and cold again, wished she hadn't told Skeeter not to come. Her body felt as heavy as the stone around her, pitted and unable to move.

Just a few more breaths, she told herself, looking at the floating canal as the sky around her darkened and faint stars started to appear, their reflections twinkling in the water. Her chest felt tight and prickly. *Then I'll go up.*

The crescent moon rose, its silvery light turning the skin on Maddy's arms ghostly. Moonlight danced along the surface of the canal like a ribbon.

Maddy caught her breath and rose to her feet. "Moonlight-on-the-Water?" she asked, hope making her fingers tingle. "Is that you?"

You are far from home, little one.

Maddy tried not to cry from relief. "I'm so glad you're here! I have to cross the Bridge, but I . . . I don't want to. What should I do?"

Should and should not are such small ideas for what the universe holds.

"Can you tell me what I have to do to get across?"

Not in words you will understand. My directions are of stars and gravity, of ascension and light-years.

Maddy wrapped her arms around herself and shivered. Her bracelet was quiet now, no pulsing or pulling.

"I'm scared, Moonlight," she said finally, in a low voice meant only for the night. "I don't know if I can do this."

I light midnight water and illuminate shadows, and yet I am only I. It is up to you to see.

"What if I don't want to?" asked Maddy. "I wish . . ." she whispered, and then stopped, somehow ashamed.

Wishes are the realm of the moon and the nighttime, said Moonlight-on-the-Water. *What is it you wish?*

"I wish my parents were here," said Maddy.

Ah. This is something unique to little ones.

"Wanting parents?" asked Maddy. That would make sense. Moons and stars probably didn't need parents, not in the same way she did.

Wishing for something that is already in your grasp, could you but see.

"No," Maddy said with certainty. She wasn't sure of very many things anymore, but she was sure of this. "This isn't about seeing or not seeing. It's just the way things are."

Everything looks different in the moonlight. If parents are love and difficult decisions and doing what you can to help all little ones, then perhaps you have them more than you think.

And just like that, Maddy was tired of mystery and showmanship, of stories and the grandness of the universe. She was not cosmic; she was human-sized. And in her human-sized world, she most definitely did not have parents.

"Stop it!" she cried, hands clenching. "Stop pretending I have parents! I don't! I think they had to be part of the circus, but no one will tell me who they are! Did you know them?"

A million glinting, quicksilver sparkles on the canal rose into the air like a flock of startled birds, then rained back down to wriggle like glowworms through the dark water. For a brief moment Maddy heard windswept laughter, the croon of a lullaby, the distant sound of a calliope. Something brushed the side of her face, tender and warm. Tears stung unbidden at her eyes.

Has not the circus shown its face to you? said Moonlight-on-the-Water. *Have not you lit the marquee and called the muse to your side?*

"Yes, but—"

Have not you understood the language of every creature and heard the circus's Heart?

"Yes!" cried Maddy. "But what does that have to do with anything?"

Moonlight-on-the-Water washed across her, soft and lovely. *Little one. You are a child of the circus. We found you, Il Circo and I, when you were small and alone and perfect. We found you on our shore, and we loved you. But we could not raise you. I am only I, ever waxing and waning, and a circus is far too grand to be a parent. But we loved you nonetheless. And so I gave you a piece of moonlight to carry on your wrist, and Il Circo gave you a piece of its heart. Then we delivered you to others of your kind to raise. We hoped these pieces of us might lead you back to us someday. And now, they have.*

Everything drained out of Maddy—anger, tears, even shock—leaving her empty. "What?" she asked, her voice shaking.

Explanations are not the realm of the nighttime.

"But—" Questions and thoughts raced through Maddy's mind, one after the other, each crowding out the next. She stared at her bracelet—which, now that she really looked, shone the exact color of Moonlight-on-the-Water.

"So my bracelet . . . it's from *you?*" said Maddy slowly. "Not from my parents?"

No human parent could give you a piece of moonlight made solid. Only I am I.

Maddy kept staring at her bracelet. She couldn't quite process it. She could understand being found by Moonlight-on-the-Water—a little bit, anyway. Moonlight *was* light, after all, and that light must have made it easier to see a baby on a dark beach. But being found by the *circus?* What did that even mean? Was the circus a person? A thing? It didn't make any sense!

And what did this say about her parents? They had left her on the beach, where she could have died! What kind of person did that? Maddy twisted her bracelet around and around on her wrist. Skeeter had said she was better off that her parents never came back for her. Was he right, after all? She almost wanted to cry, thinking about it—but only almost.

Because she *didn't* die. Instead, she was found by Il Circo and Moonlight, and they had given her the gift of magic. She still didn't quite understand it, but she understood this: They had taken care of her and made sure she was safe.

They had saved her.

"Moonlight," she said, her heart pounding with a strange and confused exhilaration. "Thank you."

I am only I, said Moonlight-on-the-Water. Although the moon was still high in the sky, it had moved enough that it was starting to dip behind the Bridge of Sighs, its light temporarily blocked and its voice fading. *I but reflect upon what is. It is up to you to see. We have missed you, little one, and the circus needs you now. We are glad you are home.*

Maddy stood still for a long moment after the moon disappeared behind the Bridge, a buzzing in her ears. And then she did the only thing she could think to do. She turned and ran up the cold stone staircase, taking the stairs two at a time, and stumbled over the threshold onto the Bridge of Sighs.

21

The Bridge smelled of loneliness.

As Maddy stepped onto the white stone floor, all the strange joy that Moonlight-on-the-Water had given her drained away, as though the Bridge had pulled a plug at the base of her heart. The air was bitter and fetid, and it trailed down her spine like damp fingers. A sourness rose in Maddy's throat but she swallowed it down.

It was a bridge. It was just a bridge, and all she had to do was walk to the other side.

She could do this.

She took a step forward. The stone was cool on her feet.

Instantly the air pushed back at her, thick and sticky, like in a dream where you have to get someplace but you can't seem to move. She took another step, fighting her way forward. The walls and roof felt as though they were closing in on her, ready to trap her in their ancient grasp.

And then the voices started.

Unwanted. Given up.

The hairs on Maddy's arm rose. The voices were icy cold, reverberating around her, but she took a deep breath and forced herself to stand taller. She could do this. She *could.*

What's the matter with you? Even your own mother didn't want you.

Like taunting kids on a playground, the voices surrounded her. Maddy pressed her hands against her ears so hard that it hurt, but it didn't help.

You can't play with us. This is a club for the kids who live here, not for you! Go find your own place to play!

The voices were moving closer, like animals hunting.

We already have too many girls here. We can't take one more, and a sick one at that. Find somewhere else.

It *hurt,* as though Maddy's heart had literally torn open, spilling out every piece of pain she had ever had. She took her hands from her ears and pressed them against her chest, forcing herself to straighten. She had to keep going. She had to. The circus was the only place she had ever felt as though she might belong.

Nice try. The words were like bee stings, sharp and poisoned. *You belong nowhere.*

Maddy cried out as the air closed in around her, the loneliness trapping her. She put out her hands and pushed, but it was as though her entire life was hardening around her, holding her in place like a moth caught in sap.

No one cares. No one wanted you enough to keep you. No one remembers you, either. As soon as you were gone, they forgot you.

It was as though her heart were crying, as though the tears were welling in her chest and not her eyes. Maddy tried counting her breath, the way that girl had taught her, but she kept losing count. And she was cold, so cold, shaking all over.

Always sick. More trouble than you're worth.

Maddy thought she had remembered how awful it had felt before, when she had first been here, but she was wrong. This was worse. She couldn't move, couldn't push back against the loneliness sucking everything out of her. Would she just get trapped here, frozen forever?

You'll never amount to anything. How could you? This is just who you are.

Maddy clenched her teeth together, holding in the sobs. If she started crying now, she didn't think she'd ever stop. It was true. Everything the voices were saying was true.

This is your life. Nothing you do will change that.

"Stop it!" Maddy had meant to yell, but the words came out small and unconvincing. She dropped her head, her thick black hair curtaining her face. She hadn't really understood when

Vanessa had said she would have to face the most frightening thing imaginable. She had thought it would be some kind of monster, but it wasn't. The most frightening thing possible was simply the cold, hard truth: She could never belong. Hadn't her whole life proved that? What was the point of crossing the Bridge of Sighs? In fact, what was the point of anything at all? She felt herself shrinking into nothingness, exactly where she belonged. All that would be left of her would be a faint, Maddy-shaped smudge.

No home. No family. No choices. No one.

Now something huge and frighteningly familiar was moving swiftly toward her. Maddy huddled down on the stone floor and curled herself up into a ball, cold seeping through her. How could she have ever thought she was ready for this?

May as well accept that no one wants you, the awful thing said as it grew bigger and more solid.

With a start, Maddy suddenly knew what it was, this thing on the other side of the bridge. She recognized it with horrible certainty. It was her own fear, and it was coming for her.

You're never going to belong anywhere.

She had to fight it. She had to, or she would never get across.

Slowly, every muscle screaming for her to run away, Maddy put one trembling hand on the wall and stood, legs unsure and shaky. She hated fighting, but she had been in enough group homes to know how to do it. Her hands balled into fists. When her fear was close enough, she rushed at it with all her might, punching and yelling, but her fists passed right through it. Not only that, but with every jab it grew larger and hungrier, more solid and real, a great, misshapen beast ready to swallow her whole.

"Go away!" Maddy shrieked, twisting and turning as her fear wrapped itself around her, clasping her closer.

She couldn't escape. A strange wailing had filled the air, and after a moment she realized it was coming from her own mouth. She tried to stop crying, tried to punch and push, but her fear held her paralyzed. And then it began to ooze through her skin, into her veins and heart and mind. Black spots pushed at the corners of Maddy's vision.

"Help!" she tried to scream, but her fear slid down her throat and choked off the word, gagging her.

Maddy's eyes darted wildly as more and more of her fear filled her entire body, slimy and thick. The far side of the Bridge of Sighs was as impossible now as another planet. But then a small beam of moonlight spilled in through one of the tiny, barred windows at the top, dappling the walls and sending monstrous shadows of her fight with her fear dancing across the stone walls of the Bridge.

"Moonlight-on-the-Water?" Maddy gasped. "Is that you?"

It wasn't. There was no water here to shine down upon, only stone, and so no one answered. But the silvery light reminded her. It reminded her of magic, of sparkle, of the daytime and nighttime circus. Of really seeing. Of the many sides of all things. And with that memory, an idea grew. Slowly, not even sure why, Maddy stopped struggling against her fear. She could still feel it pressing at her, but she gritted her teeth and closed her eyes. While it pushed against her, she thought of Moonlight-on-the-Water and the beauty that had come when she had finally seen the nighttime circus for what it was.

Would that work here?

Inside of her, something, softly, said *yes*.

Let me see, thought Maddy, eyes screwed shut. *Please. I really want to see.*

She took a deep breath and opened her eyes. At first, she couldn't even tell what she was seeing, but then her brain caught up to her eyes and she gasped. The thing towering above her, the horrible thing pinning her arms to her sides, wasn't huge at all! Not only that, it wasn't even holding her! It was there, yes, but it just floated around her like a cloud. It wasn't doing anything. *She* was holding *herself* still. She was letting herself be frozen.

She was allowing all of it.

Understanding settled around Maddy like a friend throwing an arm over her shoulder. It was *all* her . . . which meant that the thing she had to face on the Bridge, the most terrifying thing she could imagine, was . . .

. . . herself.

Oh.

And if that was true, well, she probably had to accept all of it, all of her, all of her sides. Just like with the nighttime circus.

That was right. It had to be right. Slowly, Maddy stepped away from the shadowy cloud, stood tall, and looked—really looked—at her fear. At first, it seemed to grow even larger and more menacing, and she thought maybe she had been wrong after all, but she didn't look away. Instead, she looked *into*. And then, slowly, finally . . . her fear began to shrink. The more she looked into it, the smaller her fear grew.

No one wants you, her fear tried to growl, but now it just sounded petulant and whiny. *That will never change. You'll always be unwanted. Unworthy.*

The air around her seemed to hold its breath.

"Um . . ." Maddy tucked a piece of hair behind her ear and took a deep breath. "Okay."

Okay? repeated her fear, sounding perplexed.

Maddy nodded, over and over, the motion somehow soothing. *I can accept it all*, she thought, and to her surprise, she could. Now that she could see it for what it really was—small and weak and fed only by her own self—she could.

"I accept that maybe I won't ever belong anywhere." Maddy shook out her arms, feeling energy zing down them. "Maybe Il Circo isn't my home. And that's . . . well, that's okay."

But aren't you scared? demanded her fear.

Maddy chewed her lip. "Yes," she admitted, for she was,

terribly. But somehow saying it out loud made it *hers*, made it bearable. "And I *am* lonely, although not nearly as lonely as I was before. So maybe it's not actually true that I don't belong anywhere. Maybe I could. Maybe . . . Oh!" Maddy inhaled with surprise as another thought struck her. What if her fear was part of her, just like the nighttime circus was part of the daytime? What if she needed it, and it needed her, just like Il Circo needed both parts to make up the whole, beautiful, messy, dangerous, *wonderful* circus?

"Maybe you could help me?" Maddy asked her fear, which had shrunk now to a tiny, hovering puff of gray, as insubstantial as sea spray. She took a step toward it. "When I need you?"

Really? Her fear sounded suspicious. *And you'll listen to me?*

Maddy considered this. She wanted to be honest. "Well . . . not always. But if it's really important, like I'm about to do something I actually *should* be afraid of, I'll do my best."

Hm, said her fear. *In that case, I accept.*

Her fear surged toward her. Maddy braced herself, but it really wasn't bad as it sank into her skin, just tiny pinpricks of cold like walking into a fog. She could actually feel it curl up in a little nook inside her mind.

I'll be right here, said her fear. *In case you need me.*

"Thanks," said Maddy. "I'll do my best to take care of you, too."

And then, all was quiet. Maddy wiped her damp hands on

her shorts. Was that it? Could she cross now? She took a tentative step forward.

The air let her pass.

With a whoop, Maddy broke into a run.

22

Unfortunately, the Bridge wasn't quite done with her.

Maddy was just steps away from the far side of the Bridge of Sighs when a small booth with red and purple beads hanging over the doorway dropped in front of her, cutting off her access to the other side. She skidded to stop, breathing hard.

A red neon sign buzzed noisily to life above the booth.

**WELCOME TO THE ALTER
THE LAST STEP ON THE BRIDGE.
FORTUNES READ AND RUINED
LIVES TOLD AND LOST
(ATM INSIDE)**

"Madeline Adriana?" called a woman's voice through the doorway. "Please, enter."

Heart pounding, Maddy inched forward, pulled back the beaded curtain, and peeked inside. An ancient woman sat at a table covered in a dark purple cloth with a deck of cards in front of her. Behind her stood an old, battered ATM.

"Madeline Adriana, I presume?" said the old woman.

Maddy stepped in, staying close to the swaying beads of the doorway so she could run out if she had to. She could feel her fear inside of her nodding its approval. "Yes," she said warily. "Who are you?"

"I am the last step," said the woman. "Once you pass me—*if* you pass me—you have crossed the Bridge of Sighs." She picked up the cards, shuffled them expertly, and then spread them face-down in an arc across the table. "Pick a card."

"What for?"

"To see if you can pass."

"But . . . who are you?"

The old woman burst into flames.

Maddy shrieked and jumped backward but the flames disappeared as quickly as they had come, leaving a tiger sitting placidly in the old woman's chair.

The big cat yawned. "I'm the Alter, of course. It says so right on my sign."

Maddy shuffled closer to the doorway. "I thought an altar was like a table, with flowers and pictures and stuff."

The tiger grinned widely, which was quite unsettling. "Clearly, I'm not that kind of Alter," it said, and then melted into a massive dictionary whose yellowed pages flipped open to the A's.

Maddy leaned forward. "Alter," she read. "Verb: To change, make different, or modify."

The dictionary snapped shut and became the old woman again.

"You can't pass without picking a card," she said. "It's the law."

That didn't sound right. "Which law?" Maddy asked.

"The law of entropy. Pick a card."

"Are you Fate?" asked Maddy. In the books she read, Fate was always an old woman, and she was almost always heartless.

"Fate? That old bore?" The old woman began to laugh. Her mouth grew wider and wider and her body shrank smaller and smaller, until she was nothing but gaping teeth and maw. Maddy's fear shouted at her, but then the mouth became a green dragonfly. It zoomed over the table, brushing against the cards and sending them flying onto the floor. Out of habit, Maddy bent down and scooped them up. She was about to hand them back, but then realized that one of them showed a stylized drawing of *herself*! She paused, worry rising in her, and riffled through the other cards. They were all of her! Here was one of her finding her skateboard; here was another of the first group home she had lived in.

"Why do these cards have pictures from my life?" she said slowly.

The dragonfly became a tornado that swept the cards out of her hand and deposited them back on the table in a neat stack. "Because this is your deck, of course. What else would they show?"

Maddy stared at the cards, wanting to grab them back. "You mean they tell my future? So you *are* Fate, after all?"

"Indeed not, and never suggest such a thing again. Fate is preordained, and I am anything but. I am this . . ." The tornado became a column of black, shiny rock. ". . . and I am this . . ." The black rock eroded into a large puddle of water. ". . . and I am this." The water evaporated, blanketing Maddy in clouds. "I am change, and I cannot be escaped."

The clouds rose into the air and took the shape of an older girl—a girl with a thin, angry mouth and wavy black hair hanging lank around her shoulders.

Maddy blinked. The girl was her, a her from the future, with hollowed cheeks and eyes that were sunken and bitter. "Is that . . ." The words scraped at Maddy's throat. "Is that what happens to me?"

"How many times must I tell you?" The Alter-Maddy spoke in a high, chirping voice as it folded in on itself to become a cricket. "I am not Fate. No one but you can say what you become, and nothing is guaranteed: not time, not life, not the Earth nor the sea. The only certainty is that I exist." The cricket shimmered into the shape of Skeeter, smiling at her, dimples creasing his cheeks.

Maddy started to smile back, but then caught herself, shaking her head. "It's not real," she muttered. "It's not really him."

"It is human nature to deny change, to fear it, to pretend it isn't there. That, however, does not make it any less real." The Alter-Skeeter became a small, gilded hand mirror, hanging in the air in front of Maddy. She took a step closer. Her reflection was the opposite of the other Maddy and was beautiful in a way the real Maddy knew she was not. The Maddy in the mirror had a bright, dancing quality, as though she were listening to the most wonderful story and could barely contain her laughter. It took a moment to realize what it was.

The Maddy in the mirror was happy.

"You have faced your nighttime," said the Alter-Maddy in the mirror. "Now you must also face your day."

Maddy reached out and took the mirror, bringing it closer. The Alter-Maddy in the mirror smiled at her and a bubble of longing rose in Maddy's chest. Could she be this happy? After everything, after all the loneliness, after always being different . . . was it possible? She stared at her reflection, studying every piece of the Alter-Maddy and doing her best to copy it: how to smile just right, how to tilt her head the same way, how to make her eyes this kind of crinkly happy.

After what may have been two minutes or may have been two hours, Maddy noticed something.

"You're not changing," she said to the Alter-Maddy in the mirror. "How come you're not changing?"

The Maddy in the mirror laughed. "Oh, but I am. I am always changing, all around you. But since you are not willing to let go of this change you like, you can no longer see my true form."

"Does that mean I can keep you like this?" asked Maddy hopefully.

"No," said the Alter-Maddy. "Life frozen in one spot becomes death. My very nature is change. But there is always the option to ignore the truth of what I am. Should you choose to do so, you will have plenty of company."

Like an old black-and-white film running in the background, shadowy, washed-out people began to appear around Maddy. Each of them held a small mirror that they stared at with dreamy, faraway eyes.

Suddenly cold, Maddy tore her eyes from her reflection. "Who are they? What's wrong with them?"

"These are the ones who prefer to pretend they can live in a world without change. But that is impossible, for change happens whether you choose to see it or not. And so they remain stuck in a falsehood of their own making, not seeing what is true."

Maddy stared at the pale, wispy figures and then at the Alter-Maddy in the mirror. Surely, if she held on to the Alter-Maddy, if she kept the image here and refused to see anything else, she could figure out how to become the happy girl in the reflection?

But even as Maddy thought this, she knew it wasn't true. This Alter-Maddy was an illusion. That didn't mean that the real Maddy couldn't grow up to be more like the Maddy in the mirror . . . but it *did* mean that nothing would happen as long as the real Maddy sat here, looking at an image of what she wanted to be but not actually *doing* anything to make it happen.

She wouldn't get stuck here, not now, not when she was so close. In one fast motion, before she could change her mind, Maddy dashed the mirror to the ground, where it shattered to pieces.

Immediately, the broken glass re-formed into a feathered mask, a high-heeled boot, an egg, a stack of pancakes, rotating through changes so quickly that Maddy couldn't keep up. At the same time, the ATM in the corner lit up like a slot machine.

"Good girl," said the Alter, and it became a baby elephant that wrapped its trunk around Maddy and pushed her toward the ATM. "You have chosen to go forth, and so you may make a withdrawal before you pick a card."

"But . . . I don't have any money," said Maddy.

The baby elephant turned into a large luna moth. "Not money," it sang as her name appeared on the ATM screen along with a string of numbers. Maddy leaned closer to read:

Madeline Adriana: Account balances
(Amounts shown are current estimates only)

Friendships: 3,568
Loneliness: 8,353
Courage: 13,333
Kindness: 13,799
Magical Happenings: 13,535
Health: 142
Sadness: 12,400
Family: 64
Wishes: 11,732
Conviction: 8,672
Time: 91
All balances subject to change

Maddy's teeth worked her lower lip. Next to each number was a place to input how much she wanted to withdraw—but she had no idea what the numbers meant.

"What am I supposed to do?" she asked.

The moth became two slices of bread that popped out of a toaster. "It is an exercise in choice," said both slices together. "Withdraw what you choose to carry with you."

"But how do I know what to take?"

The bread became an orange-and-white lizard. "Sometimes we can choose. Other times we cannot." The lizard bloomed into a single pink flower, then wilted and died, shriveling into a mass of dark mold. "What is important is to recognize which is which," said the mold in many voices at the same time. "Every time you make a withdrawal, you choose."

Maddy stared at the screen, her fingers hovering uncertainly. Should she withdraw everything good and leave sadness and loneliness behind? Or was this a time when she should accept it all and take everything with her, good or bad? What happened if she withdrew all the good things and had no balances left?

But she didn't really want her sadness right now. And she needed all the help she could get. With that thought, she raced through, withdrawing most of anything that sounded good and leaving everything else behind. *Health* and *Time* already seemed low, and she certainly didn't have much *Family*, so she left those as they were. Maybe she could add more later.

As soon as she had finished inputting her requests, the machine began spitting out new playing cards. Maddy caught them as they spewed from the machine, each one showing a scene from her life, a moment caught in time. Here, marked *Courage*, was when she had stood up to some older girls who were bullying someone. Here, marked *Magical Happenings*, was Maddy as a baby, the bracelet on her wrist shining as though lit from within. Here, marked *Friends*, was an image of her and Skeeter on the beach, playing tic-tac-toe in the sand. Maddy walked slowly back to the Alter's table, looking through the cards. A warm flush spread over the back of her neck.

The mold became the old woman, who held out her hand. "Cards, please."

Maddy folded them to herself protectively. "But they're mine!"

"In order to move forward," said the Alter, her hand still extended, "you must learn to let go."

"Do I get them back?" asked Maddy.

"That depends."

"On what?"

"On you. There are plenty of times in life you can make a withdrawal. Really, you can do it far more often than most people think. And if you're careful, you never lose the cards you withdraw. They just replenish."

Reluctantly, Maddy handed over her cards.

The Alter shuffled them in with the others. "Now your deck is stacked."

Maddy knew what that meant. There had been a card night at one of her group homes, so she knew that stacking the deck meant slipping extra cards into it so you had a better chance of winning.

She also knew that stacking the deck meant cheating.

"But—that's not right," she said quietly.

"Nonsense," said the Alter. "All decks are stacked. It's a lie meant as kindness to say that everyone plays with the same deck. Our deck changes the moment our parents' parents touch it, the moment we touch it, the moment our friends touch it. Life is an ongoing chance to stack the deck with whatever you choose to withdraw. Luck or friends, anger or jealousy. You choose. And then you play." The Alter became a sea lion with liquid brown eyes and fanned the cards across the table with its front flipper. "Pick a card."

Maddy stared at the cards, anger building inside her. It had been like this her whole life. The same group home leader who had organized card night used to always talk about the cards you were dealt, right before giving a lecture on Gratitude and Acceptance. *We have no control over the cards we're dealt,* he would say. Why was Maddy an orphan and other kids weren't? Those were the cards she was dealt. How come she was sick? Those were the cards she was dealt. None of it was fair, not in the slightest. Some kids got the parents cards, some kids got to be healthy, some kids had a home and friends . . . and some kids didn't. Well, for the first time ever, Maddy had a deck stacked with every good thing in her life, and she wanted it—all of it, not just one card.

In one swift move, she scooped up the entire deck, the cards slippery against each other. One of them slid from the deck and fell to the table, and the sea lion became a smooth gray pebble that pinned the card down.

"Is this your choice?" asked the pebble.

"No!" With her other hand, Maddy swept the pebble away before it could change into something heavier and picked up the card. *Magical Happenings,* it said, showing a top hat the color of midnight underneath the lit marquee of Il Circo delle Strade. Maddy smiled. That *was* a particularly good card. Even so, she didn't want to choose just one. She slipped the card into her pocket with her pills and the Ringmaster's seashell, so she could find it easily later on and look at it more closely. "Since I get to choose, I'm taking them all."

The pebble crumbled into a huge brown pelican that stood almost as tall as Maddy. "Very well. You have made your choice, and you have stood by it with conviction. Even I must sometimes bow to that, for choice is powerful. And so you may pass, and you may take your whole deck with you."

"You mean . . . I'm done?" asked Maddy, barely daring to hope.

"You have crossed the Ponte dei Sospiri," said the pelican, and it spread its brown wings wide, wide enough to break through the walls of the Bridge of Sighs, wide enough to carry Maddy easily between them. "And now I will carry you into the heart, where this and all bridges lead."

Cards in hand, joy catching at her throat, Maddy climbed onto the back of the pelican. The world fell away, the Bridge and the booth and the ATM, and together she and the Alter-pelican rose into the air and soared over canals and mountains and strange, golden seas.

"Choose to go forward," said the Alter. "Always go forward. Be willing to let go."

"Now?" asked Maddy.

"Now," said the Alter.

Holding her cards close to her chest, Maddy let go.

23

Maddy fell gently, as if she were floating. Her cards pulled out of her hands, joining together beneath her to form a long, papery slide that she rode down to land on a mat of muscle in a pulsing red chamber. It was smooth and slippery under her bare feet, and she wished she had somehow kept her flip-flops with her. Around her, the heartbeat stuttered and strained, bucking the floor beneath her feet and shaking the walls.

Tha-thump. Thadda-tha-thump. Tha-tha-thump. Thadda thump.

The Heart itself was far smaller than Maddy had expected—just about the right size to have an earnest conversation with herself. She stood, and the slide that had carried her collapsed into individual cards that fluttered around like flattened paper airplanes. One by one they landed on the floor of the Heart, where they began to burrow into the muscle. Maddy gasped and fell to her knees, scrabbling to save them—she couldn't lose her cards! Not now, not when she had just gotten them! But they had somehow embedded themselves already, and the muscle wouldn't give. Maddy didn't want to hurt the Heart, but . . . her cards! How could she get them back?

Tha-thump. Thadda-tha-thump. Tha-tha-thump. Thadda thump.

Right. Maddy sat back on her heels, the sound of the heartbeat reminding her why she was here: to call the Ringmaster and save the circus. She wasn't sure how the magic that called the Ringmaster to her would work, but this room was definitely too small for both of them. She should probably find a place the Ringmaster could fit.

Walking through the Heart was like trying to walk in a bouncy house that had come alive, only more disgusting. The walls were battered and damaged, covered in fissures and rips.

Poor Heart, thought Maddy, trying not to touch anything. *It looks pretty beat up.*

She ducked under a wet red flap into a bigger chamber where a large fissure split the floor like a fault line. For some reason, looking at it made her want to cry—and it was somehow familiar. Maddy frowned, then slowly turned to stare at the odd rips and tears in the walls. She moved closer. She knew these shapes! Here was a tear in the shape of the time she had to move away from her favorite group home. She ran her fingers over the wound and hot tears sprang to her eyes. Here was a rip in the shape of getting teased by the kids at school. When she touched it: anger and bewilderment. Here was one in the shape of asking the Ringmaster if he was her father. Embarrassment and humiliation.

What did this mean? Maddy backed away unsteadily, stepping right onto the fissure that ran across the floor of the Heart. A jolt of unbearable aloneness shot through her chest, making her inhale sharply. What was happening? She had thought that, after crossing the Bridge of Sighs, she wouldn't ever have to feel this way again! She teetered in place and then lost her balance, sitting down hard on top of the fault line. Another burst of loneliness seared through her, loneliness she recognized.

Oh.

This wasn't the Heart at the End of the World at all.

This was *her* heart.

The Alter had brought her to her own heart.

Maddy sat for a moment, unsure of what to do, loneliness washing over her. And then something scurried across her leg. Maddy shrieked and jerked her leg, but the creature grabbed on with its front paws. It was a small gray mouse, wearing a waistcoat and holding a tiny toolbox.

"Must you sit *right here*?" it said—somewhat crankily, Maddy thought.

Maddy opened her mouth and then closed it again. "Um," she began.

The mouse sighed noisily and pulled a monocle out of its pocket. "Oh," it said flatly as it fitted the monocle to one beady brown eye and looked her up and down. "It's you."

"Are you a . . . *mouse?*" Maddy croaked.

"I beg your pardon!" The mouse dropped the monocle back into its pocket. "I am a circus heartmouse, which is as different from a normal mouse as swiss is from cheddar. One of *your* circus heartmice, I might add. My name is Geoff."

"I have mice in my heart?" Maddy asked faintly.

"All circuses have mice."

"But . . . my heart isn't a circus."

"No?" said Geoff with a good deal of irritation, scurrying off her leg. "I must be terribly mistaken, even though I've lived here my whole life and would therefore be expected to know a fair bit more about it than someone who's never even bothered to visit before now. In any case, it's lovely that you to have so much time to chitchat, but I'm terribly busy and you're sitting right on my job." He looked pointedly at the fault line.

"Oh," said Maddy, flustered. She scooted to the side. As soon as she moved off the fissure, her loneliness disappeared. "Sorry."

The heartmouse flipped open his toolbox. Inside were a needle and thread the exact blue color Maddy loved. Geoff wetted one end of the thread on his tiny tongue, passed it through the almost-invisible eye of the needle, and then, carefully, began to sew the fault line together. Maddy watched as he made small, precise stitches through the muscle.

"What are you doing?" she finally asked, even though she thought she knew.

"Do be quiet and let me concentrate. It's difficult enough with these shoddy materials you've given us."

"You're mending my heart," Maddy said softly.

Geoff made an affirmative humming sound. "That's what circus heartmice do."

Maddy stood and went to the wall of the heart. Now she could see that countless nicks and tears had been carefully stitched together with the same blue thread. She ran her hands over them, waiting for some sort of painful feeling, but nothing happened.

She turned back to Geoff. "Did you fix all of these?"

"Of course not! No self-respecting heartmouse lives alone. The others are out scrounging for more thread, which, might I add, wouldn't be a problem if you supplied us with something better to work with, something that didn't snap at the first sign of strain. Something sturdier." He waved his fist in the air, blue thread peeking out. "This works fine for the little hurts. But the bigger ones, like this one here? The thread you've been giving us isn't nearly strong enough."

"I didn't know I was supposed to give you thread," said Maddy.

"Obviously. I haven't had a vacation in ten years."

Maddy touched a few more mended spots on the wall of her heart. No sadness, no loneliness. She crouched down next to

Geoff, gratitude flooding her. "Thank you," she said.

"Humph," said Geoff, but his whiskers quivered as though he might smile.

"How do I get you more thread?" said Maddy.

Geoff looked up in surprise. "What kind of a question is that? Everyone knows that mending materials grow when you pay attention to your heart and do what *it* thinks is a good idea instead of listening to everything else."

Maddy ran one hand over the section of the fault line Geoff had just sewn together. Nothing. No loneliness taking her breath away. Then, carefully and gently, she touched the tip of one finger against the non-mended part. Not-belonging and aloneness stabbed through her like an electric shock. She sat back on her heels, listening to her own heartbeat shake the walls, erratic and sharp.

"I'm going to make sure you get better thread from now on," she said. "I'm sorry it's been so weak. Does, um . . . does mending these tears mean I won't be sick anymore?"

Geoff shook his head as his paws moved with great expertise. "Mending the breaks won't change that, I'm afraid. That's something different from heartbreak. But we heartmice stay with the heart no matter what. Always have, always will."

It had never occurred to Maddy that being sick affected anyone but herself. She rose to her feet. The Ponte dei Sospiri was supposed to bring her inside the Heart at the End of the World, but it had brought her inside her own heart instead. She knew they weren't the same thing; she had seen the other Heart and it was huge, far larger than hers. But maybe she could get there from here. After all, she *was* bound to the Heart at the End of the World.

"Capt'n Geoff!" cried a small, excited voice. Another heartmouse, its paws full of thick blue thread, darted into the room, followed by several others. Squeaks and squeals filled the air. "Look! Supplies! More'n I've ever seen!"

Geoff dropped his needle and scurried away after the other heartmice, back into the chamber where Maddy had first landed. Careful not to step on anyone, Maddy followed, a smile starting across her face as she saw what was happening.

From each card that had implanted itself in the flesh of her heart, a tree of blue thread had sprouted, all of it thick and strong and glorious. Skeins of blue wrapped around themselves like tangled hair while the heartmice swarmed everywhere, chittering excitedly as they gathered up the thread: *Ho! . . . Can you believe? Well, I never . . .*

Geoff put one little paw on his heart and used the other to wipe away a tear. "A whole forest!" he said as the strong blue thread grew before their eyes. "Quick, now, lads! Snip and snap! Cut and clip! Time to mend!"

With a great chattering of glee the heartmice began to harvest the thread. It felt to Maddy as though countless caves inside of her were filling up, caves that had been empty for so long she hadn't even known they were there. It made her feel as though she could do anything.

And then, like a doorway, something opened in the side of the chamber, right through the muscle. Maddy's hands flew to her mouth. Leading away from her heart was a keyhole-shaped pier stretching over a pale blue sea, its circular end glowing gold.

Tug, went Maddy's heart—both from inside of her, and around her, too, the heart she stood in flashing with beautiful blue light. Geoff looked up from gathering thread and saw the pier.

"Well, my goodness," he said.

"Does every heart have a pier?" asked Maddy.

Geoff sniffed loudly. "Up until this moment, I wouldn't have said *this* heart had a pier."

Maddy smiled. She didn't have to ask where her pier went. She knew. For she was bound to the Heart at the End of the World and that meant it was bound to her as well—two hearts, one and the same, connected. She crouched down next to Geoff, her heartmouse who had done so much work for her.

"I'll do my best to send you better materials from now on," she said. "I promise you'll get that vacation after all."

Geoff's button eyes lit up. "I hear the lungs are nice this time of year."

Maddy kissed the heartmouse between his tiny ears, and then turned and ran down the pier of her heart. There were no lights, no circus announcements, no marquees. Just the slapping of her feet and the rushing of her blood and the pounding of her heart, both inside and out. *How can I be inside my heart while my heart is still inside me?* Maddy wondered, but before she could piece together any kind of answer, she had reached the end of the pier. Without pausing, she dove over the railing into the warm golden sea. There was no need for the leg warmers here; the warm water carried her quickly where she needed to go, right up to the Heart at the End of the World.

It was even bigger than it had looked through the Ringmaster's window, its uneven heartbeat reverberating through the water. The Ringmaster's whip was wrapped tightly around it, squeezing in time.

Thakthak-thump. Thakka-thump. Tha-thump-tha-tha-thump.

Maddy tore her eyes away from the painful-looking black whip and swam around the Heart until she found an opening, a large valve with a sign above it:

**WELCOME TO THE HEART
AT THE END OF THE WORLD.
SINCERE INQUIRIES ONLY.**

She tumbled through the valve, landing on her feet inside the Heart at the End of the World. It felt the same under her bare feet as her own heart had, but it was golden instead of red, bright instead of dark, vast instead of cozy . . . and terribly, terribly confused. The sound was deafening. It wormed into Maddy's ears and stomach and chest, rattling her painfully from the inside.

Thakthak-thump. Thakka-thump. Tha-thump-tha-tha-thump.

The Ringmaster's whip had eaten through the Heart's exterior in places, and it showed through here and there, the muscle around it raw and torn. The whip pulsed with its own rhythm as the Heart struggled against it. It was like listening to two different radio stations turned up all the way and playing at the same time, one overlapping the other until all you could hear was wrongness. Maddy's own heart was already starting to skitter and jump, trying to match the confused heartbeats around it.

Thakthak-thump. Thakka-thump. Tha-thump-tha-tha-thump.

The rhythm tore at Maddy's ears and she took a sharp, ragged breath, her own heart straining like a trapped animal. Pain shot through her chest, through her entire body, followed by a dull numbness that made panic rise into her throat. She couldn't seem to breathe.

Thakthak-thump. Thakka-thump. Tha-thump-tha-tha-thump.

Maddy took a step forward and then fell to her knees, curling up into a tight, small ball. She hadn't really understood before, hadn't really thought she needed to be in a home for sick kids. But she had never had an attack like this one. She could barely see, barely think.

Thakthak-thump. Thakka-thump. Tha-thump-tha-tha-thump.

Something wet slapped her in the face.

"Stop," Maddy said weakly. She tried to push it away, but her body wouldn't move.

The wet thing slapped her again.

Maddy cracked one eye open. One of the leg warmers had slid off her ankle and was reared like a cobra ready to strike. When it saw her eyes were open, it tapped emphatically at the pocket where, what seemed like so long ago, Maddy had stowed the Ringmaster's shell.

Thakthak-thump. Thakka-thump. Tha-thump-tha-tha-thump.

Of course! The Ringmaster! That's what she was supposed to do: call the Ringmaster so he could fix the Heart at the End of the World, which would fix her, too. She fumbled at her pocket, pulling out the shell. With her last remaining strength, she slammed the shell against her leg, feeling it crunch. But she didn't feel the sharp shards of the seashell cut her hand or the leg warmers slide back onto her legs. By the time the Ringmaster arrived and picked her up, she had slipped into darkness.

24

"My dear girl, that was beautifully dramatic." The Ringmaster's voice was cheery, but there was a note of strain beneath it. "Your swoon was perfection itself."

Maddy rubbed her eyes. She was slumped against the golden wall of the Heart at the End of the World. In front of her were the Ringmaster and Kuma, who dipped his great head at her in greeting. Maddy nodded back and rose woozily to her feet. Her heartbeat was slow and steady, even though the Heart at the End of the World shook and trembled around her as its beat raced and skittered.

Thakthak-thump. Thakka-thump. Tha-thump-tha-tha-thump.

"What happened?" she asked. "How come I feel okay?"

"I gave you one of those pills you've been carting about." The Ringmaster took his top hat from his head. "The label has washed off, of course, but I felt safe in assuming they were for your condition."

"But . . . I thought I was sick because I'm bound to the Heart." Maddy's head throbbed. "And the Heart's not fixed. So how come I feel better?"

"I am afraid, my dear girl, that magic or not, sometimes you just have to take your medicine." The Ringmaster tossed his top hat into the middle of the Heart, where it immediately began growing in size until it filled much of the chamber. "Stand back, now. Renegade hearts seldom come easily. And please—no flash photography."

Thakthak-thump. Thakka-thump. Tha-thump-tha-tha-thump.

The Ringmaster started to chant, his voice taking on an odd cadence, and his whip in the walls of the Heart began to pulse in time. Maddy could see the muscles of the Heart tighten with each pulse, as though jolts of electricity were running through them. The top hat, too, was pulsing.

Kuma padded over to Maddy and butted her gently with his head, nearly knocking her over. "It will be done soon," he said. "I am grateful."

Tha-thump. Tha-thump. Tha-thump. Tha-thump, went the top hat, steady and reasonable, coaxing the Heart at the End of the World back to its original heartbeat as the Ringmaster chanted. In the chant, Maddy could hear the lilt of Il Circo delle Strade when it was new, of the boardwalk and rides, of a circus learning its strength. It was as soothing as being rocked to sleep, as familiar as her own reflection in the mirror, and it pulled at Maddy's memory like a distant lullaby. She *knew* this rhythm, knew it inside and out. And yet . . .

Maddy twisted her bracelet worriedly around her wrist. "Kuma, is that the right rhythm?" she asked quietly. "It sounds . . . I don't know . . . like it's missing something."

Kuma turned his topaz eyes to hers, and in them was a message she couldn't quite read. "It is the original rhythm of Il Circo, as it was when we were new."

The whip contracted and released. The top hat pulsed. Under her breath, without really even realizing she was doing it, Maddy began to sing a counterpoint.

"Stop that at once!" cried the Ringmaster, breaking off from his chant. "You're confusing it!"

Maddy bit her lip as the Ringmaster started up again. His chant was ancient and simple, lush with overlays of ocean and color and miraculous feats, and yet it sat heavily on her like a hand holding her back from where she wanted to go. She could feel the Heart at the End of the World begin to match the Ringmaster's rhythm, slowly and against its will: a beat here, a beat there. The rhythm was so easy, so familiar, so welcoming . . . and so *wrong*, like a favorite jacket that was now too tight. Inside of her, Maddy's own heart protested. She shuffled closer to Kuma until she was pressed against him, his fur soft and comforting on her leg.

Thadda-tha tha-thump tha tha thadda thad-thump.

The Heart was fighting back, but it was tiring. Maddy felt it inside herself as much as in the walls around her, a battle waged through heartbeats. Even though she had taken—or, really, been given—her medicine, her own heart was starting to race again, pulled by the Heart at the End of the World. It was hard to breathe, hard to think. She shifted her weight from one foot to the other, not sure what to do. She knew the Heart at the End of the World had to be fixed, knew it better than anyone. It *had* to, or the circus would never be well again. *She* would never be well again. If the Heart wasn't fixed, Maddy would always have a life of sickness and pills and Extra Attention.

But what did *fixed* actually mean?

Thadda-tha tha-thump tha tha thadda thad-thump.

"Stop!" The words tore from her mouth, tumbling over each other. "The Heart doesn't want that rhythm! It wants something different. Can't you hear it?"

"My dear girl," said the Ringmaster between the words of his chant, "there is one rhythm and one rhythm only that can save Il Circo, and that is the rhythm it has always had. I know what is best for my circus."

"But what if the rhythm has *changed*?" cried Maddy. It felt as though her own heart were weeping. "What if the Heart wants something different? Why does it have to do what *you* want? Shouldn't it choose for itself?"

No longer chanting, the Ringmaster turned to her, his expression darkening. "Do not forget that *I* am the Ringmaster," he said. "I am the one who must keep the Heart safe, must keep us *all* safe."

Maddy shook her head, her voice rising. "It isn't right! It's not, and you know it!" She was as sure of this as she had ever been of anything. "The Heart can't stay with the rhythm you want just because *you* like it better. It can't stay what it used to be. It needs to be something different!"

"It's not a matter of what I *like*," roared the Ringmaster. "It's a matter of what the Heart *needs*. And this is the rhythm it needs, the only one it knows!"

Thakthak-thump. Thakka-thump. Tha-thump-tha-tha-thump.

"But you're killing it!" cried Maddy. She couldn't help herself. "Don't you care?"

The Ringmaster's face turned a dark, mottled red. "Care?! CARE!? I have cared for Il Circo for longer than you have been alive, longer than you can even imagine! What are you but a girl with a crush on a few pretty lights and some sparkle? How *dare* you suggest that I don't care!"

"I'm sorry," cried Maddy, her own heart racing. "But—"

Kuma pressed his weight against Maddy's leg like a warning. Fighting her panic, she clamped her mouth closed as the winged lion turned to the Ringmaster.

"You have done what you promised to do," said Kuma, his voice a low rumble. "You have protected the circus. But this girl is right. The Heart needs something else. *We* need something else. It is time for us to release it. To release ourselves."

The Ringmaster gaped at them, speechless for the first time Maddy could remember.

"My dearest Kuma," he finally said. "I cannot. You know I cannot. I have sworn to protect—"

"As have I." The winged lion left Maddy's side and padded over to sit in front of the Ringmaster, tail wrapped around his legs. Man and beast stared at each other, eye to eye. "I have been with you, your trusted companion, through it all. We are old, you and I, and yet we still have some good years left. Let us go outside, where we can live and run. Let us be free while we can."

Thadda-thatha-thumpthathathaddathad-thump.

The Heart at the End of the World was pounding faster, and without Kuma at her side, Maddy found she could no longer hold herself up. Her heart surged, bucking and fighting—her medicine was no match for this. She staggered backward, head throbbing in time to the heartbeat, and sagged against the wall of the Heart.

The Ringmaster cupped his hands around the winged lion's face. "But, Kuma," he said, almost pleading. "You want what I want: Il Circo back again, in all her glory."

"No," yowled Kuma softly, shaking his mane. "I want only my boy and a day in the sun. Let us be done here."

The Ringmaster's face crumpled and he drew his hands back. "I am sorry, my dear friend. I cannot. But as soon as I am done, I promise, we shall return to the sunshine and the sea." And the Ringmaster turned away and resumed chanting, his tone sadder than before. Kuma said nothing, but lowered himself to the floor of the Heart and laid his great head on his paws.

Maddy pressed her fingers into her temples and screwed her eyes shut, trying to block out the frightened pounding of the Heart at the End of the World, the wrongness of the Ringmaster's chant. She thought about Geoff and the heartmice and hoped they were okay. She thought about the Alter, about change and choice. She thought about being willing to let go.

"Oh," she said, dropping her hands to her sides. "You're stuck."

Kuma's ear swiveled in her direction, but the Ringmaster kept chanting.

Maddy pushed away from the wall. "You're stuck," she said again, louder this time. "Like the people at the Alter's, the ones with the mirrors. That's why the Heart wouldn't let you in. Your path has changed, but you can't see it. The circus has changed, but you can't see that either. You can't see what it *is* because you're so focused on what it *was*."

"Don't be ridiculous," snapped the Ringmaster. "The Heart must return to its original beat. That is where it belongs, where we all belong."

"You're wrong," said Maddy simply, her own heart aching. Because she knew now what had to happen. The Heart needed to become what it was supposed to become, whatever that was, no matter what anyone else thought. She understood this because, more than anything, it was the same thing she needed for herself. She hadn't known this before, but now it pulsed through every part of her being.

And just like that, something flew into the back of her head.

"Ow!" she cried as it bounced off her and landed on the floor of the heart, flopping around like a hurt bird.

It was no longer a small gray rock, but she still recognized it immediately. It had sprouted metallic wings and become glittery and shiny and—for some odd but fabulous reason—fluffy, but there was no mistaking it. It was her fondest wish, and she had called it back.

Maddy scooped her wish into her hand, cradling it as it flapped in circles. One of its wings was torn and jagged. Back when the carny had first asked her, Maddy would have said her fondest wish was for a family. But it wasn't. Her fondest wish was to choose for herself who she was and what she was going to be. Sure, she had been dealt some bad cards . . . but hadn't everyone? And it was up to her, wasn't it, to see what was true and choose what to do with it? She could choose to stack her deck with everything good she had. She could choose to see all sides of it and accept it for what it was. She could choose her own rhythm. And so could the Heart at the End of the World.

In fact, they both needed to if they wanted to survive.

Maddy stroked the furry casing of her wish, which shivered and flared and then cracked open like an egg. Something like cool fire rushed out of the shell and into her fingertips, racing up her arm and through her body. It was soothing and strong, and it filled up spaces she hadn't known were there and left her feeling certain and grateful and very, very alive.

Maddy took a deep breath. She looked at the Ringmaster as he chanted, his posture rigid. She looked at the whip in the wall of the Heart, squeezing so tightly that the muscle around it was red and inflamed. She looked at Kuma, whose head was bowed, whose great copper wings had gone limp. Then she rubbed her finger carefully against the broken casing of her wish. It was sharp, sharp enough to cut.

It was up to her. It was time to choose.

So she did.

Maddy sprang forward and sliced at the Ringmaster's whip with the edge of her fondest wish, cutting it cleanly in two. A foul-smelling black liquid oozed out. She coughed, gagging, but turned to another part of the whip and kept slicing. Black pieces of whip fell to the floor of the Heart.

"Stop, my dear girl, stop!" cried the Ringmaster, and Maddy was surprised to see tears streaming down his cheeks. "You mustn't! The only way to save Il Circo is to keep it as it was."

"No," said Maddy, her own voice choked. She hadn't realized she was crying, too. But she was doing the right thing. She knew she was. She had to give the Heart what it needed, what it wanted. It had to be able to choose its own rhythm. She sliced through the last piece of whip that was binding the Heart at the End of the World and stepped away, breathing hard. "The only way to save Il Circo is to set it free."

And then Maddy heaved the casing of her fondest wish as hard as she could right into the pulsing top hat. It slammed through the fabric, leaving behind a wing-shaped hole, and the top hat deflated like a popped balloon and collapsed onto the floor of the Heart.

For a long, breathless moment, for the space of one heartbeat, the air went still. Maddy listened, hope pressing at every part of her. And then the Heart at the End of the World gave a staggered, syncopated beat and began to race out of control.

"What have you done?" whispered the Ringmaster, and he dropped his head to his hands.

25

*Thaddathathumpthumpthuthaddathumpthaddathathumpthump
thuthaddathump.*

The walls shook as numbness raced down Maddy's limbs.
She felt her own heart lock into the too-fast beating of the
Heart at the End of the World, felt it slamming against her
ribs. She took an unsteady step and then pitched forward onto
her knees, gasping.

The Ringmaster lifted his head, and Maddy nearly cried out.
He had turned suddenly, shockingly old. Lines radiated from his
mouth and eyes, and a weariness had settled over him.

*Thaddathathumpthumpthuthaddathumpthaddathathump
thumpthuthaddathump.*

Maddy opened her mouth to speak, but the words wouldn't
come. Her own heart raced without pause, just like the heartbeat

around her. Black spots formed in her vision and she slid the rest of the way to the floor.

"Madeline Adriana," said Kuma, his voice deep and strong. "Attend to what I say."

Gasping for breath, Maddy turned to look at him. It took every ounce of strength. She forced herself to listen over the pounding of her heart.

Thaddathathumpthumpthuthaddathumpthaddathathump thumpthuthaddathump.

"When we are gone," said Kuma, "you must guide the Heart to its new rhythm. It cannot do it alone. When things have been tamed for too long, they forget how to be free."

"Gone?" asked Maddy, the word making no sense to her at all. She pressed the heel of her hand into her chest as her pulse jumped in her neck. "What do you mean, gone?"

The winged lion sniffed the air. "The doorway of time is at last clear, and I am no longer unsure whether to step out or stay in. We will age now, and die."

"What?" Maddy looked in horror from Kuma to the Ringmaster, who was staring at his hands with mild interest as they wrinkled. His face had grown haggard, his dark hair gray. Maddy gasped, tears blinding her. "No! I didn't mean for anyone to die!"

"We are no longer part of this rhythm." Kuma's own whiskers and fur were graying as well, his glorious mane growing thin and sparse. "Death comes to us all. It is no shame, and no tragedy when one has lived a good life." The winged lion unfurled his copper wings and knelt down, offering his back to the Ringmaster. "And we have lived good lives, haven't we, my friend?"

The Ringmaster was ancient now, withered and bent. His voice shook with age, and perhaps a little fear. "But who will care for Il Circo when we are gone?"

"Il Circo is no longer for us to protect," said Kuma, his voice deep in his throat. "It will find its way without us, or it will not. We have a new rhythm now, you and I. We go together into the Circus Beyond, where we shall run and play."

The Ringmaster hung his head for a long moment. Then he sighed and looked up. "You are right," he said quietly. "It is time."

"No!" Maddy cried, choking on the tears that now streamed into her mouth and dampened her hair. The walls of the Heart shook. *Her* heart shook. She pressed her hand harder into her chest, grief cutting through her. "No, please! I'm sorry! I'm so, so sorry!"

The Ringmaster brushed off the lapels of his coat, now frayed and faded. He cleared his throat with a soft, papery sound.

"Storytellers never apologize, my dear girl," he said, giving a small smile. "And I like to think I have at least taught you how to tell a bit of a story. One last lesson, if I may—never forget that even the grandest of shows must have a finale.

Otherwise, how will a new one ever begin?" Slowly, the Ring-master climbed onto the back of the winged lion, and he leaned forward to speak into the great beast's ear. "We have had quite a run, have we not?"

"The very best," said the winged lion.

The Ringmaster took a long, slow breath and looked around one last time, his eyes surprisingly bright in his now-ancient face. Then he laid a hand on the lion's mane. "Kuma, my dear friend. I am ready."

And then the Ringmaster slumped forward onto Kuma's back, and Maddy caught her breath as the colors from his tuxedo began to swirl over his skin and body, *into* his skin and body, and then into Kuma's. Soon both man and lion were one writhing mass of color: the steely blue of the ocean in storm and the green of palm fronds, the brightness of the beach in summer and the glow of the sand at night—all the shades of a city by the sea.

"My dear girl," said the Ringmaster in a distant, windswept voice, "do tell my circus I love it."

And with a sound like a sail being unfurled, like a surfboard cutting through a wave, like a heavy curtain dropping closed, the colors that had been a winged lion and his boy swirled into nothingness and disappeared. All that was left was a top hat the deep blue of midnight, spinning slowly on its brim.

"No!" screamed Maddy. Her tears puddled on the golden floor of the Heart and her own heart skittered and ached. It felt as though everything had shattered, not just around her but inside her as well. "No," she sobbed, collapsing, curling her head in her hands. "No . . ."

The Heart was racing, spinning, wild and scared. The sound of it mixed with Maddy's sobs.

But then a new sound made Maddy raise her eyes. Something was coming through the valve of the Heart at the End of the World. Something blue and yellow and . . .

"Ophelia!" cried Maddy, jumping up.

The mimic octopus tumbled from the valve, morphing into a blue-and-yellow pogo stick as she fell. The pogo stick hit the floor of the heart, bounced two times, and then flung itself at Maddy, turning back to octopus mid-fling. Maddy threw her arms around the soft body of her friend and buried her face in Ophelia's wet skin to cry. The octopus had turned the same golden color as the sea around them and she smelled of taffy and nighttime, of ocean and stars. Around them, the Heart raced, the beat growing faster and more frightened.

Thaddathathumpthumpthuthaddathumpthaddathathumpthump thuthaddathump.

Maddy lifted her head and wiped her face with the back of her hand. "Thank you for finding me," she whispered as the octopus tentacled up to her shoulder. Then she turned her attention to her bracelet, waiting for it to set the new rhythm . . . or for her own heart to tug just right. But nothing happened, other than the heartbeat around her speeding up even more.

Thaddathathumpthumpthuthaddathumpthaddathathumpthump
thuthaddathump.

Moonlight-on-the-Water had told her the circus needed her. It was now, and there was no time to waste. She had to help the Heart find its rhythm before it spun out of control.

"It's just you and me, then," she whispered to Ophelia, who wrapped a tentacle around her shoulder and flashed a determined blue.

Thaddathathumpthumpthuthaddathumpthaddathathumpthump
thuthaddathump.

Maddy closed her eyes and listened as hard as she could to every heartbeat, trying to hear the rhythm the Heart at the End of the World wanted. But the beat was too fast, too skittish, too frightened. Maddy couldn't hear the spaces, couldn't hear what needed to happen. If only she could slow it down a little . . .

Her eyes flew open. Of course—her pills! They were for slowing down hearts! Would they work here? It was worth a try. Maddy fumbled for the bottle in her pocket, hands shaking, trying not to jostle Ophelia too much. She pulled the pill bottle out, and with it came the playing card from the Alter, the one with the top hat and marquee. Ophelia reached for the card as it spiraled to the floor.

"It's all right, you can leave it," said Maddy hurriedly as she twisted the cap off the bottle and poured the remaining white tablets into her hand, counting them quickly. Twelve pills. Would that be enough? The Heart at the End of the World was more than twelve times as big as her own heart. It was a thousand times bigger, a million times maybe. But all she needed was a tiny slowness, a little opening.

"Put these behind you!" she cried to Ophelia, tossing half of the pills to the octopus. Ophelia grabbed them out of the air and spun around, planting them quickly into the wall of the Heart behind them. At the same time, with all her might, Maddy threw the remaining pills at the front wall of the Heart.

For a long moment nothing happened. Maddy clenched her hands, willing it to work. And then the Heart seemed to take a great, shuddering breath and began to slow.

Thadda-tha thump-thump-thu thadda-thump. Thadda-tha thump-thump-thu thadda-thump.

Maddy let out a sigh of relief and sent a mental thank-you to the tired county doctors who had helped her more than they would ever know. The heartbeat was still too fast, but at least she could hear the rhythm. She glanced at Ophelia, who had turned a hopeful yellow, and then closed her eyes again and listened.

Thadda-tha thump-thump-thu thadda-thump. Thadda-tha thump-thump-thu thadda-thump.

And now she could hear it, the spaces where something was missing, where the new rhythm needed to go. It had to be just right, though. Maddy thought about drummers and contortionists with unpronounceable names, about transparent muses and turquoise octopus tears. She thought about marquees and piers and the promise of new acts. And as she did, she realized she knew exactly what the rhythm had to be, for it was like listening to herself.

"Ta chukka ta ta chukka, ta chukka ta ta chukka," she sang to the Heart. Ophelia turned into a squishy drumstick and tapped along on Maddy's shoulder. "Ta chukka ta ta chukka!"

The Heart trembled. *Ta chukka*, it began, and for a brief, glorious second, Maddy's heart, too, clicked into place, giving her strength. But then the Heart slipped off beat.

It needed more. This rhythm was good, but it wasn't enough. Maddy thought about the Race Thru the Clouds and chainsaws that liked to steal your food. She thought about bridges and Alters. She added all of this into the mix, into the way the rhythm dipped and swelled. She tapped out the beat on her leg, Ophelia drumming along: "Ta chukka chukka ta ta chukka. Ta chukka chukka ta ta chukka!"

Ta chukka chukka, replied the Heart, but still the rhythm didn't stick.

"Let's split up!" Maddy cried, and she moved to one wall as Ophelia jumped from her shoulder and moved to another. Maddy slapped her hands against the muscle; Ophelia morphed back to herself and used all eight tentacles to hit the wall of the Heart in time.

The Heart was trying, but the rhythm wasn't quite right. Something was still missing, some essential piece. Maddy closed her eyes and called up the wildness of the nighttime circus, haunting yet necessary, and used it to create a deeper counter rhythm. She added a backbeat of the celestial timescale, a shimmering overlay of Moonlight-on-the-Water, a drenching of newness, of life, of the crashing sea. Ophelia followed, picking up the new rhythm easily. The Heart strained to match the beat, but it still needed something else, something more.

Maddy concentrated as she watched Ophelia pound the walls of the Heart, and suddenly a rush of pure love filled her. And in that moment, she knew exactly what the final piece was, the piece that would make this rhythm right: friendship. Skeeter with his dimples and funnel cakes; Ophelia with her silliness and shape-shifting. Maddy added that in now, weaving it underneath the other beats to hold them all up, an unshakable foundation of trust and laughter and time shared. Ophelia meeped and drummed along, colors rippling over her skin.

Maddy shouted out the new, complete rhythm as she drummed: "Ta chukka chukka ta ta chukka ta! TA CHUKKA CHUKKA TA TA CHUKKA TA!" Her bracelet started pulsing, too, beating in time, urging the Heart to join in.

And the Heart did.

Ta-chukka thump, went the Heart, folding the new rhythm into the old as though that was where it had lived all along. *Ta-chukka thump, ta-chukka thump, ta-chukka thump, ta-chukka thump.*

"Yes!" shouted Maddy as the Heart settled in, as the new heartbeat rolled through the walls, as Maddy's own heart answered with the same *ta-chukka thump*. Maddy wasn't sure whether the rightness flooding through her belonged to her or to the Heart at the End of the World. She wasn't sure whether it even mattered. She turned around and grabbed Ophelia into a hug, tentacles and arms and happiness everywhere.

Ta-chukka thump, ta-chukka thump, ta-chukka thump, ta-chukka thump.

Ophelia scampered up to Maddy's shoulder. Together, they listened for a long moment.

Ta-chukka thump, ta-chukka thump, ta-chukka thump, ta-chukka thump.

"Okay, Heart," said Maddy. "I think we're good."

With one tentacle, Ophelia tapped Maddy on the shoulder and pointed. The playing card that had fallen to the floor of the Heart, the one with the top hat and marquee, had lifted into the air. Maddy stared as it twirled over to land on the Ringmaster's top hat, which began to glow a beautiful sky blue, Maddy's very favorite color. Then the top hat, too, rose into the air, and the hole left by Maddy's fondest wish mended itself.

The air eddied and rolled.

And then a bank of white lights blazed to life around the perimeter of the Heart. Ophelia shimmered into the same sky blue as the top hat while a sudden swirl of glitter showered down around them.

"Hello, Maddy," said the top hat. "I am so glad you and Ophelia found each other."

The voice didn't quite come from the top hat, but didn't quite come from anywhere else, either. It was neither male nor female, neither high nor low, and it held excited whispers, pinpricks of apprehension, a gilding of expectation. Maddy knew instantly that she was talking to the spirit of the circus itself. On her wrist, her bracelet shone the exact color of Moonlight-on-the-Water.

"Hello," said Maddy as Ophelia pulsed softly on her shoulder. "You're . . . you're Il Circo delle Strade."

"Oh, Maddy." The soft blue glow brightened. "I wasn't sure you would recognize me. Look at you, so grown up. And you still have your bracelet!"

At the mention of her bracelet, something hard pressed at Maddy's chest. She hadn't really had time to think about what Moonlight had told her, about being found on the beach as a baby. She should be grateful . . . and she was. She *was*. But she didn't want to be bound—not to anything—without her permission. Not even something as wonderful as the Heart at the End of the World.

"Of course I still have it," she said, a little more bitterly than she intended. Ophelia wrapped a tentacle around her shoulder. "It doesn't come off."

"But of course it does," said the spirit of the circus.

"It doesn't!" cried Maddy, heat flaring through her. "I've tried!"

The spirit of the circus laughed, the sound a mix of joy and fierceness, of day and night. "Did you honestly *want* to take it off?"

"Yes!" said Maddy hotly, but even before Ophelia had given her a questioning look, she knew it wasn't true. She hadn't wanted to take off her bracelet, not really. She had wanted the magic and how special it made her feel. It was the best part of her life. And it had led her here. "I mean . . . maybe. But that's not the point! The point is I should be able to take it off, if I *did* want to. I should have the choice."

Circus laughter danced around her. "But you do. You always did."

"No, I don't!" Maddy didn't want to be angry but the words came flying out of her, the words she needed to say. "I've never had a choice, not about any of it! You found me on the beach, but you didn't keep me. I didn't choose that! You sent me away, the same way everyone always has!" Tears sparked behind her eyes, but she blinked them back, taking comfort in the octopus on her shoulder sitting quietly and listening. She would not cry. She wouldn't. She twisted her bracelet around her wrist and added in a whisper, "Why doesn't anyone want me?"

Ophelia turned a sad gray.

"I don't mean you," said Maddy to the octopus, wiping at her eyes. "I mean . . . I mean parents. Someone to take care of me."

The top hat floated closer, its blue glow softening. "Oh, Maddy," said the spirit of the circus "Oh, little one. We wanted you. We wanted you dearly. From the moment we saw you, that's what we longed for. But it is not in the nature of a circus to raise a child, and Moonlight-on-the-Water is only Moonlight-on-the-Water, light and beauty and mystery. Neither of us could touch you or hold you or keep you safe. For I am not always safe, Maddy. You know this." The glow of the top hat darkened briefly. "Moonlight and I, our hearts swelled for you. Since we could not give you a home, we gave you pieces of ourselves. Moonlight-on-the-Water wrapped a piece of itself into a band of silver, never-ending, always the right size for your perfect wrist and always illuminating what *is*, should you choose to see. And I, I tucked a piece of my Heart inside of you so you would know my love and, if you wished, follow it home when you were old enough. Twelve years is not a long time for us, though I know it is for a little one. And for that, I am sorry."

Maddy's brain felt fuzzy, slow and stupid. "But . . ." she said, "but you *bound* me! Without me knowing!"

The top hat reared back in surprise. "That isn't a binding, little one."

"It's not?" Maddy stared from her bracelet to the top hat and back again. On her shoulder, Ophelia began to cycle from gray to red to a soft circus purple. "Then . . . what is it?"

The top hat brushed sweetly against her cheek and the Heart around them seemed to hold its breath. Inside Maddy, her own heart did the same.

"It's *love*," said Il Circo. "The very best of all my circus tricks. What connects my Heart to yours, little one, is simply love."

Maddy closed her eyes, scrunching her face up for a long moment. She couldn't think straight. "But . . . it made me sick!"

The top hat tilted toward the floor, a sadness seeping from it. "That was never intended. I did not know my rhythm would need to change so, and I did not know that need would make you sick as well. By the time I understood this, I was too ill to fix it. And you were so far away at that point, too far for my circus magic to reach. This is why we arranged for you to be sent to the Venice Beach Home for Children, where you would be close enough to me to see my magic and to choose if you wanted to return."

"But if your circus magic couldn't reach me," said Maddy slowly, "then what are all the things I've been seeing my whole life? I thought all that magic was from you."

The top hat lifted back up. "Oh, little one," said the spirit of the circus, the mischievous smile back in its voice. "Do you really think I am the only magic there is? Each and every place has its own magic. Not all of them have a marvelous circus, of course, but they make do with what they have. Because you chose to see magic in the first place, you saw it all—not just mine. As soon as I understood that my illness was making you sick and that we needed each other to heal, I asked for help from the places you lived, and they used *their* magic to draw you close enough for me to call you on my own."

"Then . . . my heart . . ." Maddy began, trying to make sense of it. "My illness . . ."

"You are no longer sick, little one."

Maddy knew that—she could feel it—and yet hearing it still sent a warm shiver through her. "What about the tugging? Is that . . . is that me, or was that you?"

"The pull you feel in your heart comes from you and you alone." The spirit of the circus paused. "The piece of my heart in you might have augmented it, I suppose. But if at any point you had chosen not to see the magic in the world, chosen not to follow the call of the heart inside of you, the tug would have grown fainter and fainter. That is the way of hearts; they must be listened to in order to grow. And had you made that choice, we would have left you alone, as one sometimes must when love is true. The piece of Moonlight-on-the-Water you wear on your wrist would have dimmed and fallen off, and the piece of my heart inside of you would have shriveled and grown silent. It would have been hard for us, so very hard. But love is not always easy."

Maddy looked down at her wrist, at the beautiful, magical bracelet she had worn her whole life. It had never occurred to her to ignore the magic around her, to let herself be convinced she was making it all up. It had never occurred to her not to follow the pull in her heart. Someone else might have, perhaps. But not her.

"I didn't know I was choosing anything," said Maddy quietly. "It was just who I was."

The top hat shone. "Oh, little one. Sometimes our most powerful choices are the ones we don't even know we've made."

Maddy nodded. Il Circo was right. She *did* have a choice. She had, all along. And she loved her bracelet, loved who she was, loved the magic that was all around for anyone who chose to see.

"Thank you," Maddy said to the spirit of the circus who loved her as well. "For saving me, and for calling me back. And, thank you," she said to Ophelia, "for staying with me now, and being my friend." Maddy took a deep breath and looked back at the top hat. She thought she knew the answer to her next question, but she had to ask anyway. "Do you know who my parents are?"

"No, little one. It was only you we found that night on the beach. There was no one else in sight."

Maddy nodded again. But instead of the sadness she had expected, what she felt was a strange sort of closure that was oddly comforting. She had known this all along, really. Her parents weren't coming back for her; not now, not ever. Perhaps it wasn't fair, and perhaps other kids got different cards. But wasn't there magic in every deck, whether you were loved by parents or by a circus, by Moonlight or by friends you had found on your own? She could choose her own family and her own home. In fact, she already had. She reached up her hand, and Ophelia twined her tentacles around it.

The top hat's glow was dimming. "I cannot keep this form much longer. Take the top hat and put it on, and it will carry you out of my heart and back to the rest of me. There, if you wish, you can take my name and make me your home."

"I'd like that," said Maddy, but she still had one more question. "Can you just tell me . . . who *am* I? Everyone in the circus keeps asking me, and even *I* don't know."

"Ah," said Il Circo, its voice starting to fade. "That is easy. You, Madeline Adriana Strade, are simply and beautifully *you*. That is all you ever have been, and all you ever need to be."

Maddy had never had a real last name before, and it felt like a missing piece inside of her had finally snapped into place. Trembling slightly, she reached out with a hand that was wrapped in tentacles, and together she and Ophelia took hold of the top hat. It went limp as soon as they touched it, the spirit of the circus swirling away.

"Wait!" cried Maddy. "When will I see you again?"

The voice of Il Circo drifted back to her like distant applause. "You will see me wherever you look," it said faintly. "I am so proud of you, my love."

And then it was gone.

Top hat in hand, Madeline Adriana Strade stood in the center of the Heart at the End of the World with her dearest friend on her shoulder. She turned in a slow circle, listening to the rhythm sound exactly as it should, both inside and out. For the first time ever, she could feel her entire life unfold in front of her with endless possibility. And although she hadn't really known it until this very moment, Maddy loved possibility.

A small smile lifted Maddy's lips as Ophelia settled contentedly on Maddy's shoulder, shifting back to blue with yellow spots. Maddy turned to the Heart.

"See you later, Heart," said Maddy. She held up her arm and tapped her silver bracelet meaningfully. "You know how to find me if you need anything." Then she looked at the octopus on her shoulder. "Let's go home," she said.

With tentacles and hands, she and Ophelia placed the top hat on her head.

26

It was morning.

A whole night had passed without sleep, but Maddy wasn't even tired or hungry—and somehow, the yellow flip-flops were back on her feet. She and Ophelia touched down on the floating wooden dock in the canal just in time to hear the splash of a tail slapping water, followed by what sounded suspiciously like an Italian swear word.

"Hi, Isabette," called Maddy.

Isabette glanced up from trying to unwrap a loop of fishing line from her fin. "Ah. It's you. And you've brought the Ring-master, I see."

"Oh . . . um . . ." Suddenly embarrassed, Maddy pulled the top hat from her head and twisted it in her hands. Ophelia launched herself from Maddy's shoulder to splash into the canal, jetting happily to the bottom. "I found him. But I didn't bring him back. He and Kuma . . ."

"I do not mean the Ringmaster *past*," said Isabette, yanking at the fishing wire. "I meant the Ringmaster *present*. Did you think there was only one?"

"Um . . ." Maddy hesitated. "Yes? Kind of?"

The mermaid rolled her eyes. "Pensa! Think! The Race so much as told you when it brought you where you asked to go."

"What are you talking about?" said Maddy. "I asked the Race to take me to the Ringmaster, and instead it dropped me on the Bridge of . . . the Bridge of . . . oh . . ." She broke off. She had been so proud of how she had worded her question at the Race Thru the Clouds, so careful to specify she wanted to find the Ringmaster of Il Circo delle Strade and not some other circus. But she hadn't thought to say it had to be the *current* Ringmaster.

The Race had taken her to herself.

"Oh," she said again, quietly.

"Oh, indeed." Isabette tore the fishing line from her tail and swore at it once more for good measure.

"But . . . how can I be the Ringmaster if I'm not even old enough to be in the circus?"

The mermaid shrugged. "New Ringmaster. New rules."

Maddy looked down at the top hat in her hands.

Isabette raised a perfectly arched eyebrow. "Ah," she said thoughtfully. "Yes. Well, it is up to you, of course."

Happily hydrated, Ophelia chose this moment to shoot back out of the water, hitting Maddy squarely in the chest with a wet *squelch* before tentacling up to her shoulder.

"You'd best go," said Isabette. "Everyone's waiting for you on the pier. They know they need a new Ringmaster, and it seems they've chosen you. Should you decide to accept, that is."

Ophelia clapped her tentacles together, but Maddy just nodded, top hat in hands. Joy and sadness, excitement and fear were swimming around inside her like brightly colored fish. Slowly, though, an idea took form, an idea that might make all this work for her. Interestingly enough, inspiration *did* feel a bit like a light bulb going off in her head. She thought of the Ringmaster and showmanship, of stories and circus acts, of decrees and bindings. Then, feeling only slightly awkward, she swept the top hat across her body and took a deep, dramatic bow. Ophelia held on with seven tentacles and saluted with her eighth.

"Ciao, Isabette," said Maddy as she straightened.

For the first time ever, Isabette actually smiled. "Ciao, bambina," she replied.

27

Maddy ran, Ophelia draped tightly on her shoulder. They ducked around tourists snapping photos, around families with coolers, around couples holding hands. They ran down the street where the nighttime circus gathered, past the mural of the nighttime muse, right to the mouth of the pier itself. At the far end of the pier, the strange white fog was rolling in as the smell in the air shifted, becoming saltier and wetter and slightly metallic. Like before, the lifeguard climbed down from his tower and began warning people about another freak storm.

No Ringmaster's voice welcomed Maddy this time as she dashed past the lifeguard onto the pier. Waves were crashing, tourists shouting as they gathered their things and hurried to their cars. Ophelia held on to the top hat with her tentacles to keep it from blowing off Maddy's head.

Mist was swirling in faster now, and the light at the end of the pier shifted to pale green. In it, Maddy could see the drummers gathered. When they saw her coming, the lead drummer gave a short, sharp cry, and they began to play. The rhythm bounced and echoed, and Maddy recognized it as the new rhythm of the Heart at the End of the World—although with a little something extra as each player added in a twist, a backbeat, a piece of themselves.

Ta-chukka thumpa thump eh, ta-chukka thumpa eh-eh-eh, ta-chukka thumpa thump eh, ta-chukka thumpa eh-eh-eh.

Maddy's heart flew.

She locked her steps into the rhythm as the wind picked up, whipping her hair and a few tentacles into her eyes. Waves smashed over the pier, splashing onto the concrete, as people flowed past her in the opposite direction to escape the storm— but not everyone. A few people stood frozen, looks of wonder on their faces: a little girl with her mother, their matching dark braids glistening in the mist; an elderly person with a walker; three rowdy teenagers.

New Audience! thought Maddy, and she felt like fire, light and hot and crackling with life.

The end of the pier turned golden, the same color as the Heart at the End of the World, lighting up the crowd of performers that was growing bigger by the second. There was Adela holding Edith the chainsaw, Dov and his snakes, the Ichthyquilibrists, Barton the carny, and of course Vanessa, along with so many others Maddy hadn't met yet but knew she would love . . . and hoped would love her, too.

And then, from above, a whoop of joy as a boy on skateboard swooped out of the fog. Maddy thought her heart might burst with gladness.

"Skeeter!" she cried.

"You did it, Octogirl!" Skeeter's face was alight, dimples in full force, the red and gold sparks flying behind his board leaving colored trails in the fog. "You must have, because, look!"

He swooped past, using his feet to spin his skateboard onto its side so he was standing on its edge. Then he somehow wound it around his legs in a stunning sort of dance, grabbed it with both hands, and kicked up into a handstand.

Maddy clapped so hard her hands stung. Ophelia clapped, too, smush-y tentacle claps. "A new trick! Skeeter, it's brilliant!"

"Hurry, you two!" cried Vanessa. "It's time!"

The air smelled coppery and electric. Skeeter landed beside her, and Maddy reached one hand out to him and the other to Ophelia. Hand-in-hand-in-tentacle, they rushed to Vanessa's side as the end of the pier began to glow blue. A drummer shouted and another answered, and the rhythm rose, vibrating Maddy's entire body as the waves vibrated the pier, as the heartbeat vibrated the circus.

"Link up, now!" cried Vanessa, and everyone did, linking to the person on either side however they could, all connected. Ophelia shifted into an umbrella as a giant wave rushed through the water, flashing with magic. The wave grew and grew, and then crashed over the top of the pier and onto all of them. The force of it pulled everyone apart and bowled them over, and they came up laughing and sputtering and drenched in glitter. Sparkles of silver and blue covered the performers, the railing, the concrete, the octopus umbrella. Glitter sparkled in Skeeter's black hair and on Maddy's eyelashes. Ophelia shimmered back into herself, the glinting specks on her skin catching the light and throwing beams everywhere as if she were an eight-legged disco ball.

With a sound like a heavy curtain opening, lights blazed to life around the end of the pier.

"Are you ready?" asked Vanessa.

Next to her, Skeeter squeezed her hand once, tightly, and then let go. Maddy smiled and held out her arm for Ophelia, who shimmied onto her shoulder.

"Yes," said Maddy. Everything around her seemed to sharpen and focus. "I'm ready."

And Vanessa grew solid, as real and present as any muse could hope to be. Her hair floated like seagrass in a current as the sky flashed to a silvery blue and the leg warmers on Maddy's legs slithered off, twining together. Vanessa pulled a single strand of hair from her head and wrapped it around the leg warmers, which became a baton the exact shimmery hue of Moonlight-on-the-Water. Holding the baton, Vanessa turned to Maddy, and the pier grew quiet.

"Madeline Adriana Strade," said the muse, "we have chosen you as the Ringmaster of Il Circo delle Strade. From the moment you touch this baton, it is your job to make sure the circus is strong and dynamic and extraordinary. You are promising to love it, to protect it, and to keep it safe."

"And to let it grow," Maddy added, and all around her the circus performers murmured their agreement as Ophelia nodded. "Don't forget that part. The circus has to grow."

"Right on, Octogirl," Skeeter said, close to her ear.

Vanessa smiled, a deep, warm smile. "Yes. And to let it grow. Do you accept?"

Maddy reached out and took the baton, which fit perfectly in her hand. "Of course I do," she said, and she gave the baton an experimental swish.

With a sound like a million spotlights, the marquee blazed on.

IL CIRCO DELLE STRADE RINGMASTER: THE DELIGHTFUL SIGNORINA M. A. STRADE

It felt like grilled cheese on a cold day, like laughing until you couldn't breathe, like coming home. Ophelia turned into a noisemaker and made a squelchy bugle sound. Wind swirled over the pier, lifting the specks of glitter into the air where they shifted into thousands of floating bubbles swirling with color.

Adela's chainsaw came to life and reached out for one.

"Edith, no!" Adela said firmly.

Maddy began to laugh. Using her baton, she popped the bubble closest to her and a round of applause filled the air. Suddenly all the circus folk were laughing and popping bubbles—even Josi. Edith whirred happily, cutting through more and more bubbles until there was an ovation, a roar of appreciation, everyone taking bow after bow and slapping each other on the back. On Maddy's shoulder, Ophelia got up and took a bow herself.

Down the pier, the New Audience Maddy had run past—the ones who knew that the storm was something more than a storm—were moving closer. One of the teenagers had slowed to help the elderly person with the walker, but all of them were staring wide-eyed, grins breaking across their faces.

Skeeter's voice carried over the applause. *"Theydies and gentlethems, elders and wee ones, and everyone between and betwixt and more than the sum of their parts . . . join us as Octogirl, Queen of the Skateboard Cephalopods, Ushers in a New Era of Il Circo delle Strade!"*

Maddy smiled. But as the performers kept bowing and cheering, as someone called for Maddy to make a speech, she shifted uncomfortably from foot to foot. She might be the Ringmaster of the best circus in the world, but she still hated Extra Attention.

It was time to announce her plan.

She took a deep breath and looked at Vanessa. "As Ringmaster,

I can do whatever I think is best?"

Around her, the performers quieted, all of them watching Maddy. Josi stopped smiling and crossed her arms over her chest.

"Of course," said Vanessa, sounding surprised. "You can set forth decrees or create a new binding or . . . or whatever you want. It's part of the job."

"Nothing like that," said Maddy. "In fact, can I . . . can we, I mean . . . not have bindings at all?"

"I kinda love my tattoo, Octogirl," said Skeeter.

"No, sorry!" said Maddy. "I don't mean get rid of the tattoo! I mean . . . can the tattoos just be, I don't know . . . a sign of love for Il Circo and not really a binding at all? If, um, if everyone is okay with that?"

A happy murmur rose from the crowd.

"Certainly," said Vanessa softly, and a shimmer passed over the pier like a collective exhale. For a moment everyone's tattoo—at least the ones Maddy could see—shone deep midnight blue, then settled into the metallic copper color of Kuma's wings. People laughed, showing their new tattoos to each other.

"Anything else?" asked Vanessa.

Maddy took off the top hat, its sky-blue fabric the exact color of her favorite kind of summer day, and twisted it in her hands. Her bracelet shone in the mist. She thought about how to say what she wanted to say, took another deep breath, and looked up. "It's just that . . . well . . . you all have things you're really good at . . . performing, obviously, but all the other things that go into making a circus run. And I'm new, so I'm going to need a lot of help with pretty much everything. Um . . . would any of you like to help? With anything at all?"

There was a moment of silence. Then one of the drummers raised his hand.

"I love to cook," he said tentatively. "I could oversee the menus in the café."

"That's perfect!" said Maddy, and Ophelia turned crisp and powdery, like a funnel cake. "Anyone else?"

One of the Ichthyquilibrists—Maddy was pretty sure it was Emmon—pushed to the front of the group. "Can I make sure New Audience knows where to go?" he asked breathlessly. "I think people are so *funny!*"

"Of course!" said Maddy. "I think there's some New Audience here right now. Want to start with them?"

"Oh yes!" Emmon turned and ran to meet the six people making their way forward, taking perfect leaps as he went. He reached the little girl first, bending down to lift her up and spin her around.

"And," said Vanessa, eyes shining with tears as she pulled her gaze away from Emmon and the New Audience, "while I inspire the acts, perhaps I could be a little more proactive in finding them? I do so love discovering new performers." The tears rolled down her cheeks to plop onto the pier, where they turned into tiny octopuses. Ophelia made a low cooing sound and waved at them as they scooted across the concrete and tumbled into the sea.

"Vanessa, that would be wonderful!" said Maddy.

And suddenly everyone was clamoring to help.

"Can someone write this down?" called Maddy, turning from person to person, saying, "Yes; that's great; thank you!" Ophelia shot a spray of blue-and-yellow ink into the air, and Vanessa dipped her finger into it, reached up, and wrote in the air to list each person along with their new job.

"Octogirl?" Skeeter's voice was as quiet as she'd ever heard it. "Could I, um . . . maybe I could help you announce the acts sometimes?"

"Oh yes, *please!*" cried Maddy. "Skeeter Chen, Fastest Boy on Wheels *and* Master of Ceremonies! That's *brilliant!*"

And just then, time stuttered. Not enough to stop, not even enough to hiccup, but enough for Maddy to hear a distant roar and, perhaps, an even softer whisper in her ear: "Well done, my dear girl, well done. A new rhythm, indeed."

A particularly large bubble wafted over to Maddy. She blew on it gently, taking care not to pop it as her breath sent it out over the sea. Maybe it would find its way to the Circus Beyond.

Something pulled at her shirt collar. Maddy looked over as Ophelia turned into a blue-and-yellow-dotted question mark.

"You already have a job," she said to Ophelia, and warmth spread through her. "I belong to you and you belong to me. We do this together."

Ophelia's skin turned a bright sunshiny yellow. She wrapped all eight tentacles around Maddy and squeezed. Then she tentacled down Maddy's body and over to the pier railing, where she shimmered and stretched into two short words.

"Hm," said Maddy, tipping her head to one side as she read. "I don't know . . ."

"It's Eye-talian, doofus!" screeched a seagull as it dive-bombed into the crowd, causing several performers to duck and cover their heads. "It means 'The End.' Didn'tcha learn *nothing* this whole time?"

"I know what it means," said Maddy. She placed the top hat back on her head and reached out to Ophelia, who leaped from the railing to her spot on Maddy's shoulder. "What I was going to say, before I was interrupted—" The sound of seagull laughter came from above, followed by a very rude noise that made everyone giggle. "—was that maybe that's true. But maybe . . ."

Maddy paused. She smiled at Ophelia, at Skeeter, at the whole circus. And then she reached up and tilted the top hat at a jaunty angle, the way the Ringmaster used to do. ". . . with a little sleight of hand, a dash of circus magic . . . well, maybe this is just the beginning."

AN AUTHOR'S NOTE ON
VENICE, CALIFORNIA; OCTOPUSES;
AND OTHER DELIGHTS

While the real Venice, California, might not house a circus as organized as Il Circo delle Strade, its real-life history is just as colorful . . . if not more! It was designed to be a gathering place for artists, musicians, movie stars, and the people who loved them, and was built to look like Venice, Italy. The entire city was originally canals rather than streets, where people traveled by canoe or gondola. It had multiple piers and amusement parks, a swimming hall that held five thousand people, dance halls, parties, and of course, the famous Venice boardwalk, where performers from all over the world came to show their tricks. While most of the canals were paved over in the early 1920s after the city of Los Angeles annexed Venice, the town remains a fabulous circus of a city. Even now, when Venice is known more for tech companies than for counterculture, the beating heart of the original Venice is still there, pure and strong. Whenever I head for a skate on the bike path, I always think of it as *"going to join the parade."*

Here are a few places in Maddy's Venice that actually exist. Feel free to look them up online if you'd like!

1. The Ballerina Clown—I know, I know. Who builds a three-story-tall ballerina clown and hangs it on the side of a building? An artist named Jonathan Borofsky, that's who. I positively adore this creepy clown, although I know plenty of people who are so disturbed by it they won't even drive down this street.

2. The Venice Art Walls and Cones—On any given afternoon you can see street artists painting new art on these concrete structures. From the Venice Art Walls website: "Free to graffiti artists, street artists, and any other creative minds, we are open all weekend on a first-come, first-served bases." All artists over the age of eighteen are guaranteed a spot to paint. Like Vanessa, I love to stop on my skates and watch these artists work.

3. The *Venice Kinesis* mural—The inspiration for Vanessa! This is one of the most famous murals in Venice, created by one of its most famous artists, R. Cronk. This mural is a re-visioning of a re-visioning of the original mural, also by R. Cronk, entitled *Venice on the Half Shell*. *Venice on the Half Shell* was an art parody of a famous Renaissance painter named Botticelli and one of his paintings, called *The Birth of Venus*. The woman in the *Venice Kinesis* mural always seemed iconic of a certain Venice feel, so it seemed natural to give her a name and make her the muse to the entire city.

4. The Venice Pier—This keyhole-shaped pier has been shut down more than once when high storm waves damaged its foundation. If only the waves had been glitter rather than water. . . .

5. The Abbot Kinney mural—Abbot Kinney really is the visionary who created, designed, and paid for the entire city of Venice, and he really does have a mural on a brick building. Because this city was all his idea and built with the fortunes he made as a tobacco magnate, he feels like a grandfather to everything that happens here.

6. The *Angel of Unity* mural—This mural of a faceless woman diving sideways is on the side of a building right by the Venice Pier. Painted by the artist Rassouli, it's also graced by a Rumi quote that says, "Reach higher. Reach for your spirit." This mural and that quote always make me feel strong and safe and wild and free, all at the same time. No wonder, then, that the impressionist form of the woman became my inspiration for the nighttime face of the muse.

7. The Venice canals—All that's left of an entire city of canals are a few square blocks, but what a few square blocks they are! I've seen the Venice canals go from unpaved, run-down, smelly waterways with roving packs of geese that would attack you if you tried to pass, to the overpriced homes-for-the-famous they are now . . . and I have loved them with all my heart no matter what.

8. The Race Thru the Clouds Roller Coaster—This coaster really did exist in Venice, and it really was a race . . . in fact, it was the first racing roller coaster in the western United States. Two tracks went side-by-side with two different coaster cars riding them in a race to the finish. Now a tribute building stands near where the coaster used to be, designed specifically to evoke the swirls and dips of the Race Thru the Clouds.

9. The gas mask mural—This is the mural Maddy passes in the Race Thru the Clouds. What I love about this mural is: 1. When it was new, it looked so real that, from a block away, it was easy to think there was an actual person suspended on the side of the building. 2. It's painted by R. Cronk, who is, as mentioned, probably the most famous muralist in Venice, California, and 3. It's a self-portrait of the artist, meaning that R. Cronk painted himself painting the word "Venice" on the side of a building. Yeah. Pretty spectacular.

10. The Bridge of Sighs (The Ponte dei Sospiri)—This is a famous enclosed limestone bridge in the original Venice, the one in Italy. Originally commissioned by a royal family to connect their palace to the prison, today it has a much more romantic use: it's said to bring good luck if you kiss your loved one while passing under the bridge in a gondola.

11. The tuxedo bunny mural, the cheetah-wolf-unicorn mural, the man in the spangled bathing suit and his snakes, the bike path, the person on the unicycle with their hair gelled into horns, the person in the tree costume, and, of course, the drum circle—These are all real, too, as are many of the other things mentioned in passing in the book. The murals were painted, respectively, by artists Max Neutra and Diana Garcia. The man in the gold-spangled Speedo with his snakes has been a mainstay on the Venice boardwalk for ages, although I don't know his real name so I made one up. The tree person used to wander randomly around Venice, in the most spectacular costume and in character, at all hours. As for the drum circle, well, that's been part of Venice for as long as I can remember, a joyous gathering of drummers and dancers filling the air with rhythm.

Another thing that really exists is the mimic octopus, and what these octopuses are able to mimic in real life is nearly as incredible as the Hollywood Sign! Look them up online and be amazed. Also, the marine biologist in me has to add this small fact: octopuses don't actually have tentacles. They have arms. In scientific terms, a tentacle is longer and has suckers only at the end, while an arm is shorter and is suckered all the way down (like Ophelia and all octopuses). But "tentacle" is so much more fun to write, so I have taken poetic license with that.

Another thing I took license with is the fact that, much to its chagrin, Venice is not officially a city. It's a beachfront neighborhood in Los Angeles. There is always a small, dedicated fringe movement toward Venice cityhood, though, so maybe one day again . . .

Acknowledgments

Getting to the point where you can hold a published book in your hands takes an entire circus—as well as some pretty strong magic. I call this book my love letter to Venice, CA, but in truth it's also a love letter to all the people I've been lucky enough to find in my life.

First off, to my brilliant and kind agent, Ammi-Joan Paquette, thank you for loving Maddy and Il Circo delle Strade as much as I do, and for staying in my corner no matter what. Knowing you has brought much joy to my life! To my wonderful editor, Tara Weikum, thank you for seeing potential in me and in Maddy and for taking it to the next level. You've made Il Circo so much stronger and this whole process a delight. I knew we were the right match when I sent you an eight-page answer to a simple question, and instead of rolling your eyes, you took it and ran! I love your feedback, I love your approach, and I love being on a team with you. To assistant editor Sarah Homer: thank you for your keen eye and careful reads. Chris

Kwon, huge kiss-the-ground thanks to you and your whole design team for wrapping this book in magic, and to everyone at HarperCollins: I wish I could thank you all in person—I still can't believe I get to be part of this publishing house. Big beach thanks also to LA photographer Bria Celest, for capturing my wanna-be Ringmaster self in an author photo that makes me grin.

Artist Petur Antonnson made me cry happy tears when I first saw his spectacular cover. Thank you for bringing everyone to such perfect life, and for including the iconic Windward Avenue in the background. The buildings shown on the cover were part of the original Venice, and they still stand today. In fact, the building on the left now houses one of my favorite coffeehouses, Menotti's Coffee Stop, where I wrote a good chunk of this book. A big thank-you to Nicely and the whole crew at Menotti's for keeping me supplied with the world's best mochas as I sat typing and watching all of Venice go by. As a note, Petur included this building in the cover illustration without even knowing my connection to it. Luck . . . or a dash of circus magic? I'm going with the latter.

The Society of Children's Book Writers and Illustrators (SCBWI) taught me pretty much everything I know about writing for kids and gave me a gazillion wonderful friends. Thanks especially to Kim Turrisi for championing this book in the early days, and to Wendy Loggia and Jennifer Azantian for making me feel like this was something real. A warm, sent-to-the-heavens thank-you to one of my early mentors, Cubby (aka Hubert Selby Jr.) for the magic words you said to me all those years ago: *I love it. What happens next?* I know you've been hanging with all the cool kids in the Circus Beyond, and I hope you get to meet Kuma and the Ringmaster, 'cause I know they'd love you as much as I do.

I did not coin the amazing phrase *theydies and gentlethems*. I found it while searching for a nonbinary show welcome that still felt iconic, and then wanted to see if I could find who came up with it so I could credit them. This led me to an Instagram account called theydies.and.gentlethems, which in turn led me to where they had first seen the phrase: in a tweet from J Srimuang (@thaibrows). J Srimuang let me know that yes, they had thought of the phrase on their own and popularized it when their tweet went viral, but had since seen they weren't the first person to use it, and therefore didn't really think the credit should be theirs. So I'd like to say it was inspired by J Srimuang, and also send a huge thank-you to both these lovely humans for taking the time to respond so kindly to a random person reaching out to them.

To my chosen family: I love you more than I can ever say. There's no way to list everyone I love here, but a few must be mentioned. To Allison Canady Martinez, my BOP (buddy-old-pal) ever since we were four years old. Seriously, who would I be without you? To the best pirate crew a gal could ask for,

Bloody Cuddles/Dawn Fratini and Capt'n Itchy/Collyn Justus, for the years and years of love and silliness and laughter and tears and all of it in between, from me, the Dread Pirate Curly. To Frances Sackett, Rita Crayon Huang, and Edith Cohn, aka The Pudding Sisters—wow. Did I ever luck out getting to be in a writer's group with you three! You brighten my life and make me a better writer and human. Edith, thank you for insisting on the right ending for this book (and for letting me name a chainsaw after you); Rita, thank you for your huge heart and for understanding me and my backward writing process (and giving me someone to talk to about it); Frances, thank you for instant best-friendship, for the first line of this book, and for always being there for me and for my writing in every way. To Lee Wind, for writing mornings and kindness and love and for being the lighthouse. To Daniel Stewart, for his lion's heart and deep, gorgeous spirit. To Kevin Sharkey, for the way you think about the world and for the best stories, cocktails, and laughter ever. To Lisa Occhipinti, for impeccable aesthetics, mocha mornings, and nonstop support. To John Servilio and Rick Austin for brilliant conversation and sublime humor. To Sara Falugo, for parallel lives and shared paths. To Jamie Bellermann, for late-night conversations about writing. To Liz Delaney, whose off-hand comment years ago, about wishing she could find more stories for her kids that reflected the values found in yogic traditions, helped shape this book. To Fred Samia the person, for your creative eye and kind, inclusive heart, and to Fred the writing group, for encouragement and joy. To Heidi Bourne, for down-to-earth friendship, humor, and mindfulness teaching, and to Jill McKee, for dancing with me through Venice back in the day. And to the two dear ones I lost this past year, Tracy Hill and Kati Cesareo: I love you. Thank you for sharing your life with me for as long as you could. Your lights, both of you, pulse through this entire manuscript.

My outlook on the world wouldn't exist without my mom, Judie Snyder, and her love for all things interesting and beautiful and unusual. Thanks, Mom, for introducing me to the arts and then conveniently forgetting to tell me I shouldn't try to make a living from them. (Ha!) Thanks to my dad, Gary Snyder, for the hilarious plays you wrote when I was a kid that let me see writing was fun. To my big brother, Keith Snyder, thank you for your humor and for being the example that this was possible. To Susan Walker, thank you for your straightforward midwestern goodness. Thank you to my nephews and nieces—Bear and Ash Martinez, and Zachary and Nicholas Snyder. You are all brilliant and amazing and I adore you. Thank you to my Other Mother and Other Father, Andrea Canady and Richard Canady, for adopting me as their second daughter when Allison and I became inseparable, and thank you to my whole Davis family for being so fabulous in every way.

Another "I LOVE YOU" screamed from the rooftops to the hundreds of writer, yoga, and creative friends—in addition to the ones above—who have inspired and encouraged me along the way. Here are just a few of those very many people, in no particular order: Deborah Kagan, TaRosa Jacobs, Jason June, Laurie Young, Mara Bushansky, Brad Keimach, Bruce Coville, Alón Sagee, Bruce Hale, Beenish Ahmed, Calvin Harris, Kat Shephard, Virginia Allison-Reinhardt, Michael Reinhardt, Steve Valdez, Jenny Howard, Lori Polydorus, Firas Nasr, Max Strom, Moses Goldstein, Tanynya Heckymara, Anna Cherekovsky, Xander Bernstein, Dunja Vitolic, Kirsten Cappy, Vicki Wawerchak, Juliana Bolden, Jen Kushell, Ginny Ryder, Tracy Lee Curry, Steve Dennis, Richard Ford, Lisa Rocchetti, Heather Carter, Paula Fellbaum, Owen Hurley, Lonny Grafman, Janine Melzer, Megan Rosenbloom, Betsy Rosenthal, Javanne Golub, Demetra Brodsky, Rhonda Kennedy, David Boren, Michelle Raff, Nate Occhipinti, and Jamie Elmer. Huge thanks also to the communities of writers that are Splendid Mola and the Writers Happiness Movement, for the constant reminder of how many of us there are reimagining the world into one built on a foundation of kindness, community, and the arts, day in and day out. Thank you to all my Venice neighbors and friends, and to my beloved Venice itself for constantly filling my heart with so much delight. Particular thanks to the sea and the boardwalk, the dolphins and sea lions, the bike path and my skates, the pelicans and the pier, Small World Books, and every single street performer. Without all of these, my life would be much less joyful.

There are two parts to the grand finale of the gratitude

show. First, my heart and my love to Bob Johnson, the behind-the-scenes rock that lets the magic happen. I love you wildly, and this book wouldn't exist without you. And next, thank you to everyone, everywhere, who steps into the nighttime to seek and chooses to see what is true. You are my people and we do this together.